Also by Margaret Schweitzer

Fiction
The Copper Kettle
Miss Putnam's Garden

Non-Fiction
Unlocking the Blue Door

"Billings Bridge (DbJm-34):
A Paleo-Indigenous Site near Thunder Bay, Ontario"
(Peer reviewed scientific paper)

For Rachel and her sisters,
because families matter

Table of Contents

Foreword	ix
Chapter One: England, 1890s	1
Chapter Two: Voyage to Canada, 1905	15
Chapter Three: World War I, 1914	23
Chapter Four: France, 1915-1916	37
Chapter Five: England, 1917	51
Chapter Six: England, 1918	71
Chapter Seven: Toronto, Ontario, 1919	81
Chapter Eight: Sault Ste. Marie, Ontario, 1929	95
Chapter Nine: Port Arthur, Ontario, 1935	107
Chapter Ten: Scotland, 1941	121
Chapter Eleven: Scotland, 1942	139
Chapter Twelve: Scotland, 1943	155
Chapter Thirteen: France, 1944	173
Chapter Fourteen: Scotland, 1945	189
Chapter Fifteen: Port Arthur, 1946-1947	201
Chapter Sixteen: Toronto, 1950s	217
Chapter Seventeen: Toronto, 1972	229
Epilogue	251
Afterword	259
Bibliography	269
Acknowledgments	273
About The Author	275

Foreword

This is the most challenging book I have written to date. It is something that has been on my mind literally all of my life. It wouldn't be true to say that I obsess over it (or ever did) and now it's time to get to the heart of things.

My mother's father, Frederick James Dawson, was a man I never knew, never met. He died before I was born. Frederick remained a figure of mystery for me, like a person seen too far away to identify. His wife, my grandmother, was an imperious and distant woman, not one given to hugging children or providing personal details of family history. She died when I was eighteen, leaving me no further ahead in learning about the man she'd married some sixty years earlier. For many years I believed that they'd divorced in middle age, but that turned out not to be the case. My mom had not been close to her father, and whenever I asked her about him, she shrugged off my questions as if he hadn't mattered much to her.

I have always been interested in familial roots, and having only the sketchiest information about a direct ancestor grated on my sense of personhood. Over the course of a few years, I ruminated on the idea of writing a book about Frederick. Impossible, I reasoned, how could I accomplish such a task for somebody I didn't know and had virtually no stories of? Still, a decade earlier in the city library, a technician had looked up some information for me from the 1921 Canada Census, and there was Frederick, his name written in the beautiful cursive script of the time. He had lived.

This tale does not fall into the category of non-fiction novel, as Truman Capote offered with his *In Cold Blood*. I would call it historical fiction or perhaps fictionalized biography, based on a threaded trail of proven facts. Neither seems adequate by definition. On the other hand, I now have tantalizing glimpses of my grandfather's life, just enough to begin filling in the blanks between what is recorded. A veteran of two world wars, an adventurer, a proud man always in motion. The more I discovered about him, the more intrigued I became. Writing a version of his story is still daunting, even as I commit these words. Very difficult, unwise, risky. And yet.

As human beings, we want to discover the tribe that spawned us. We need to know where we come from and who our people are. They live on, both in and through us. I present this work as one possible interpretation for the life Frederick lived. It is not likely to be as accurate as I would prefer, yet it is still a possible narrative. I cannot present it as biographic *précis* because my information is incomplete, but neither is it entirely fabrication; it lies somewhere in between. I began with a fairly comprehensive record of his military service in the two world wars of 1914-1918 and 1939-1945. Going by what was contained in the records, I added possible details that would flesh out the gaps and create a supplement to the limited knowledge that I had handed down to me by my mother. A reference section will detail where the facts originated. The rest is my imagination. At the end of the book, I've included two more chapters, one about my interpretation of his personal life and the other regarding research challenges.

Margaret Schweitzer
December 11, 2024

Murillo, Ontario

Chapter One

England, 1890s

Enfield, in the County of Middlesex, England, is an ancient place. It is noted in the *Domesday Book*, the great survey of England and Wales completed in 1086 at the behest of William the Conqueror, also known as King William I. Royal Enfield Chase was part of Enfield Wood, of the Forest of Middlesex, which encompassed lands as far south as the River Thames, almost thirteen imperial miles in distance from north to south. William I gifted the manors of both Edmonton and Enfield to Geoffrey de Mandeville after the Norman Conquest; this event is also referred to as the Battle of Hastings. De Mandeville was named the first Earl of Essex.

More recently in history, a Tudor palace for Queen Elizabeth I, the Virgin Queen, was built at Enfield, but it was not really a palace, resembling more a manor house for Her Majesty's comfort while she visited and hunted in the nearby deer park. She was the daughter of Henry VIII and Anne Boleyn, and so from early days, Enfield was no ordinary locale. It could be a ride of two hours to London by horse, depending upon conditions. And the horse. One wonders if riders even then sensed the narrative of their time, worn into the soil of Roman Londinium: soldiers laden with weapons, trades workers with their tools, magistrates in their robes and leather footwear. Perhaps not. The distance was some thirteen thousand paces taken by a typical soldier, according to the Romans.

Also in Enfield, a boy was born at home, on March 7, 1894. It was a cold day and rainy. The baby was wrapped in a shawl and held tightly by his mother while the household took pause at her confinement. A grand babe, the ninth of ten children born to his parents as it turned out. His mother held the child quietly, making soothing sounds while asking him to stay with her, imploring his two siblings who had already died to watch over him and keep him safe. Mary and infant, the blessed duo.

As soon as he arrived home for his tea that day, John Dawson looked in on his wife and new son. A handsome baby with his mother's fair looks. John sighed, relaxing momentarily; no one could know what life might bring, and something bad could happen if one let down one's guard too soon. He shook himself mentally and reached out a hand, touching her shoulder.

"He's *álaind*," John whispered. Beautiful. Saying the words, he heard the ghost of his own mother's voice. *Buachaill leanbh*, baby boy. John felt a brief stab of grief as he reflected on his present joy, while thinking of his ancestors' grief in communal silence after thin wails. People who had survived the famine were too weak to bury their dead. Even when John was a child, his family encouraged him to leave the Irish earth that had formed him. *Go away, lad,* they said, *go away and make something of yourself. The land has emptied out, there's nothing for you here.* As he later began the long walk from Portadown to Belfast, it was the colours and images that stayed in his mind, not anyone's words. Pinkish tinge of limestone in the quarry, grey metal sky of winter, impossible green of spring: these would form his lifelong memories. Never again would he witness the hunger of previous generations that remained in the faces of his countrymen, no matter how much they ate. Starvation had touched them inside where no one could reach. At first he enjoyed the walk off his island as the distance stretched out before him. He caught a lift on a dray for the last two miles, his legs tired. A steamship to Liverpool, John's first time on the water, and he stumbled trying to stay upright in the wind on deck. His stomach tied in knots of fear as he got further from the coast, a thing he pushed down. Accents from all over the counties, melancholy songs, a baby's cry. John shook his head now, returned to the presence of his newly born son and wondering where his emotion had bubbled from, perhaps only acknowledging the passages of his life. He saw the yearning in Mary's eyes, willing the child to survive. She carried the sorrow of the other two lost to them, same as a sack of potatoes that she couldn't set down as it weighed upon her shoulders. And in the midst of these sad thoughts, she and John were quiet in each other, marveling once again at the miracle of birth. She looked up, with all the hope and joy and fear of a mother's love plain on her face.

"What will we name him, John?"

John frowned. "James?" He cleared his throat. "For my father."

Mary's breath caught; their baby James, the first namesake, had died in infancy. No use in tempting fate again. But she still loved the name. "James for his second name. How about Frederick? Frederick James."

John went silent. He didn't know that his wife had visited a country healer in secret with her sister, when she'd said she was going to visit a sick parishioner. Mary was determined to see her baby live to adulthood, consulting the healer for advice in stopping the devil from taking this child. The woman had told her that she would have a son, a strong boy who would be a leader. She was to name him Frederick without question. Mary held her breath for one moment, two, then exhaled softly as John agreed.

"*Sea*, we'll call him Frederick James, then. If that's what you wish."

"Aye," she answered, "It is."

John went back to work after his tea, a short walk from their rented home. He measured his paces, a skill learned as a carpenter. Everything determined by the ruler, be it a wooden stick or a man's arm. John had a head for numbers and it stood him well in his career. He smiled, thinking of their address on Manor Road – as if he or his family would ever own a manor house. They would be tenants forever, so it seemed. Still, he didn't regret leaving his homeland and all the talk of war from the Fenian Brotherhood: get the goddamned English out of Ireland for good, preferably by force, the bastards. John was not a man of war. He'd read in the newspapers that things were better now, with emigration decreasing. Tenant farmers were being allowed to buy their own lands, something unheard of in his grandparents' generation. Now he had a family of nine children; he still considered the two that had died as living. Something niggled inside as he walked, an ominous feeling that shifted about in his brain. It was as if he were getting a message from Mórrígan, the Celtic goddess of Irish folklore, about fate and wartime battle. This omen, a tangible thing for John, represented anxiety and fear of death, and it had traveled down the lines of his forebears for centuries, all the way to him. He recalled his mother's angst whenever a flock of crows flew over, insisting it was Mórrígan who sent such a sign and nothing else. One young relative who had laughed at the superstition had died the following day. Now here it was again, a tenuous note attached to his newly born child. John shook his head and took up his hammer. Silliness of the mind, he decided, it was only that.

Later that night as the household grew quiet, Mary eased herself into bed, the baby gently sleeping in his cot beside her. She looked him over carefully.

"He's a bonny one."

John smiled, touching her arm. "Yes, a fine lad for us."

"Reminds me of my uncle Alexander already."

"Let's hope he doesn't have his temper, eh?"

"Oh, you," she giggled. "You know how proud he was to be a Scot."

The light grew darker around them. "Tell me, Mary, are you happy here?"

She took a moment to answer. "I'm happy with you, happy with what we've got."

John sighed. "Sometimes I want more for us. More for you."

"I'm not sure what you mean. Aren't you happy?"

"Yes, but I'm getting older now, thinking about the future."

"That's not like you."

"I know. That's part of what's bothering me."

Now Mary sighed, tired from the day. "Let's get some sleep. This wee one may be up in an hour or two."

John turned on his side towards his wife, tucking his arm around her waist. To him, she was still the beautiful girl who had taken his breath away the first time he saw her. Now as then, he wanted to give her the life she deserved, something more than the one that had been handed to them. He begrudged their rent of five shillings per week when outbreaks of cholera and dysentery were as frequent as the rains. John drifted off to sleep, dreaming of living a life of freedom, somewhere else.

From the time before he could crawl, Frederick could not or would not be still; anything moving fascinated, and he had to learn what made it go. Both of his parents noted a restlessness in their son, different from his siblings. As another winter set in, chilblains abounded on the bodies of Enfield's children. The youngsters scampered behind the coalmen who were bent forward under heavy hessian sacks. Occasionally a lump fell out of a small hole in the weave, and it barely touched the ground before it was snatched up, sometimes causing a scuffle of ownership. Frederick watched this from the front window of his home, thinking that delivering individual loads of coal like that was a waste of time. He wanted to devise a system where the coal could be brought directly to the cellars by a machine. He watched the blackened faces of the workers, smuts surrounding their noses and mouths.

In school, the boy fidgeted constantly, earning him weekly (and sometimes daily) raps of the cane. There was talk of the Boer War, and this held his attention, stories from far away in another land. It wasn't so much the killing as the battle strategy that he was interested in. At last, the schoolmaster spoke of it since he had a brother serving with the British Army in South Africa. Frederick sat very still to listen. Afterwards, he and his friends played mock war in the streets and hills nearby.

"Shoot him!" shouted Harry, lifting his stick high.

"Aahhh," moaned George, falling over dramatically in death.

Frederick stayed near the back, planning the best way to win. He nudged Arthur forward. "Go around the side of that tree where they won't see you. I'll head straight in, and as soon as they turn towards me, you attack from the side."

Arthur bit his lip, lowered his head and ran. It was a pitched battle with no clear winner in the end, but the boys all had fun. An hour later, they split up, happy and tired.

At tea, Frederick asked his mother, "Ma, why does Mrs. Edwards call me Mick?"

Mary went still, her eyes narrowed. "When did she do this?"

"Yesterday, and the day before that, too. I told her my name is Frederick, but she turned away. Is she hard of hearing?"

"No, son," Mary sighed, "Her hearing is perfectly fine."

"But. . ."

"Now then, it's a bad term for someone from Ireland."

He sat up straighter. "I'm not from Ireland, I'm from here!"

"Aye, you are, but your da's from Ireland."

"What does that matter?"

"Some can't accept others for who they are. They think that where you come from is all they need to know."

"So it's a bad word?"

"Aye, and the best thing to do is to ignore it. When you make a fuss, they'll come at you more."

"I'll get my friends to kill them with lances."

"No, you won't. I'll go and talk to Mrs. Edwards. She's no better than the rest of us."

The boy loved his war games, exhorting his mates to mimic the great British soldiers that he'd learned about in class. Marshal, Nelson, Gordon. Frederick would huddle his friends around to explain battle tactics before standing up and giving Nelson's rallying cry: *England expects that every man will do his duty.* It gave Frederick the shivers when he said it (one of the few things that he ever remembered from school). His father, John, watched the boys for a few minutes once and sadness entered his thoughts on realizing that he'd wanted none of his family to be English. Now his later children had been born here. He would not surrender his identity, not for anyone. After the potato famine of the 1840s, it was all they could call their own. *Dul ar aghaidh,* the priest had said so many times to those who were left. Go forward. Leave the dead in their graves and carry on.

John had landed in Liverpool during the time before his marriage. Seeing the docks that seethed with activity made him dizzy. He couldn't understand the Scousers' accent for weeks, and a few spat on him as Irish, but soon enough he had a job unloading ships from the West Indies, West Africa, Canada, and Brazil. It was backbreaking work and the men were run like slaves, never fast enough, never strong enough. John spent months in exhaustion. He was good with his hands and with building things, and for a time he thought he might be a ship builder. However, the noise, smoke, and dust assaulted his senses without cease as he longed privately for home and the quiet fields of his childhood. As soon as he heard of work in Leeds building houses, he struck out on foot to make his way there. Within a month or two, John felt more sure of his footing in life and was able to relax a bit. A few times he even considered going home for a visit. There was little leisure time, but his wages were steady – he envisioned building his own house one day. For now he rented a tiny room barely large enough for a bed and wash basin. A shared privy reeked at the end of the lane. He didn't go to church regularly or to public houses but did get out every so often for a walk on weekends, along the River Aire.

On a bright spring day in 1874, John marveled at the new cast-iron bridge over the river, realizing how much had changed in the past years. The bridge gave him a sense of renewal and promise, that he could make something of his life, just as his da had told him. The work had been regular and John was known as a conscientious and careful carpenter around the county, not one to take short cuts or to cheat anyone. He'd sent a letter home the month before and was still waiting for a reply. On this day, he felt better than when he'd first arrived in this unfamiliar land, better than the time when he'd looked back at Ireland's receding coastline from the steamer deck. And almost as if his mood had conjured it, a young girl was crossing the street at the opposite end of the bridge. She carried a basket under her arm. An ankle-length dress followed the line of her form, neither loose nor snug, in a shade of blue that complimented her fair hair, tied back with a bit of cloth. A girl in service, tidy and purposeful. John stood intrigued, watching her. He'd seen dozens of eligible women in his life but none that interested him like this one. She stopped momentarily before turning in his direction, and he raised his hand without thinking. Only then did he take a step towards her, then many steps, never taking his eyes from her face, afraid that if he looked away, she would vanish. She paused before moving to the side of the road and waited for him to join her.

John blushed. "It's a beautiful day," he said, catching her blue eyes very briefly before looking down, reminding himself not to speak Gaelic. After three years, he still thought in it. His fingers twitched, wanting to shake her hand in greeting as would be proper. He left his hand at his side as shyness overtook him.

She smiled and replied in Gaelic, "*Halò. Feasgar math*." Then in English. "Good afternoon. I hear your accent."

He grinned, glad to hear familiar language. "You're not from here then, either."

"Girthon, near the sea. Kirkcudbrightshire. It's why I come to the river whenever I can. I imagine following it all the way back home when I feel lonely."

John's heart turned over slowly, listening to the Scottish lilt in her voice, the soft broad vowels.

She smiled again, her teeth even and white. "I must go now. My mistress is waiting for me."

"Will you come again?" John asked.

"Aye, I try to get a moment to walk on my half-day. M'lady is at the dressmakers and sent me. . ." She stopped. "It doesn't matter." The girl turned to leave.

"Wait," he urged, reaching his hand towards her without touching. "Your name?"

"I'm Mary. Mary Wilson Smith," she offered in formal tones.

"Pleased to meet you. I'm John Dawson, from County Armagh."

"Well, John Dawson, perhaps we'll meet again." She blushed briefly at her own forwardness and walked away without looking back.

John thought about her for the rest of that day, the fact that where she was from and where he was from were not that far apart, separated by the Irish Sea. He thought of the Fates, and whether he was chosen to be in this place at this time. Later that evening, John returned to his room. He wanted to be a practical man, a logical one, but his mind had other things in it, from the world of faeries and demons, things that frightened children. He hoped to see Mary again.

By the age of nine, Frederick was lithe and athletic, determined and stubborn. He wouldn't give in during arguments, even when he was wrong. The boy had a natural confidence that was uncommon for his age. He was never anxious, and if he were, hid it well. His interest in war games continued, and he had his own squadron of soldiers, selected from his friends in the street. They had mock battles at weekends, where Frederick was always the leader. Some boys from immigrant German families ganged up on them, which Frederick delighted in. He would trounce the scoundrels, showing them that God favoured the British, then and always. The children of Russian Jews were less interested in war games, and the English boys pursued them with insults, goading them into skirmishes. When no one else took part, the group split into English and Irish as obvious warring sides, given their history of animosity. A newcomer took pleasure in teasing Frederick.

"Oi, Mick there! Me da says you lot are ungrateful bastards. Ye should all be drowned in the sea." He threw a bit of sod, striking Frederick in the shoulder.

"Says who, eh?" Frederick shoved the boy backwards where he kept his ground.

"Is that all ye've got, then? Pansy like ye, wearin' skirts instead of trousers. No wonder yer Prince Charlie lost, har har."

"Shut up!" Frederick felt his temper getting the better of him.

"Papist Paddy. Yer ma's not even English, either. Yer a bloody foreigner."

That did it. Frederick punched him hard in the mouth and the boys fell to the ground together. The others formed a ring around them, shouting encouragement. No one came to break up the contenders and the fighting turned serious. Scratches and gouges came from fingernails, and grunts tore from angry mouths. Frederick's opponent grabbed a sharp stick from the ground and plunged it towards Fred's face. At the last instant, Frederick turned his head to the side and pulled back. The stick caught his cheek, tearing the skin in a bright red line as blood spurted.

"Hey, what're you lads doing? Trying to kill one another?"

It was Arthur's father, heading home. "Stop that now. Get up and behave like gentlemen." He pulled at the other boy first, separating them. The boy spat at Frederick.

"Bloody Mick. Why don't ye go back where ye came from?"

Frederick surged toward him once again but the man held him back.

"Go home now. Go on, get out!" Arthur's dad shoved the other boy away.

The youngster left with a handful of supporters beside him.

"Are you all right? That's a nasty scratch you've got."

A trickle of blood oozed down Frederick's cheek. He rubbed a dirty hand through it. Arthur's dad rumpled his hair. "Best get home to your ma now. She won't like the sight of you."

And indeed, his ma did not. Mary pursed her lips as she cleaned the fresh cut, thinking of the bonny baby he'd been, now with a mark on his face that looked permanent. Sometimes when days were harder, she remembered John's talk about starting again somewhere else.

At the end of March 1901, the census taker came around and dropped off the forms to be completed by each family on the street, as designated by law. In January of that year, King Edward VII had taken the throne upon the death of his mother, Queen Victoria. A new era was underway, one of hope in the future and increasing confidence in technological innovation. Mary Dawson laid the forms aside as she waited for her husband to come home.

"Frederick, keep an eye on Walter while I hang up this washing."

"Aww, can't Joseph?"

"Nay, son, I'm asking you."

"I'll take him out with me."

"All right, but don't get him dirty. I've just caught up on everything."

Frederick took his little brother's hand and together they quickly found a puddle to play in. Frederick pitched small stones into the water while Walter laughed at the splashes, soaking his coat sleeves as he searched for the pebbles. When they were all gone, Frederick tossed in bits of wood, telling Walter to pretend they were treasure. Their father found them not long after, the toddler muddy and wet from the waist down. He sighed, thinking of how quickly time went by, the last of his children growing fast. *Tá na laethanta imithe go luath*, his dead mother told him. The days are soon gone. As John and Mary filled out the forms in that evening's quiet after the young ones were in bed, the familiar feeling that he'd experienced from close to twenty years before nagged at him.

"Hard to believe that our Elizabeth has already left us. It's only a year now but seems longer. I miss her," he said wistfully.

"Aye, but she's doing well in service, better than most her age."

They filled in the form's spaces with neat letters. John was a carpenter foreman now, after numerous moves to London boroughs, following where the work was. Daughter Maggie was a laundry soaper, son John a plasterer's apprentice, son Alexander a butcher's apprentice. They all still lived at home; no wonder there was so much washing every week. Mary placed her hand softly over John's.

"Is your heart heavy, then?"

John turned his eyes to her and smiled. "I'd be lying if I said no." He cleared his throat. "You're right, I know that we're grateful. Our children all have work."

"But it's not enough for you, is it?"

"You know me too well, my dear. Ever since I left home, I haven't been able to stop thoughts of emigrating further, across the ocean."

"To America."

"No, to Canada. I saw a leaflet only yesterday, of how Canada wants people just like us to go there. British people who want land, who want to be free of class divisions. Did you know, the acres available for farming are almost endless in the west of the country?"

Mary chuckled. "We aren't farmers, John."

"No, but farms lead to towns, and they need all kinds of people with skills. Imagine, one day we could have our own land, our own home. . ." He sighed heavily.

"You can't live your whole life wishing."

"If we do decide to do this, we can't wait much longer. I'm already forty-five."

"How much will it cost?"

"Over a hundred pounds for all of us."

She sucked in her breath. "So much money."

"But it's a permanent move. One that could change our future."

Mary said, "I'm tired. Let's go to bed and think on it some more."

Chapter Two

Voyage to Canada, 1905

The crossing was new to them and not something a typical family from their London borough did every week. However, the freshening ocean breeze came as a blessing after the stifling heat of the city's record temperatures that summer of 1905. In early August, the Dawsons disembarked Liverpool on the *SS Dominion*, a carrier of more than eleven hundred passengers. While talking to the purser, John learned that the ship had been originally launched in Belfast a dozen years earlier, and he reflected that his first voyage to England in 1872 had brought him to Mary. John's legs still felt soft on the rolling sea despite the passage of years, though he managed to not be sick. The Atlantic crossing took nine days in good conditions before they landed at Quebec and took their first footsteps on foreign soil. Neither John nor Mary was a student of history, but they knew of the earlier wars between England and France. Here, the Dawsons heard French spoken for the first time, to them an incomprehensible language. The family milled together in the allotted area at the docks, craning their necks to see the Citadel. Frederick exclaimed with excitement, "A castle!"

"Aye, it is, son, and a fine one at that," said his mother.

"Can we go there?"

"Nay, lad. We have to pass through immigration."

John closed his eyes a moment, reliving his months at the Liverpool docks thirty years earlier. Much of what he saw here was the same: stevedores moving kegs of molasses, huge squared timbers, grain, fish, metal ores, and spices. He mused on how much his life had altered since those days, yet here he was, an immigrant again. *Téann an t-am i gciorcal,* he recited silently in Gaelic. Time goes in a circle. The dialect was harder to remember now, slipping away in single words. He no longer spoke it aloud and never to his children. They were Irish, Scottish, English, and now? Something else again, Canadian. He couldn't fit their lives around it, couldn't apply it to their family, waiting on the dock. Perhaps in time.

Soon enough, the family was directed towards the immigration sheds.

"How much longer, Da?"

"Not long, son. Another day or so."

"Is this where we're staying? I can't understand what they're saying."

"Our ticket pays to Hamilton. We take the train from here."

"A train!" The boy could barely hold himself still.

Some hours later, they all loaded up again, their cases stored in the baggage car. None of them had ever been on such a long train before, and tired as they were, excitement still fueled the younger children. As darkness wove together the last thoughts of day, they settled together in a single large compartment while Mary hummed a lullaby to soothe them all to sleep.

The next morning found them traveling along an expanse

of flat cleared land with pockets of trees here and there. Their bodies swayed gently, now used to the motion. Cups of tea were handed out by porters along the cars. Looking out the window, Frederick saw farm workers in fields, draft horses and wagons, not so different from his home country.

"See, Ma? They're like us."

"Aye, dear, we're all cut from the same cloth."

"Do they talk French here, too?"

"I don't know, perhaps some do. We aren't the first to come from England, mind."

"Are there soldiers?"

John chuckled. "Not in the fields, lad. No war here that I've heard of."

"I'm going to lead men in war."

Mórrígan shadowed John's soul at his son's words and he shivered involuntarily. A sense of doom covered him briefly like a mist. He turned his eyes to the train's window and saw a flock of crows fly up as the carriage rocked by on the tracks. Turning back, Mary met his eyes, something pleading in hers.

By late afternoon, the train eased into the station at Toronto, where they would switch to another train for Hamilton. They exited their car, glad to feel solid ground beneath their feet. Young Walter stumbled on the way down the steps. Hours later they were still there, tired, hungry, and thoroughly sick of waiting.

"Where's the train? How long are we to be here?" asked Mary.

"I'll go and ask a porter," replied John.

Frederick and his little brother stared openly at the black man that their father approached. The rest of the family shuffled about, covering their mouths and noses from a gust of dirty wind. John returned with the news that the train they were waiting for would be another six hours at least. Uncharacteristically, Mary's patience thinned dangerously. "We've come this far, what's the difference? It's all Canada." Her words clipped under the strain.

"Yes, but. . ." John said.

She interrupted, "We're starting over and none of us has work yet. How do we know what's in this Hamilton? What if we're better off here?"

"We can't get a refund on the ticket, you know."

"I don't care about a bloody refund!" Mary pressed her lips together quickly. "Oh, I am sorry, forgive me."

They stood indecisively but not for long. "Look, Da, Ma. Look at the sign." Frederick pointed.

Not far away, there was a mounted wooden placard declaring *York County, est. 1792*. In smaller letters below, it said *formerly Dublin*.

"Where?"

The boy exclaimed, "York and Dublin! See?"

"Well, I'll be." John scratched his head. He did believe in omens.

"Why don't we start right here instead?" asked Mary.

And so they did.

John wasn't used to skipping a four o'clock tea break in his new country during the week. He disliked having the noon meal followed by long work hours before supper at seven in the evening. It was one more thing to get used to. The family rented a house on Merton Street, almost as far north as the street car would travel from the Lake Ontario waterfront. At weekends John loved to stroll in the nearby farm fields as the city still felt some distance away. On rare occasions, Mary joined him.

"Ah," he sighed, "It's lovely here in spring."

"Aye." She looked down as they walked.

John stopped. "Are you sad, then?"

"I was thinking of my mam." She wiped a tear. "You know, I wanted to throw away the letter when we got it and pretend it never arrived."

They'd received notice the previous winter of the woman's death. John took his wife's hand. "It's hard, I know. But we're here, and that's what we must think on. The children like it; they adapt better. All except for school, according to one." he said.

Now Mary smiled. "I don't think Frederick will ever make a good student. He can't sit still for a moment. I wonder what will become of him?"

"He's a smart boy, just needs to harness his energy in the right way."

"He was telling me about some flying contraption in the United States. I can't imagine what that is. It sounds like madness out of a fantasy tale."

"No, it's true. A machine that's heavier than air but can stay aloft with an engine. Something about air currents on the wings," said John.

"Well, I hope our son stays away from that nonsense, it sounds very dangerous."

"As long as Frederick can do his letters and some mathematics, he can go far."

"I notice he likes geography and mechanics. He's good with his hands and fixing motors. And he thinks things through without losing his temper, at least not for a little while."

"No Latin and Greek for him."

"Certainly not!" Mary laughed.

They stopped walking, hearing the sounds of a whip-poor-will in waning daylight.

"It's your mam," John whispered, "People here say the bird knows of death."

Mary shuddered and took his arm. "Let's go back."

Frederick roamed a mile or more at a time away from his family's home. His new friends often came with him, but he wasn't bothered by going alone. It had taken him only a short while to get used to the open spaces and clean air of his new country and he reveled in it. Usually he was on foot but was known to borrow a pony when the opportunity presented itself; he always returned the animal to its shed when he was done with it.

This day found him away to the east, a long way gone. He was attracted to the sounds of clanging metal tools somewhere in the distance. Drawn like a wasp to rotting fruit, Frederick kept walking until he saw a workshop attached to a blacksmith's forge. A heavyset man with his teenaged helper was building something. They worked without speaking until the man noticed their audience. He put the hot metal bar into the water trough, which hissed its compliance, before setting down the tongs and straightening up.

"Well, then, lad. Are you lost?"

Frederick inflated his chest, saying, "No, sir, not lost."

The teenaged helper smirked. "A Limey, no less."

The man nodded his disapproval to the helper, turning his head. "What part o' England are you from?"

"London. But I'm here now," the boy replied, as if it weren't obvious.

"What d'you want wit' us?"

"Is it all right if I just watch?"

"What for?"

"I'd like to see what you're making. Is it an airplane?"

The man chuckled. "No, son, not an airplane." He scratched his chin, then added, "A more powerful motor car, that's what I'm aiming for."

And so Frederick returned many times to the shop, watching the chassis take shape, his questions stilled inside but bursting to emerge. Just by paying attention, he learned many things about powered motion and thrust, weight and drag and lift. He paid attention to the tools, what they were called and how they were used. The helper no longer called him Limey.

"Da, d'you think we'll ever have a motor car?"

John held his teacup against his lips for a moment before answering. "I don't think so." Seeing the shadow cross his son's brow, he added, "But you never know."

"I want to ride in one. I want to drive one."

"D'you know somebody who could let you ride?"

"No, not yet." Frederick brightened. "But I'm learning how to build one!"

"Those are your new friends, are they?"

"Yes, they let me watch what they're doing."

"What sort of car do they want?"

"A fast one!" Frederick laughed. "They want to enter a speed race."

"Well, there are worse things to do than building cars."

"The man, his name is Mr. Jones, says there's a business not too far away that builds cars. He calls it the McLaughlin Carriage Company, in Oshawa. Where's Oshawa?"

"Oh, it's about thirty-five miles from here, to the east."

"Can I go there?"

John set down his tea. "You're pretty keen, then."

"Yes, Da, I want to work with motors."

"I've heard there may be a trunk line put in soon, so you can travel there by train. But it's not built yet."

"Oh." Frederick frowned.

"You can become a mechanic, you know. Then you can build your own car."

Two years later, the *Silver Dart* airplane took the first ever powered flight in Canada at Baddeck, Nova Scotia. Numerous articles were written in the *Toronto Star* newspaper, accompanied by drawings of the craft. Frederick was beside himself with enthusiasm and interest. More than anything, he wanted to fly airplanes. He contented himself with working on motors in the meantime and eventually qualified as an automobile mechanic. Mr. Jones had taken his protégé on full-time as soon as he'd finished secondary school.

The following year found the Dawson family moved to Leaside Junction, a hamlet and rail siding created in 1881 by the Canadian Pacific Railway. This rural location had been chosen as a maintenance facility for the company, its level farmland conveniently close to the Toronto waterfront hub, about five and one-half miles distant. John built the family's new home at 131 Laird Drive, using lumber he'd purchased from a former military jail that was dismantled close to his recently purchased property. Another move, another adjustment, but they were doing well; both John and Mary enjoyed more rural environs, especially John. Somewhere in the back of his mind, he always looked for the fields of Ireland without even realizing it. He had plenty of carpentry work as growth continued apace in the city, where he took the streetcar back and forth daily. There were few neighbours in the beginning and plenty of wild creatures in lush surroundings to keep the landscape interesting. Water from wells was clean and the blue summer sky endless. John's mind was pleasantly at ease for one of the few times in his life. Frederick had to only walk across to street to his employer, where a shop had been opened by the McLaughlin Carriage Company in a series of arrangements with the American entrepreneur, Billy Durant.

Chapter Three

World War I, 1914

The second decade of the new century brought political unrest in Europe with the Balkan Wars, labour strife, and economic decline in the United Kingdom. It was followed by the Dublin lockout of 1913, an industrial dispute between twenty thousand workers and three hundred employers. James Larkin and James Connolly were heroes to the few Irish men John knew in Toronto, one from County Clare and the other from Sligo. He didn't drink with them, didn't drink, in fact. But John knew what was happening in his homeland through the newspapers. The Irish Citizens' Army, a paramilitary group, had been organized and led by Larkin, Connolly, and Jack White, all of them republicans and socialists. John couldn't fault the men for their goals of improved conditions and pay for workers. It was a coming of age story that appealed to the downtrodden. Funny, he thought, that Larkin was born in Liverpool and Connolly in Scotland, yet the two men were a powerhouse in Ireland.

White was the only one born in Ireland. John yearned for his mother's language, knowing that he hadn't heard Gaelic spoken since he'd arrived in Canada, and only wisps of it blew through his mind during moments between sleeping and waking now. It was as if part of his past were slipping away, slowly but surely; none of his children knew the language. And then things in the world changed again, with the murder of Archduke Ferdinand in June 1914. Great Britain declared war on Germany in August of that year. Soldiers from the colonies were obliged to support the British Empire, and this included Frederick, now twenty years old.

"Ma, Da, they're taking volunteers right away. I'll train in Quebec, at a place called Valcartier."

His parents exchanged worried glances.

"But, son, are you sure? Maybe wait a few weeks; the war is expected to be over by Christmas."

The young man shook his head. "No, I went to the armoury this morning. I've joined up."

His mother moaned involuntarily and covered her mouth. Another one gone, another one like her two children years before, another son to be missed. John looked at the floor and sighed. They knew he wouldn't listen to anything they said.

Frederick stood up tall. "I'll be fine, don't worry. The train leaves on Monday afternoon. It's the new camp not far from where we got off the ship at Quebec. There're marching drills, target practice, and other things. I may not even get overseas if it's over that quickly."

"Have you got your papers?" John asked.

"Yes, here they are." Seething with excitement, the young man proffered them. His childhood games of war were continuing on a whole new level, and this time it was for real. In the crowd at the armoury, he'd met a veteran of the Boer War. They'd talked for fifteen minutes and Frederick had almost asked the man for his autograph. He wanted to know everything about the fighting and how the war had been won. And so the recruit left his home to join the Canadian Expeditionary Force. His medical examination described him as fit for duty: one-half inch under six feet tall, fair hair, blue eyes, scar on left cheek. Frederick couldn't wait to begin.

Valcartier camp was set up very rapidly in response to the declaration of war. The site encompassed a large stretch of farmland along the east side of the Jacques Cartier River sixteen miles northwest of Quebec City, and it covered more than twelve thousand acres. In the few weeks since war had broken out, Valcartier had been transformed into a camp housing over thirty thousand soldiers in tents as they prepared to go overseas. Frederick arrived in late August along with hundreds of others, soon numbering in the tens of thousands. Not long after arrival, the men learned who their Minister of Militia and Defence was: Major-General Sam Hughes. The man was everywhere, never still for an instant, and he put his plans for a fighting force into action more impressively than anyone else could have. In a stirring impromptu speech, Hughes exhorted the recruits, many still teenagers, to give it their all, to make their country proud as they squashed the Hun under their feet. Listening to this, Frederick thought of his home country as England, not Canada. He wondered where his childhood friends were, the ones he'd played war with. If he made it overseas, he imagined meeting the boy who'd cut his cheek with the stick. As the crowded camp grew even more congested, he kept company with a group of fellows who'd formed a bond around the Orange Order. Almost to a man they were British born, flecked with a handful of Canadians. They teased him that his da was not from Ulster, but anyone with Irish roots was good enough for them. Frederick enjoyed the sense of camaraderie.

Reveille sounded at daybreak, the bugler a diminutive

corporal from Saskatchewan. The newly enlisted men slept in tents, on ground muddied from so much disturbance. It rained over five inches during September, and everything was a soup of muck. Hauling themselves over to the mess tent, one grumbled, "I hope the grub's better than the sleeping quarters. I had a drip into my boot all night. Just found it now."

"At least you got boots. Mine won't make it to Saturday." Another lifted his foot to show the worn, hobnailed boot, one sole hanging loose, his woolen sock covered in wet clay.

"When do we get uniforms?"

"Who knows? Everyone's still in their civvies," a third man said, nodding around them. "Only the corporals and up have them. We're just privates."

"Mind your privates!" One laughed, clutching at his groin with a high-pitched voice.

They shuffled along in a great snaking line. It began to rain again.

"Crikey, mate, does the sun ever shine here?"

"Should'a brought me rain gear," remarked a tall, dark-haired youth. The others stared at him.

"What did you say?"

"Rain gear. For the rain, like."

"Whe're you from?"

"Newfoundland."

"Where's that?"

"East of here. It's an island."

"Are you part of the Empire?"

"For sure, b'y, for sure. It's the oldest colony, don' y'know."

"I can hardly understand you," another grinned, giving him a playful shove. "What're you doing here?"

"Was workin' on a barge in the St. Lawrence an' decided to join up, is all."

"Ah," the man accepted.

"All sorts here, then, Ned," one said to another. "From all corners of the land."

"There's a group of Frenchies over on the west side of the camp. Wonder why they'd want to join up? Don't seem like their war."

"Hmmm. Could be running from wars at home, eh?"

A man spat into the sucking gunk around their feet. The sound of someone shouting, quickly becoming hoarse, caught their collective attention. A corporal strode along the line, his face red with effort.

"Get in line, you cherries! Stand up properly, what's the matter with you?"

No wonder he was hoarse, as not more than ten percent of the men paid any attention. Between the rain and hunger, they didn't immediately respond to orders, which made the corporal all the redder. Frederick stopped talking and straightened up, his height giving him an advantage over some in front. The line was moving, albeit slowly; nothing to be done for it. The corporal gave up, fuming, and squelched away to another group already in uniform. A few of the recruits had brothers or cousins serving in existing Scottish regiments from Victoria (50th Gordon Highlanders), Vancouver (72nd Seaforth Highlanders), Winnipeg (79th Cameron Highlanders), and Hamilton (91st Argyll and Sutherland Highlanders). These men would be joining the battalions to be sent overseas along with members of the Royal Canadian Regiment (infantry), Lord Strathcona's Horse (armoured), and the Royal Canadian Dragoons (armoured). Lastly, the privately raised and equipped Princess Patricia's Canadian Light Infantry battalion would round out the ranks of the First Canadian Division. Frederick remembered Ma telling him once that her father had taken her to listen to a piper from the Scots Guards. Something stirred in him, thinking of this. The story of Culloden that he'd learned as a boy, tainted as it was by the English interpretation in school, making the Scots out to be cowards, or so he recalled. He hungered to be at the front, to live out his destiny. Frederick wondered if there would be pipers at the European fronts. Ma said the soldiers of long ago in the highlands could do anything, their bravery was legend. She'd recounted that the Jacobites were raised quickly from the clans, proud men who fought to the death. Frederick daydreamed about this and yearned to meet a Scottish soldier. He felt kinship with them in a way that he couldn't clearly define and wondered if any of his ancestors had been at Culloden.

The men recommenced chatting before nodding at the corporal's back. "That's a sergeant, right?" one asked.

"Look for the chevrons on the sleeve, it tells you the rank. Three for sergeant, two for corporal."

"Who told you that?"

"My uncle went to Royal Military College in Kingston."

"I bet he's too smart to come here."

At the end of three hours, almost everyone had been fed his ration of bread, coffee, beans, and cheese. It was eaten quickly as rumbling grew about the lack of potatoes, meat and vegetables that were promised during recruiting. A few talked to one of the cooks, who assured them that the rest was coming, only delayed, and word spread throughout the crowd.

By ten o'clock, the new men were formed into platoons to begin drill training, using wooden cutout pieces in place of the actual weapons that were not yet available for everyone. Between thousands of feet pounding the sodden ground amid shouts of corporals and a brief letup in the rain, a semblance of military order was birthed, or at least conceived. Everyone's lower legs were the same greying brown colour of mire – whatever trousers they wore were soaked through to the skin. There was no way of drying anything save a bit of sunshine and wind. Target practice began in the afternoon at the world's largest firing range at the time, fifteen thousand targets. There were too few rifles to go around, so shooting was done in rotating shifts as long as there was daylight. Trappers and farmers among the recruits proved the best shots, with a small number noted as potential snipers. The Ross Mark III was the firearm outfitting every soldier, Canada's pride in its home-grown weapon of choice, independent of the British kit. Great Britain had pressured the Canadians to use their Lee-Enfield rifle in battle, to maintain common equipment strength among all troops of the Empire, but to no avail. Sam Hughes had the rifle he wanted for his troops. Frederick fired a gun for the first time in his life, ripples of excitement running across his abdomen. He lay spread-eagled on his stomach, a short distance from the man beside him, and the man beside *him*, and so on. Turn of the torso at a thirty degree angle away from the forward line of body symmetry, elbows braced, butt stock tucked tightly into the recess below the coracoid process, breaths managed. This is what Frederick worked on most of all, timing and controlling his breaths. In a short while, his targets were better, although not as good as some he saw. He wanted to be as adroit as the crack shots among them. Bayonet drills were done daily. As Frederick drove his weapon into haystacks while shouting, he wondered what it was like to kill a man; he thought he could do it. The days of playing war as a boy were over.

By the end of the first week, some uniforms arrived in wooden crates but not enough for everyone. More long lines formed as the men picked up their tunics and trousers, caps and puttees. They joked that there were two sizes only, too big and too small. At last everyone had a proper set of combat boots, known then as ammunition boots. For some, it was the first new set of footwear they'd ever owned. Soldiers were sorted into the corps where they'd been enlisted, and Frederick answered to regimental number 36069, Divisional Supply Company. Time seemed to speed up, especially when the contingent prepared to sail for England in early October 1914. Motor transports, artillery, troops, horses, and so much other cargo was loaded, unloaded, and reloaded on vessels in the St. Lawrence River. At last the flotilla of ships, spreading miles in length, left the Gulf and entered the Atlantic, escorted by British warships on the twelve-day crossing in smooth seas. Intending to land at Southampton originally, their destination was changed to Plymouth after reports of German submarines being detected in the English Channel. Back home, John and Mary Dawson worried about their son, and John felt Mórrígan hovering in the air. He'd never told his wife that he'd first sensed the omen on the day of Frederick's birth. One could not change one's fate.

The First Canadian Division landed in England to great welcome and relief. The Dominion had produced enough soldier recruits to ease anxiety in the motherland. Unloading so much war materiel on that scale was a lesson in re-organization, if not disorganization. Horses and weapons and men and equipment were shuffled and reshuffled like so many decks of cards before some semblance of order permitted further loading onto trains. Troops took the seven-hour journey to Amesbury Station (Wiltshire) before disembarking and marching to camps awaiting them on Salisbury Plain, where they would spend the next sixteen weeks. Frederick's group was sent to West Down North Camp, some six statute miles from the village of Amesbury on the River Avon and a mile closer to the ancient monument at Stonehenge. They arrived during a rainstorm. Not long after, members of the Newfoundland Regiment joined them, known as the First Five Hundred.

As they set up cots in their training quarters, the tent walls sagged from the weight of water. It had poured for days on end prior to their arrival. Frederick's feet were soaked through and chilled within minutes. "D'you know how long we'll be in this camp? Will we be moved?" he asked another soldier.

"I heard a few months, but I'm not sure. Depends on the war."

"I didn't come here to drown," grumbled a third man.

The ground inside the tent was a floor of ooze, sucking at their boots as they moved around, placing kit bags on top of other gear in an attempt to keep them dry. The Plain consisted of a large chalk plateau covered with clay turf, preventing water from draining the impervious layer beneath. Everyone was tired by nightfall, and the rain continued all night. Next morning found the squadrons formed up to begin marching drills and tactical manoeuver exercises. This was supplemented by bayonet drills, trench digging, and animal care, as the horses hung their heads and shivered, up to their fetlocks in cold water. By early evening, Frederick stood in the mess line, waiting for boiled potatoes and greasy beef, hiding his misgivings as he scuffed along the queue.

"Christ, they should've brought us boats to get through this," one said.

"Guess it's good training for the trenches."

"We'll be swimming there, mate, if this is what to expect."

Frederick thought of his mother's baking and simple, hearty stews, his mouth watering in memory. He remembered her attention when he came home for tea as a youngster, her hand lightly touching his head as she smiled and set down his plate of food. He would not think of that now. His stomach rumbled. The night before he'd left home for Valcartier, his father and he had drunk a pint of beer together. Homesickness tugged at him as rain lashed the sides of the tents. By the end of the first week on the Plain, he suffered painful muscle spasms and could not feel warm no matter how he tried to alleviate his discomfort. Other than cursing, no one else nearby had expressed anything like Frederick experienced, so he kept silent. The training would continue through the winter, this much he already knew. When the temperature dropped with the months of the calendar, sleet cut through the air like needles, and the thin crust of ice on the ground broke easily from the thousands of feet churning up the mud. Sleep came in fits and starts, sometimes from exhaustion, sometimes from stress. Frederick lay awake on one of many nights, listening to the quiet sounds of masturbation from another soldier. Every morning the men struggled to dress in their damp, muddy uniforms, unable to get them clean enough or dry enough to be comfortable, and many wore the uniform to bed. Sliding in the muck during drill that first week, Frederick went down into the water, twisting his knee as he scrabbled to keep his balance. There was no sick parade for him, just more marching while he gritted his teeth in pain, the knee swollen and stiff. Weapons practice had to be cancelled a number of times when the riflemen could no longer see their targets in the rain. The new Ross rifle, pride of Canadian sponsors, was not up to battle standards, frequently misfiring and overheating when conditions at the front were simulated. It did prove worthy in terms of sniper marksmanship. The British army's Lee-Enfield rifle was more suited to trench fighting. Now the Canadians understood the difference between the two weapons.

Command of the Canadian Expeditionary Force was provided by Lt.-General E.A.H. Alderson, a veteran of the Boer War. The Canadians were a freedom-seeking lot in general, and some chafed at the idea of snapping to attention and following orders whenever it was required. In their distant lands of home, they had the freedom of living in open spaces and forests without constriction. They sneaked away for beer and local delights at nearby taverns whenever possible, indifferent to the consequences; anything was better than the boredom and mud of their training grounds. Going absent without leave (AWOL) was a growing problem for the officers in charge. Frederick infrequently participated in delinquent activities as he struggled to feel at home on the island of his birth. His spoken accent had diminished since childhood, and he felt in between two distinct worlds, not belonging entirely to either. As bad as circumstances were in the camp, he was anxious to get into battle. Survive that and return to Canada, those were his priorities. He wanted to work with motors and fly airplanes, not drown in cold muck. Frederick wondered if he could get to London somehow, despite his military commitment. It was eighty-five miles away, too far to walk, and he couldn't get a horse easily. And what would be the point? To see his former neighbourhood again? He'd heard about young women handing white feathers to eligible men who hadn't joined up yet, the coward's mark of shame.

It rained without cease for eighty-nine of the one hundred and twenty-three days that the Canadians were on Salisbury Plain, the worst winter in more than thirty years. There was nowhere to dry uniforms, nowhere to escape the cold and wet, and inevitably, soldiers became ill. Billets were sought in nearby villages. Men were also moved into wooden huts where possible, which promoted the spread of more viral disease. Given the situation on Salisbury Plain that first winter of the war, officers noted that the Canadians would have been better off completing their more advanced training at Valcartier, where physical conditions were much better. After four months of marching, weapons training, and learning to live together in a semi-aquatic environment, the group was reviewed by King George V and Lord Kitchener in early February 1915. The war was about to begin for the Canadians as they prepared to leave for Flanders, Belgium. Frederick and his fellow soldiers packed up their kit for the last time.

"It can't be any worse over there than it is here," one remarked.

"At least we're not getting shot at," said another.

"I've heard there've been plenty killed in Belgium already."

"You mean ours?"

"Nope, both sides."

"Well, I'm sick of it here. A change will be good."

"Fred, you're quiet."

"What? Oh, just thinking."

His mate chuckled, "Shouldn't be doing too much of that. We just got to do what we're told."

"Maybe, but I've no intention of being anyone's sitting duck."

"You're in divisional supply, right?"

"Yeah. Loading and unloading trains and wagons all day."

"War couldn't run without you."

A soldier from the neighbouring tent joined them as they lugged their duffels outside, careful to keep them up off the soggy ground. He nodded to Frederick's group.

"I hear we're leaving before first light."

"Be good to get out of this bloody cold, even for a few hours."

"Hear anything from the front?"

"Very little. Makes me nervous."

"The brass wants to keep morale up."

"That's easy until you get killed."

"Don't talk like that, you'll jinx us."

"No more than those poor bastards who died here."

"Who?"

"You know, the guy with meningitis, and there was another one. I think he fell into an old well and broke his neck."

"When your number's up, eh? Their war ended early."

The men milled around for some minutes before forming into ranks for the march to Amesbury Station. After that, a train would take them to their points of disembarkation. Frederick moved away briefly by himself, scanning the horizon. He saw nothing different and yet recognized the life change that was imminent. In his mind's eye, he watched his parents worrying across the Atlantic. He'd surrendered his last letter home to the censors yesterday, to be sent to John and Mary now that the soldiers were leaving for the front. Frederick was glad they couldn't visit him and yet he wished that they had. He wanted them to see him in uniform, looking like the leader he'd always dreamed of being. He could strip down a rifle in seconds, though his marksmanship wasn't that much improved since Valcartier. Learning to ride a horse properly wasn't difficult, and he felt sorry for the beasts as they struggled in the mud, same as the men. The company vet had had to shoot more than one with a broken leg. In his imagination, Frederick could picture men in battle without remorse, but it pained him to think of the horses. Wouldn't they be frightened? What about the ones that got wounded by bullets? He'd learned how to lead them with loaded wagons, and the roads were bad, but what if there were no roads at all? A clod of earth hit him in the shoulder, startling him.

"C'mon, Fred, lad, you can dream about girls on the way over."

A soldier held his cupped hands under imaginary breasts, saying, "What I'd give for a handful before we take care of Jerry."

"Don't worry," added another, "I'm sure the villages of France will be happy to supply us with young ladies." He winked.

The first returned, "They've got mobile brothels that travel with the troops, y'know."

"Really?"

"Sure. Men can't spend all day upright in the trenches."

"Some women like it upright."

The corporal strode towards them, his hand up. It was time to go.

Chapter Four

France, 1915-1916

The men were loaded onto vessels of every kind: steamships, cattle boats, merchant ships, whatever was available and ready. Transports of horses, war materiel, officers, and thousands of soldiers made their migration from Avonmouth (Bristol) to St. Nazaire (Brittany) on the west coast of France. They took the long way around, avoiding the English Channel due to German submarines. Seas were rough on the journey, leading most onboard to become ill. Frederick kept his nausea down for part of the trip, remembering his father's tale of leaving Ireland long before, but he did not repeat John's feat of arrival with a full stomach. As with so many others, the young soldier heaved up for hours. Only the lucky ones cast their vomit into the sea – the rest were in the holds. Horses shifted and occasionally buckled as they struggled to keep their balance down below. When they landed at the French port, the war was a lesser priority for the time being with the smell of sick everywhere. After disembarking onto solid ground, preparations were begun for the long traverse northeast that led the men to the killing fields of Belgium. Empty trains were waiting for the ships and ferries that brought munitions in a steady line, one after another.

A few hours' rest and some food brought Frederick back to himself, his stomach settled, although he'd been unable to sleep. He sobered at the thought that he was near to the war now, in the same country, and it was no longer a theoretical proposition. Men died at the front, men were broken, men never came home. Frederick felt very far from his family, from the little shop of Mr. Jones and his attempts to build a fast car on a summer's day. Everything had been left behind to come here, to start a different life, one he thought he'd wanted. Now he was no longer sure but kept his considerations to himself. It was incredible, the sheer volume of provisions that would supply the front. Frederick's unit, the Canadian Army Service Corps, had been initially formed in 1901 with a mandate to provide transport and administrative support to the Canadian army. From small beginnings, by 1914 the corps consisted of three thousand men in eighteen companies. Frederick hadn't been especially keen about enlisting into that service yet neither was he disappointed in not becoming an infantryman. Recruits were assigned where they were needed or had transferable skills. He'd written the words "Auto Mechanic" for his trade on his application as motorized transports were foreseen, if not widely used, and mobile repair would be necessary. The young soldier had learned enough about engines already to give him confidence. As soon as the war began, railroads throughout Europe became critical links in operational success. Every single day, an infantry division required twenty railway wagons packed with rations, motive power, medical supplies, coal, mechanical parts, and ordnance. By the end of the war, fifty wagons' worth was needed daily. Letter mail was viewed as a necessity in maintaining a sense of dignity and care among the soldiers. The knowledge that someone was waiting at home for their safe return made the horror somehow more manageable. Once supplies were removed from the light railway, they were loaded onto donkey- or horse-drawn wagons, which frequently bogged down in the mud and ground churned up from artillery shelling the closer they were to the front. From drop-off locations at forward areas in well protected dugouts, soldiers on the front lines then fell back to retrieve the supplies. Uniforms became threadbare and torn, sleeves loose, tunics missing buttons, puttees ripped. Clothing replacements were provided along with everything else. All of this was ahead of Frederick. He looked back at the horses now as they were led from a holding area towards the rail cars, fretful in their new surroundings; the crossing had been hard on them. A shot rang out as one animal with a broken pastern was put down. The veterinarian officer holstered his pistol, his face without expression. His priority was to keep as many of the animals fit and healthy enough to keep returning to the front, over and over again. More than twenty thousand horses would serve, and they died just as surely as their human counterparts.

Shouts and commands crossed each other as rain began in earnest. Someone grumbled, "Christ, I hoped we'd left this behind us."

Another observed, "I hear it's been raining here for a month." He palmed a cigarette, squinting.

Frederick held out his hand, asking, "Share a fag?"

"Nay, jus' take one." The man offered his open pack.

Frederick inhaled deeply, resisting the urge to cough. He'd smoked before but in entirely different circumstances. This was his first time as a soldier heading into war. He wondered if he'd survive, as anxiety pulled at his edges. He wondered what his little brother, Walter, was doing at this very moment. Would he ever see him again, or any of them? The rain came down harder.

"What route are we on?" someone asked.

"Dunno," another answered.

"Not a spy, are ye?" The smoking man chuckled and nodded at Frederick. "What d'ye think, then?"

Frederick shook his head. "This is my first time on the Continent."

Another joined the two. "We head straight east to Orleans, then north to Paris. From there it's on to Amiens. After that, I don't know. They're building feeder lines to get us up close."

"Who told you that?"

He turned his head half-way back to indicate who. "Sergeant with the horses."

"Must be hell for the poor beasts," Frederick said.

"They don't care, as long as they're fed."

Close behind, a corporal shouted, "Private Dawson! You're headed to Normandy and not for a holiday. Grab your kit and report to the warrant officer."

And so the young man traveled to Cherbourg with others of his unit, where they transferred eighteen-pound artillery shells from ferries to rail cars for days. He couldn't know that one hundred million of the shells would be fired by Great Britain and her Allies over the course of the entire war, averaging forty-three per minute for four years. With all combatants combined, something in the neighbourhood of one billion shells were loosed in the war that would be over by Christmas. The unexploded ones outlived Frederick.

It took almost ten hours to travel from Nantes, France, to the safest distance from the Ypres Salient in Belgium. Trains slowed the last miles, as if they were machines with the human quality of watching for danger. Soldiers went silent as the ground itself seemed full of dread, and the teenagers among them sobered to think that a free world's fate might rest on their shoulders. It was one thing to strut in safety on home soil and quite another to stand face to face with the enemy. No one spoke of desertion, when the penalty for cowardice was the firing squad. They were preparing for the first British offensive of the war; it was March 1915 and it rained. The Germans were dug in and had no intention of giving up one inch of territory. Artillery bombardments left thunderous booms in the atmosphere. From his post in Hazebrouck, fifteen miles behind the front lines, Frederick swallowed his fear as he would continue to do so throughout the war. He would do what was expected of him – if he were capable of more, all the better, but certainly no less than the minimum. A sense of foreboding settled in his mind. He shivered, thinking that he might kill a Hun. One could not predict the exact circumstances but it was possible. He couldn't admit his fear to himself, let alone anyone else. Divisional supply men were not issued with firearms, and there was a story going around about a British officer who'd been disarmed by the enemy and shot with his own pistol. Frederick heard that German field guns could reliably hit a target at eleven thousand yards, over two miles' distance. Men simply vanished into a red mist, and there was nothing left to gather up. In his situation now, Frederick wasn't sure about himself, wasn't sure about anything. Both Allied and German positions had remained stagnant for months. Between the shelling from both sides, the ground itself became largely impassable for man or beast. Snaking, flooded trenches led to siege warfare more than anything else. It was a wet spring in northern France, just as the previous winter had been in England.

Initially, enlisted men and officers were rotated on a forty-eight hour basis to forward locations along the front lines, in order that they first gain experience of genuine battle. As the situation changed, Canadians were then moved to French trenches which were much less secure in terms of enemy fire. These ones had been used as latrines and were full of rats and lice. Rotting corpses lay close by in no-man's land, some in the same trenches where they had died. Along the Ypres Salient, German artillery rained down thunder on Allied positions as casualties mounted; many thousands had already been killed or wounded. Two months after the Canadians had arrived from England, human beings became guinea pigs of the first poisonous gas attack in the world, courtesy of a German chemist named Fritz Haber, in an attempt to end the stalemate. Algerian and French soldiers holding the line fled the greenish-yellow cloud of death as they retreated in terror. Those who couldn't run fast enough grabbed at their throats as they coughed without cease, drowning in their own blood. The cloud began to dissipate as it drifted nearer to the Canadians, and a medical officer, Captain Scrimger of Third Brigade, determined that the gas was chlorine and ordered the men to urinate on their handkerchiefs and tie them over their mouths and noses. This was meant to allow the gas to crystalize before it could be breathed in. The method worked to a degree, as soldiers suffered runny noses, watery eyes, and difficulty breathing, rather than the quick death of the unfortunates ahead of them. More gas was used in the days to come, leaving the men weakened and demoralized as each foot of ground was contested. Frederick's company was run ragged as they tried to keep the front lines supplied. Goals were moving targets those days, trying to ensure that ordnance was where it should be, when it was needed. The lines of battle snaked back and forth and his nerves became badly frayed. One event seared itself in his mind and was as fresh weeks later as the moment it had occurred.

    Their horse had buckled just as they reached the supply depot behind the lines, and the beast fell in front of the heavy wagon, rendering it useless. Frederick and two other soldiers struggled to unload as quickly as possible in the chaos of shelling. He was deafened by a blast not far away and then surprised moments later by an Allied soldier running towards them. The young man (really, a boy) had a wild, glazed look in his eyes and carried his rifle by its strap, the barrel striking his leg repeatedly. Frederick thought the soldier might be wounded but he was moving without apparent difficulty. As the two other supply men concentrated on passing boxes of ammunition between them, not looking, the fellow stopped, chambered a round in his weapon and shot himself in the side of the head with his gun planted upright in the mud. Frederick could not comprehend what he'd just witnessed. Mute, he turned back to the wagon where his comrades carried on as if nothing had happened. Splatters wet the side of Frederick's face, and he wiped the back of his hand across his mouth, tasting dirt and blood. His fingers caught something sharp embedded in the skin of his cheek, a piece of the boy's tooth.

"C'mon, Fred. Hurry up! Never mind him."

Frederick felt a catch in his throat, his breath stopped. This was the first death he'd observed, and he hadn't expected to see it in these circumstances. The weeks that followed blended seamlessly into a version of Rimsky-Korsakov's orchestrally frantic *Flight of the Bumblebee* as the two sides contested over a hill there, a wood here, the men like ants scurrying without pause. Allied commanders did not have timely communication between their battle groups, resulting in delays and positional mistakes that cost lives. Lack of overhead observation had the same effect, and failures added up when compared to the more tightly executed German tactics in some cases. Still, the Canadians were brave; there was no doubting their courage. Frederick spent his days and nights on the verge of exhaustion. When he had a chance to rest, he couldn't relax enough to sleep. He'd lost weight on tinned bully beef and biscuits, his stomach frequently in knots between bouts of diarrhea. The war was nothing like he'd imagined: filth everywhere, unending rain, death part of a normal day, the seeming pointlessness of it all. Constant deafening explosions left everyone jumpy, especially the horses and donkeys. There wasn't time for grand speeches from officers, the sort he'd heard at Valcartier and Salisbury Plain. When Canadians had served in the First Battle of Ypres in 1914, they'd been on the front line for twenty-four consecutive days, and Frederick lost count of his own days now. He thought he'd feel proud and strong, when in reality his only priority was to survive from daybreak to nightfall. His arms and legs were bruised from trying to lead the horses safely when they panicked. When a wagon bogged down in mud, the operation slowed to a standstill, and more than once, he'd carried supplies on his back to pick-up positions for the waiting infantry. He saw the need in the soldiers' eyes, that and a vacant look when they were too exhausted to care. The teenagers who'd joined up were boys no longer. Frederick forced himself forward with his colleagues, day after day, wagon after wagon. He bathed no more often than once every ten days and learned to ignore the body odour. Dysentery, tetanus, and typhoid outbreaks were common. At least he was above the ground. He'd listened to stories about the tunnelers, "moles" they were called, engineers who worked to blow up enemy trenches from below. The idea of it left him weak with claustrophobia. Nineteen-fifteen was the worst year of the war for Britain and its Allies. Frederick was twenty-one years old and could obtain leave back to England within one year. One year.

On a rare sunny day with a brief break in artillery barrage, Private Dawson sat more or less comfortably on a hump of dried mud, smoking, with his back against a wagon wheel. The horse snuffled through its bag of feed, head low. Frederick sighed, inhaling on his cigarette. His mind was empty of horrors for once, and thoughts of his family had been put in a place where they were safe, their latest letter in his tunic pocket.

A fellow soldier collapsed beside him, his own cigarette in hand. "How lucky we are, mate. Time for a proper fag in the sunshine." He let out a long breath and closed his eyes.

"Yeah," Frederick answered. They smoked in silence for a minute or two.

"D'ye ever wonder how we ended up here?" The man squinted through his smoke.

"It's not what I thought back in Canada."

"Ye've got a bit o' accent; where're ye from originally?"

"Enfield. Emigrated in 1905. How 'bout you?"

"I's a Brummie, born an' bred."

"Never been up that way."

"Well, ye wouldn't now, would ye? You's in the south are too good for us," he chuckled.

They continued smoking, relaxing for the first time in days. Frederick felt his eyes grow heavy. He could fall asleep and wake up into a different reality, his head beginning to nod. The man nudged his shoulder.

"Got a girl waitin' for ye back home?"

"No."

"Nay? Good lookin' lad like ye?" The soldier grinned.

Frederick narrowed his eyes. "I'm no pansy."

"Hah," his companion laughed, "Never thought that, mate."

He then offered, "Soon as we return to the world, like, I'll ask my Sally to marry me."

"Oh, yeah?"

"Sure thing. She's a grand lass, a beauty an' all."

"Got a photo?"

"Nay. I had one but it fell outta me pocket an'. . ." He stopped, his face clouding over.

"S'all right, it's okay," Frederick covered for him. They had both seen things they wanted to forget.

"Met Sally jus' before we come over, met her at a dance."

"Dance? Where was that?"

"In the church hall, the one in Amesbury. Didn't ye go?"

"No, I didn't."

"At the Methodist Chapel, it were. We got sandwiches an' tea and talks with the young ladies in between a few turns on the floor. Under watchful eyes, o'course."

Frederick reflected on the fact that his parents were protestant, Church of England. It had seemed important that he adhere to his family's faith background at first, but given his current situation, the idea had become ridiculous. He asked, "How many of you went from the camps?"

"Oh, maybe thirty of us, I'd say. Ye should've come, too. It were nice, considerin' where we are now."

"I won't argue with that." Frederick remembered that time as freezing and wet. He hadn't been feeling sociable.

They finished their cigarettes at the same time and stood. One of Frederick's knees locked and he crooked in pain for a moment.

"Ye all right then?"

"Aye."

"Aye," he repeated. "Sounds like a Scot to me."

"My ma's from there." He straightened fully, pulling down his tunic. It was only since he'd arrived in France that he began using his mother's words occasionally.

The soldier held out his blistered hand. "I's John, by the way. Just started here. They sent me up the line a few hours ago. Me hands are still stiff, sorry."

Frederick shook the man's hand briefly. "John is my da's name. I'm Frederick; Fred, most call me."

"Well, then." He nodded as he began to leave.

Another shipment arrived on the train, ready for unloading. The two men took a step in the same direction before John turned and said, "When I got here, the corporal said ye's a good 'un, Fred," using his name for the first time.

Frederick looked away, embarrassed. The man continued, "He said ye do all yer required to an' then some. The men look up to ye."

"Oh, yeah? Let's go." And Frederick walked away from him, ending the conversation.

"Ye'll be an officer before ye know it!" John laughed.

The sunshine held for most of a day before rain returned. Over his months supplying the front lines, Frederick had found the place in himself where he could continue. He'd already seen dozens of men on the verge of breakdown, or past it. None in the field blamed them, none who knew war. Good soldiers died when their Ross rifles jammed, some being shot even as they cursed their weapon's failure. Frederick could swear that he'd noted more than one smile on a corpse, happy to have left the hell of their world. He did his own job that encompassed so much: evacuating the wounded in wagons returning empty from the line drop-offs, driving the motor ambulance, and fixing its engine when it broke down. He cared for the horses and donkeys, repaired sections of railway track, changed endless wagon wheels, dispensed the rum ration under the watchful eye of a sergeant, and more than once assisted fellow soldiers in their writing letters home (not all were literate). Once as he drifted into sleep, he remembered the soldier John's words about a dance in Amesbury. Frederick imagined being in a church, in the quiet, looking at pretty young women, sitting in clean clothes; he could barely draw the images in his mind. If he survived the war, he would go there, to a dance. A world at peace was a distant memory now. No one talked about the war ending, and many carried talismans of a great variety, believing they would keep them safe for the duration. Some days, Frederick felt like an old man, his joints aching in the damp.

Other days he enjoyed the camaraderie of a group of comrades as they endured the impossible. There was fun at times, practical jokes and card games, a way to find a smile, a chance to put the rifles down. Speaking with someone over tea before carrying his lifeless body by nightfall. Everything was temporary, lived in moments and no more. Frederick developed a nervous tick in his left eye. He was promoted to corporal, his efforts recognized, based upon merit and performance, but also to replace a corporal who'd been killed while being a stretcher bearer. It was the way of the war.

February 1916 ushered in the Battle of Verdun, the longest military campaign in modern history. Through the months of that bloody year, approximately three quarters of a million men were killed, missing, or wounded on both sides. It was not uncommon to see body parts dangling in torn tree trunks, what few trees were left. Soldiers who suffered direct artillery hits ended their lives in a fine wet spray. Rats chewed day and night on the flesh of those who, not so long before, ran freely at home and full of life. The needs of the infantry were enormous and never-ending. Supply division worked around the clock, and there was never time for a cigarette break. On July 1 of that year, the Newfoundland Regiment was decimated at Beaumont-Hamel, at the beginning of the Battle of the Somme. When he first heard the news, Frederick went to his knees, overcome, remembering the tall young recruit from Valcartier whose manner of speech was barely understood by the others. He was sure that the same soldier must've died with all the others. He couldn't sleep at all for a few days, pushing himself to continue his duty as his spirit failed. This was the time when he realized that he could not go on any longer – it felt as if the human species was deliberately sending itself to extinction. He'd written to his parents a month earlier and they hadn't answered. Were letters even getting through anymore? What did anything matter when the world was ending? He hadn't seen the Brummie John in days, and perhaps he'd also died somewhere. It wasn't the thing in the field to form attachments, otherwise grief could not be borne. Frederick struggled to keep the spirits of his unit up, to do his best because there was no other option. He thought about his own death, feeling sorrow not for himself but for his parents. He'd seen so many die, calling for their mothers, one calling for his dog, plenty in silence as the stare to infinity appeared in their eyes. It didn't matter, having a few days away from the front, because he couldn't get beyond the war no matter where he was. Frederick tried thinking about going back home, back to being a mechanic. Tools and engines didn't kill one another, they worked in a symphony of motion, of metal parts, tubes, and springs, all collaborating to make a vehicle go forward. A number of times, Frederick had looked skyward to see a Bristol reconnaissance biplane. He yearned to be up there, away from the mud and death on the ground. Yes, airplanes were also shot down, but he was more willing to die in that way than share the fate of millions of others. One very rainy and cold day in the spring of 1916, a raven flew over his head out of nowhere, unnerving him. It cawed repeatedly as if to get his attention, circling over him twice. Back in Toronto, John Dawson shivered at the same moment; it was the Mórrígan, forecast at his son's birth. By September of that year, Frederick had been promoted to the rank of sergeant, and he applied for a temporary commission in the Royal Flying Corps. He could only hope to be successful. There were no guarantees as to how much longer he would be able to cope with his duties, no matter what England expected.

Chapter Five

England, 1917

Monday, March 12, 1917. Sgt. Dawson sat outside the office of Lt. W.W. Fisher, acting Adjutant General at the British army base at Shorncliffe, Kent. Frederick was as relaxed as he could be for the meeting, having already been approved in terms of his personal character and physical fitness for a temporary commission with the Royal Flying Corps. Away from the battlefields yet so very far from whom he'd been before the war. He still was not used to sitting in a proper chair and not constantly itching with lice. Frederick's body was clean, his eyes clear. His hearing was no longer what it once was, but he'd got away, he was no longer in France. The quieter sounds of life in a different context were something he hadn't adjusted to. A typewriter's key strokes, a door opening, conversation in normal tones. Thunder frightened him. After receiving his initial approval soon after New Year's, he'd been granted leave back to England. Time seemed to speed up then, and Frederick's dream of flying airplanes was much closer than his daydreams about it had been in the muck and blood of his army service. The sergeant major at Service Corps had praised him for doing his duty above others, of risking more for the men; he'd never actually spoken to Frederick but relied upon the unsolicited words of others in completing his written report. Here at Shorncliffe, Dawson was considered British rather than Canadian, as if the previous dozen years of his life were merely an interlude in a foreign land. Frederick tugged gently at his uniform collar as ague threatened to derail him this important day. He was a victim of trench fever as so many millions were on the battlefield. A bacteria transmitted by body lice, it left sufferers with headaches, fever, muscle aches, and dizziness. Some endured severe pain in the thighs and legs, particularly in the shins. It was a mystery early in the war, until its secrets were finally unraveled in 1918. Frederick had endured bouts of fever and had been off duty a number of times in France, but his suffering was no greater than anyone else's. Following a few days of torment, he normally recovered and returned to duty, multiple times. Now that he'd left the Continent, he didn't expect to experience symptoms any longer; however, the familiar signs of illness were upon him once again.

On his leave, he'd chosen to return to Amesbury, two years after his training with the Canadian Expeditionary Force on Salisbury Plain. The surrounding small towns and villages had financially benefited by providing respite for military troops. In his uniform, no one questioned Frederick as he walked along the high street, stopping for a rest and simple meal at the New Inn. He'd been feeling well that day and enjoyed the warmth of the building's interior, a log fire burning against a gloomy day outside. The landlord's wife bustled about in the kitchen, taking his order for shepherd's pie and a pint of ale. His mind roamed everywhere and nowhere at once, the images of war always behind his eyes. There was no way to erase them. After ten minutes, a young woman came with his food. Frederick hadn't thought anything of her, aware of her presence, just a typical serving maid like any other. As she drew near, he noted her height, almost the same as his own, and as he looked into her face, inhaled softly at her beauty. Her eyes met his for the briefest moment before she set down the plate and ale. Thick dark hair and darker eyes, skin as smooth as porcelain, sensual mouth, strong nose – she didn't look at him again as he stared. Black Irish, Da had called them, women with those looks. Centuries before, Moorish folk had come to the isles, leaving behind their genes expressed by the colouring that stood before him; no pale English rose this one. Frederick moved his forearm towards her and she smoothly slid away from the table, turning her back. He didn't see her anymore as he finished his meal and left.

Sitting became intolerable outside the adjutant Fisher's office now and Frederick stood stiffly, his right thigh muscle seizing in pain. Today of all days. He would have to hide his discomfort, holding his jaw rigid until the spasm passed. Frederick drove other thoughts into his mind, to take away from his troubles. He remembered seeing the Black Watch regiment of Scotland at the front and later someone told him there was a Black Watch regiment there from Canada as well. Ma had told him of the piper she'd listened to as a child, and he wondered if they played the same tunes then and now. Many pipers had died in the war already. Moments of deaths flashed through his mind's eye, the smell of congealing blood, death rattles in a throat, broken arm of a stretcher, splinted by a rifle with its stock shot off, just enough to carry the wounded back across the line to safety. Some soldiers slipped away soundlessly and others thrashed as if wrestling the beast. He was safe and warm at the moment but the war occupied his brain and he was still in France. Frederick no longer believed in safety.

Firm boot-steps sounded on the other side of the door before it opened.

"Dawson?"

"Sir." Frederick clicked his heels together and saluted. Sweat ran down his back, pooling at his waist under his service dress jacket.

"Come in, let's have a chat."

Within weeks, Frederick was based at 34 Training Wing, Stockbridge, Hampshire, where he flew from air fields at Lopcombe Corner and Chattis Hill. The Sopwith 1 Strutter biplane proved a reliable craft and quite easy to fly for the student pilot. Now a Second Lieutenant, Officer Dawson at last felt some of his stress dissipate in the slipstream as he practiced take-offs and landings for hours each day. His fever had finally abated and he permitted himself some contentment as the little craft left the ground, almost eager to get into the air. The war seemed a long ways away and was less prevalent in his thoughts, at least for the time being. After six hours of instruction, Frederick took his first solo flight, noting that the training field was only fifteen miles from the town of Amesbury and the girl he hadn't forgotten at the inn. He flew with confidence in his new role, and the skill seemed to come naturally for him, as his instructor noted in the log book. Those first hours alone in the sky were the best he'd felt since leaving Canada. He'd graduated to flying a single-seater Sopwith Pup (Scout) which he liked even better. It felt like an extension of his body, and he simply willed the airplane to wherever he wanted to go; there was no need for strong-arming the controls. Staying within the airspace boundaries as his training required, he could see Stonehenge in all but the worst of weathers. There was something about the monument that calmed him, either the great age of the stones or perhaps their circular permanence in the landscape. War was insanity yet the huge blocks were real and would outlast the war.

A few times, he found himself crying while in the air, that and occasionally laughing, finally experiencing the psychological relief he so badly needed. A soldier could never show weakness, that's what he'd been taught, but alone in the beauty of the sky, there was no one to see or judge him. The sorrow and shock of what he'd witnessed near the front lines for almost two years settled in a place where he could touch it and not be drowned. He had been drowning when he left France.

His Pup touched down gently, its wheels almost kissing the grass before he taxied the craft to park. Rising up from the seat to deplane, Frederick took a deep breath and looked towards the end of the airfield. In a few hours he'd be in the air again. His leather boots sank into the soft ground as he stood by the warmth of the engine.

"Nice landing, Dawson, you've aced those, I think," said his instructor, smiling.

"Aye, I mean, yes. Thank you," Frederick answered.

"We'll get you started on navigation on Monday. How're your map reading skills?"

"Pretty good. I need more practice."

"And you were a mechanic before joining up, is that right?"

"I worked on motor cars back home. I drove the ambulance in France and kept the engine serviceable."

"Good, that's good. You're just what we need. You'll be doing artillery spotting and scout work as soon as we can get you trained."

"How long with that take?" Frederick asked.

"They want at least six months, if not more, but there's a real need for you chaps now, more than ever. Since you're doing so well, I think we'll cut it down for you."

"Yes, Flight Sergeant."

"Okay, then. Take a few hours off and report back at fifteen hundred hours." The man turned to leave.

"One minute, Flight Sergeant. Will I be issued a dress uniform?"

The instructor squinted at him. "Somewhere you need to be?"

An unwelcome blush coloured Frederick's cheeks and he rubbed his face, hiding it. Now the instructor smiled. "A girl, is it?"

His blush deepened as the flight sergeant chuckled. "I thought so. Where is she?"

Frederick felt comfortable enough to confess. "She's at the New Inn, Amesbury."

"Ah, a serving wench."

Frederick bristled and began, "No. . ." but was interrupted.

"Nay, don't fret lad. You'll have your time to see her. But don't get serious over a girl; we need your attention in the war. Time for all that later."

"Yes, Flight Sergeant."

Frederick took a relaxed walk around the airfield, daydreaming about his lass as he thought of her, although he didn't even know her name. She could be promised to someone else. At the age of twenty-three, he felt a yearning for a partner like he'd never known before. Growing up, it was all motors and adventurous friends and getting used to a new country. The war had consumed everything since, and he needed to create a space for something else. Someone else. He wished he could see his parents again. No one knew how long the war would last and no one talked about it ending. It would soon be three years since the beginning and millions had already died. It didn't bear thinking about, yet it was the only thought in the minds of so many.

Two weeks later he got a leave pass for twenty-four hours and took the train to Amesbury. It was a lovely day in spring, with sunshine after a light rain. The winter had been hard with heavy amounts of snow from time to time. Frederick wore his pressed uniform and called in at his destination, the New Inn.

He wasn't sure whether the young woman would be there but he was used to taking chances. As he had months earlier, he ordered shepherd's pie and a pint of ale. This time someone else brought his food, another girl, shorter and not nearly as pretty to look at. He thanked her as she set the plate down and nodded with a slight smile.

"I was here before and there was a tall girl with dark hair. D'you know her?"

The girl blushed. "You must mean Kathleen."

"Aye, that's her." He pretended to know her name. "Is she here today?"

"No, she's gone to see her friend, Alice."

"Oh, will she be back later?"

"No, sir." The girl blushed again. "Alice is in London."

Frederick paused, "It's all right, she wasn't expecting me today. Can I leave a message?"

"Surely, sir."

"Tell Kathleen that Frederick stopped by and looks forward to seeing her again."

"Is that all?"

"Thank you. I'll enjoy my pie now." With that, he dismissed the girl, who hurried away, turning her head to the side as if for one last look.

The pie was delicious, almost as good as his ma's. He ate with relish, thinking of the tins of bully beef and biscuits he'd lived on so recently and hoped to never see (or smell) again. No matter about Kathleen, he wasn't about to give up. Frederick enjoyed a cigarette before catching the return train two hours later. During the ride with few passengers, he found his thoughts skittering everywhere, like a moving picture running before his eyes. There were images of death and dying, men pushed past their physical limits, also the sweet beauty of a tin whistle played while he and his unit waited for the trains of supplies. He'd worked all locations between the Channel coast and as close to the front lines as anyone dared to go who wasn't actually fighting. The muscles of Frederick's back and arms were growing softer again, now that he no longer worked on the wagons and hauled frightened horses through mud for hours on end. Occasionally shivers tore through him, leaving sweaty tremors behind, and they still came to this day. He was grateful that no one at flight school had picked up on them yet. He was in the right place, he was sure of it, and planned to graduate just as soon as he was able to. What a great relief and joy it was to soar above the ground, to see things from high up, as if he were one chosen. Frederick would not squander his opportunity, and he was glad for his change in circumstances. It was temporary only, on loan during the war, but with any luck, the words "for the duration" on his acceptance meant that he would end his time in service as a pilot. The thought of dying in an airplane held no fear compared to his constant anxiety in the rats, blood, and lice of ground war. There was something poetic about meeting death in air combat or by accident, and he was unafraid. The flight sergeant was a good man, one who recognized him for who he was. He spoke with an Irish accent, something the army hadn't got out of him although he'd been in England close to twenty years; he'd told Frederick this as they waited for fog to clear one morning. This was also when Frederick heard about the Easter Rising the previous year, when Irish nationalists launched an armed revolt against British rule. James Connolly's Irish Citizen Army joined the Irish Volunteers in their leaders' efforts to proclaim an independent Irish republic. There was street fighting and long-range gun battles, but in the end, they were no match for British artillery. Connolly was wounded before being arrested when it was all over. One month later, he was one of six rebellion leaders executed by firing squad; they'd all signed a new Proclamation of the Irish Republic. The flight sergeant's words failed him temporarily as he crossed himself for the hundreds of his own country who had died. What was the point of war with Germany, when those from his homeland were killing each other? No matter where the Irish were in the world, their hearts remained on their island, he told Frederick, as if it weren't obvious. Suddenly in his mind, the student pilot was at home with his parents, listening to Da reading the papers about the Irish Republican Brotherhood. All in a place he'd never been to. Perhaps one day he would go there to understand the Irish soul. Da always seemed tied to spirits, something he sought to hide. Ma was the practical one.

The train began slowing as it neared Salisbury station. Without deciding beforehand, Frederick made the spontaneous choice to get off at that location and walk the half-dozen miles back to Lopcombe Corner airfield via the London Road. The day was fine, still sunny with a pleasant breeze hinting at summer's warmth to come. He enjoyed walking on firm ground, smoking at his leisure, and eating decent food. Thoughts of Kathleen roamed through his memory as he stepped down onto the platform. There were other soldiers there, only a handful. He nodded to them as he walked past. A cramp seized his back and he sat ramrod straight on a bench until relief came. Frederick wondered who Alice was in London, the friend that Kathleen had gone to see. Did young women travel without chaperones now? Had she been alone? It felt as if he'd missed the world going by when he was in France. A matronly woman settled beside him on the bench, holding her traveling bag in her lap.

"Are you from here, then?" She smiled at him.

"No, I'm on a day's leave, just visiting." He wished she would go away.

"Ah, then." She noted his uniform. "What service are you with?"

Frederick mentally gritted his teeth. "I'm learning to fly,

near Stockbridge."

The woman swelled. "Oh, that's wonderful! I've seen the planes flying – they're marvelous but very dangerous, I'm sure."

"Not as bad as that." He wasn't going to give her any more until an idea came to him. "Say, I have a friend going to visit a young lady in London. Can you tell me, are women working there now?"

"Oh, yes, I'm surprised you didn't know. They're doing all kinds of things, with the men all gone to war. Let's see, there are lorry drivers, mechanics, radio operators, even spies, I've heard, but that's hard to believe, isn't it? Not the sort of work for anyone of proper breeding. Of course, the great majority of them work at the munitions factory in Woolwich. Personally I don't think women are strong enough for that kind of thing, but we're in different times now, aren't we?"

His back pain loosening and more than ready for silence, he stood. "Thank you, and good day." He tipped his hat.

As she started to say something else, Frederick took one step away, then another, and it was easy to be on his own.

April arrived with more inclement weather, sleet and rain and snow. It reminded Canadian servicemen in Europe of the misery of Salisbury Plain two years before. Aircraft training was delayed a number of times, as pilots waited for breaks in the low clouds. It was canceled for two entire days once after a snowfall, as the landing field was cleared by hand. Finally a spell of bright conditions returned as the flight sergeant and his pupil walked together to the two-seater for his map navigation test. They turned back at shouts from the open hangar.

"Wait! Wait!" A young clerk ran towards them, holding a piece of paper.

"Yes, what is it?" the flight sergeant asked, his clipboard held under an arm.

"Here sir, I mean, Flight Sergeant." He held out the paper,

leaning forward with his hands on knees to catch his breath.

The instructor held the paper, moving his mouth silently as he read.

"News of the war?" Frederick asked.

"Well, I'll be," the sergeant answered.

The young lad stood up straight. "We did it! We did it! The Canadians."

"Eh?" said Frederick, "What's that, then?"

Now his instructor smiled. "Look at that, Second Lieutenant Dawson," addressing him formally. "Your Canadian Corps has taken Vimy Ridge. It's about time we had some good news."

Frederick heard nothing as his mind cast back to the 1915 failed attack that left thousands dead. He'd helped some of the wounded as they sprouted blood from machine-gun fire, bodies leaking like sieves. A soldier with his foot gone. One stretcher bearer shot while he evacuated a man, the stretcher dropping the patient out onto the ground as he slumped face-first into the mud, suffocating.

"Come along, then, Dawson!" his instructor said brightly. "You look as if you're a thousand miles away."

The clerk piped up. "First pigeons just returned a few hours ago, confirmed by Morse code."

"Thank you, son," the sergeant replied. "You may go now."

"Of course." The young man couldn't keep the grin off his face as he turned and jogged back to the hangar.

"This is worth a pint or two, first victory in a long while," the sergeant offered. He broke into a broad smile. "So what d'you consider yourself now, English or Canadian?"

Frederick laughed. "Somewhere in between."

His instructor slapped him on the back. "Let's get you qualified before the war ends."

Frederick's opportunity to see Kathleen arose on Empire Day 1917, when Amesbury was hosting a fête at the village hall with tea and dainties, children's dances, recitations, and all manner of patriotic activities. It was a time to celebrate the great nation's family around the world. As every child was taught in school, the sun never set on the British Empire. The young pilot had visited the New Inn once more since he'd missed his girl the first time. Frederick had been so bold as to enquire for her when a different person served him, and so Kathleen came into the room, stopping when she saw who he was. In the briefest moments available, he'd asked her to come walking with him, this tall girl of such dark beauty. She murmured yes before following her mother's call from upstairs and leaving him a second time with no conversation. Frederick was intrigued and more determined than ever to get to know her. Since returning to England, he'd grown used to young ladies bolding smiling at him, baring their teeth, their eyes lit up with hope of his attention. Kathleen, whoever she was, gave an air of non-acquiescence, where he would have to earn her affections. If they never met again, he would be the one with regrets. He wasn't about to give up, and his luck had turned with news of the celebration. She and her sisters helped with the serving for the first hours before handing off their duties to another shift of workers. As arranged, he met her at two o'clock sharp outside the inn and offered her his arm when they set off. One or two nodded to her with her handsome pilot; she nodded in return but didn't speak. They strolled along Church Street and stopped on the bridge over the River Avon.

Frederick inhaled deeply. "What a lovely day to be out."

Kathleen looked at him briefly. Unlike many of her suitors, he was taller than she, something she approved of. "T'is," was all she said.

Water rushed under the stone bridge, its current powerful from the recent rains. Frederick smiled. He was just where he wanted to be, in the sunshine with a pretty girl.

"Is it your parents who run the inn?"

"My father's passed away, and we help keep it going with our mother."

"I'm sorry. And who is we?" he asked.

"There are four sisters including myself. I have three brothers as well."

"Goodness, a fine family for size." They started moving again, turning to the Stonehenge road. Frederick began again, "D'you work full-time at the inn?"

"No," she replied, "I've been teaching at the primary school for two years. I'm not to keep company with men." She giggled for the first time.

"Oh?"

"It's one of the rules."

"Is that what we're doing? Keeping company?" He smiled broadly, tucking her hand more firmly into the crook of his arm. "Well, let's keep company then."

They walked together for thirty minutes and she learned that he would be finished training in a few weeks and sent to France. "When will you have leave to return?"

"I don't know. I expect some months later."

"You've heard of Albert Ball?"

"Yes, of course. He's known everywhere and has been awarded the Victoria Cross. Near the top of the list for number of enemy kills. I'd like to meet him."

"Such a brave young man, the best pilot ever they say."

"We'll see about that." He squeezed her gloved hand, then added gravely, "There won't be many better."

All too soon for both of them, the promenade was over. Frederick held the door open for Kathleen as she was returned home to the inn. "I'll come again as soon as my training's over, all right?"

"I'd like that," she replied. They touched hands very briefly before parting.

The same week that Frederick passed his written exam and flight test, he was posted to Gosport, Portsmouth, a half-hour flight south of his Hampshire training base. He received certification on the Nieuport 17 airplane before flying one to France three days later. Frederick hid his initial sense of intimidation at flying for the sole purpose of shooting down German planes and soon found that he loved his time in the air when going crosscountry. There were other aircraft to fly as well – the Sopwith Pup and Camel, plus the Bristol Scout – and he carried out reconnaissance missions and learned to use an aerial camera before participating in combat. Pursuing an enemy fighter or trying to avoid one took all his attention, and he reminded himself constantly to check his fuel gauge in between firing the Lewis gun or else risk running dry before landing. On the ground, Frederick was friendly enough with other pilots, but with an average life expectancy of eleven days to no more than a few weeks in their line of work, no one got too close to anyone else. Everyone smoked and few conversed socially. It was an altogether different form of war, Frederick decided, having the opportunity to look down on the battlefields while remembering looking up at the planes that had flown over them the previous year. He'd wanted to become an airman and now he was. Days and weeks passed quickly and no one had shot him down yet. Frederick carried his good luck charm with him at all times, a locket that Kathleen had given him when he'd asked her for a memento before he left. He intended to marry this girl as soon as possible, and his first leave pass was granted in late September. Returning to Amesbury, he spent one night at the New Inn, anxious to speak to Mrs. Corp, Kathleen's mother, so that arrangements could be made. The woman was both accommodating and all business at the same time; Frederick could sense the same traits in his intended. Wedding banns had enough time to be read (three Sundays in a row) before the marriage could take place, making the date November 6, 1917, for their nuptials. After surviving his second tour as an RFC pilot, Frederick returned to wed his Kathleen, in a small ceremony in the ancient Anglican parish church of St. Mary and St. Melor. The ceremony was witnessed by Kathleen's younger sister, Amy, and Herbert Wright, Mrs. Corp's nephew. On that day, Canadian troops captured the village of Passchendaele, Belgium. There was no honeymoon, as Frederick returned to France two days later.

Late autumn brought discontent to the new bride, still living with her family at the inn, missing her husband and afraid for his life. So many had died already, and now he was in the most dangerous role of them all. She tried to fill her days with purpose but was absent-minded in tasks, snapping at her sisters. Each afternoon Kathleen went for a walk by the river, remembering her infrequent strolls with Frederick only a few months before. Perhaps she'd rushed into marriage without enough consideration, but she couldn't deny her pleasure in seeing the looks of envy on other young women as they walked about. He was a handsome man doing an exciting job for the war effort. It was her duty to wait at home for his safe return.

For his part, the early elation of being a scout and combat pilot had worn thin. Adrenalin gripped Frederick the entire time he was aloft, leaving him exhausted later. His autoimmune function worked in overdrive, possibly contributing to the new and painful condition of rheumatism. That and flare-ups of trench fever gave him bouts of shivering and sweats; at times his headaches were severe enough to keep him grounded. The young pilot worried constantly about being branded a coward. He'd already met pilots Mick Mannock and George McElroy, both of whom he considered heroes. Once after a bad scare courtesy of a German Fokker pilot, Frederick soiled himself just before landing safely, unsure whether his physical disgrace was from stress or from ingesting the spray of castor oil from the engine.

He soon took to the accepted habit of downing shots of brandy or whiskey as soon as he landed, his knees painfully swollen. Weather reports, map reading, German Zeppelins, accuracy in dropping bombs, being shot at by anti-aircraft artillery, around the clock flight operations; the conflict never ended. Frederick had long since left behind the impressionable boy that he'd been in Valcartier, brimming with anticipation to go to war. Occasionally, he was able to work on airplane engines when he couldn't fly, a gratifying break from the flight stress and a chance for more rest. There was little pushback from the mechanics as they respected his skill with motors and his obvious experience. Despite being an officer, Frederick had no qualms about sitting with maintenance crews when they enjoyed a smoke together. Everyone knew that pilots were killed regularly and another pair of hands was welcomed. Over the coming weeks, his physical symptoms worsened, and back spasms terrified him into believing that he would be unable to control his machine safely in the air. Determined to carry on, he flew more hours, to the point where he occasionally needed assistance to deplane after landing. The last straw was a vicious bout of ague in December, as Frederick shivered uncontrollably during flight and barely landed without crashing. He'd had enough and saw the medical officer to apply for sick leave. Taken off the line, the young pilot felt a complete failure. Frederick wanted to fly. He'd put up with everything so that he could fly, and now it was over, at least for the time being. Christmas was coming, and he hadn't got leave to return to his wife. She'd sent a letter a few days previously, professing her love and wanting him to come home, adding that she couldn't bear to be without him over the holidays. An armistice had been signed by Russia and the Central Powers, and those who dared to think, hoped that perhaps, just perhaps, one could envision an end to the war. Frederick mulled this over constantly, unable to get it out of his mind. He yearned to be warm and dry for a twenty-four hour period, something that he hadn't experienced often in the past three years, to be in a place without the noise of war. He wanted to be a proper husband to Kathleen and make a life for both of them. There was so much to consider and he was so bloody sick and sore most of the time, it left his spirit in tatters. Frederick understood that he was a changed person because of the war, and he could not return to who he had been in Canada. In the end, he spent Christmas Day near Popperinghe, west of Ypres; he'd last flown there on December 11. Just before New Year's 1918, he crossed the English Channel and reported to Caxton Hall (Westminster, London) and received his first medical board examination. During this time, Frederick stayed at the Dean Hotel on Oxford Street. The symptoms listed for Second Lieutenant Dawson were: myalgia, rheumatism, trench fever, anemia, tremors, headaches, inability to sleep, severe pain in back, knees, and thighs, and poor circulation. The report ended with an assessment of degree of disability, followed by a recommendation for Frederick to recuperate on the south coast of England. Instead he was sent immediately to Furness Auxiliary Hospital in Harrogate, near the city of Leeds, some two hundred miles north of London. His mood deepened with every mile further away from Kathleen, after their brief encounter at the Dean Hotel as he waited to be sent north. Kathleen had come to see him there but left after less than an hour. She didn't touch him and said that she was going to see her friend, Alice, at the munitions factory. His wife walked away confidently in all her graceful beauty, not looking back, her skirt daringly short at mid-calf, hat set just so on her regal head. Gone was the serving girl at the New Inn.

Frederick James Dawson at about age twenty-five.

Kathleen Mary Corp at about age eighteen; the name is in her own handwriting.

Chapter Six

England, 1918

Frederick's interval at Harrogate was where neurologic symptoms of trench fever caught up with him, leaving behind depression and anxiety that took hold for days at a time. He also suffered a persistent rash on his torso, and in his worst moments, imagined that he might have been better off being shot down over France, rather than continue living in his present condition. Kathleen would not be visiting him here, and he didn't know how long he might stay. The war could continue for months or even years, with him spending all or most of it in bed. Frederick's physical tremors had finally abated, and the food and care he received from optimistic nursing sisters encouraged a confident recovery. Pain in his back and thighs eased, allowing him to go for walks eventually, with a cane at first and then unaided. He'd told the medical officer in London that he'd be glad to continue serving in a warmer and drier climate, which unfortunately didn't exist in Europe. The weather remained consistently colder and wetter than normal, contributing to the misery of all parties in the war. With time on his hands and little to occupy them, Frederick read the newspapers daily, both new and older editions, whole stacks of them. There he learned of the Canadian indigenous sniper nicknamed Peggy, properly Francis Pegahmagabow. The article said that he'd traveled overseas from Valcartier in early October 1914, in the same convoy that Frederick had gone with. Frederick didn't remember seeing any Native Indians (as they were then called) at all at the training camp, expecting them to look or act differently from the rest of the recruits. The Germans were said to be terrified of this sniper Peggy, whom they believed was actually a ghost. The man was credited with more kills than anyone and had been decorated. Frederick was impressed and would like to have met him, recalling the lack of his own target shooting skills. He also read about the troopship *Tuscania* being torpedoed in the Inner Hebrides, and women being given the right to vote in parliament, though without the same equality as men. Everyone at the hospital was talking about one or the other event. In his boredom, Frederick also wrote letters home, and it seemed to take ages for his parents' letters to get back to him, routed through London. The things they talked about were literally a world away. His moods stabilized and his nightmares of France became less frequent. Frederick began to fantasize about secrets trysts with his wife, since no conjugal visits were permitted in Harrogate. As his health continued to improve, he grew frustrated and impatient to be back in the world.

In March, Frederick returned to the Dean Hotel, to await word of what the Royal Flying Corps would do with him after his recovery; for the time being he was in limbo. He wrote a number of letters to the air ministry personnel office, trying to discover their plans for him or at least get them to hurry up with an answer. Finally, in late April, he received notice that he would be posted to where he had started out flying, at 34 Squadron in Stockbridge, Hampshire. He was forthwith assigned to be a training instructor for new pilots. Part of him was glad and another part wished he were returning to France. Baron Manfred von Richthofen, the German air ace, had been shot down and was dead. American troops had arrived in Europe and the tides were at last turning in favour of the Allies. Events of the war changed by the minute, and Frederick felt very much sidelined.

Settling in again at the training base took less time than he thought, since he'd graduated from there only the prior year. And yet what had happened to him in that year had aged him far more than twelve months might have done in a different life. His walk was stiff occasionally and his back acted up every so often, but overall, his health was much improved from when he'd left France the previous winter. Frederick enjoyed a drink and a smoke, the same as the other men. He enjoyed not having to worry about being shot down multiple times per day, where here the greatest threat to personal safety was caused by the actions of inexperienced student pilots. Flight training was also being set up in Canada, at Camp Borden in Ontario, one hundred and twenty miles north of Toronto. A letter arrived from John Dawson that spring, asking his son whether he might apply to be an instructor there? The carefully worded pages betrayed only a little of John's anxiety over his son, and Frederick had told his parents almost nothing of his health concerns and recovery. With Kathleen close by again, he did not want to return to his North American home until the war was over. It took three weeks before he got his first two days' weekend leave, and he took the train to Amesbury without delay. The village was busy, where army officers and other ranks strolled through the streets, making the most of a sunny day. Australians and New Zealanders undertook training on Salisbury Plain now, as well as Canadians. Frederick took the only empty table at the New Inn and ordered his usual shepherd's pie and pint of ale. He could hear kitchen noise from where he sat and had to restrain himself from getting up to look for Kathleen – he hadn't contacted her to let her know he was coming. Other patrons in the room were a boisterous lot, with laughter and ribaldry keeping the staff busy and the serving girls on their guard. A table of officers smoked furiously, their heads bent together in low speech. Just as he was about to give up on his wife's anticipated presence, there she was, entering the room with someone else's order. Frederick began to rise from his seat, when he saw a look that passed between her and one of the officers. It was over in a second, but there was no mistaking what he'd witnessed: a flash in her eyes, almost daring desire, before her face closed down. She noticed Frederick and nodded, breaking into a wide smile without embarrassment, as if he were anyone else and not her lawful husband. In spite of his silent dismay, he stood, waiting for her to come to him. She set down the order and took the steps to his table.

"What a nice surprise! You didn't tell me you were coming," she said.

They stood together awkwardly for a moment. He would not kiss her here. Another order shouted from the kitchen broke their reverie. "I'm needed," was all as she turned.

"Wait. Are you working tonight?" he asked.

"I'll be here until eight o'clock." Kathleen took a step away from him.

"We'll go for a walk then," he spoke with authority.

"Yes." And she was gone.

Their walk was tense and he felt a reluctance about her, something indefinable. They were married, what else could she possibly want? She didn't appear to need him as a wife should, or that was his impression. He didn't ask about the scene at the inn, didn't threaten or cajole her into submitting to him. They kissed briefly before he returned alone to the platform, smoking while waiting for the train.

Back at the airfield, he continued to be bothered by the exchange she'd shared with the army officer, whoever he was. He wanted to dismiss the situation but could not, and it ran in a continuous loop through his mind. Frederick and his wife had not had enough time to be together the way he wanted that weekend, away from everything and free for each other. He'd believed that by surprising her, she would rush into his arms and into the marriage bed that they'd shared so little of. It was the damned war, affecting everything. It wasn't his fault that he was sent to recuperate at Harrogate and not either of their faults that she didn't visit him there. He would contact her again in a few weeks, suggesting they go to Brighton for a day, war or not. Frederick's self-esteem was knocked about and he was very uncomfortable. Kathleen should have waited patiently for his return, no matter how long it took, not entertain the idea of attracting (or being attracted to) another man. He worked the student pilots hard, pushing them to perfect take-offs and landings, over and over again. His reputation on the flight line became that of a strict taskmaster. At last Kathleen and her husband took a few days together, visiting Bournemouth in mid-June. On a Sunday evening they listened to a concert on the pier, enjoying fine weather and each other's company. Frederick set aside his unrest while they were there, settling into confidence in his marriage. They would have children, they would be a family; he both wanted and needed her near him. The war couldn't last forever. One month later, another pilot instructor from the base visited Amesbury, a popular and nearby spot to unwind from grueling work hours for military servicemen. He came to see Frederick as they walked back to the hangar together after the training day had ended.

"Another week to go. Let's hope some of these youngsters will get air time."

"What d'you mean?" Frederick asked.

"The war, of course. We may just get them proficient and then there's no use for them. We *are* making gains, you know."

"I doubt anyone wants the war to continue."

"I didn't mean it that way." With steps to go before they separated, the instructor stopped as Frederick continued ahead. Then he stopped as well, looking back.

"Anything wrong?"

"Look, old boy, it may be none of my business, but. . ."

Now he had Frederick's full attention. "Out with it, man." His voice carried an edge.

"I was relaxing in Amesbury, you know, just walking around, and I saw your wife." He'd seen the full-length photograph of Kathleen that Frederick kept in his room. Fetching and tall, alluring in her dark beauty.

Frederick waited for him to continue. "So?"

He looked down. "Well, she was with someone, an army officer from the camp."

Frederick asked quietly, "What were they doing?"

"Walking arm in arm, down by the river."

"What did you do?"

"Nothing. What could I do? For all I knew, they might have been related to one another, cousins or siblings."

Frederick stood fuming, his face fierce. A cuckold, that's what he was. Shame engulfed him, an affront to his manhood.

Embarrassed, his companion said, "It might be nothing, they didn't touch or kiss. They were just walking together."

Without another word, Frederick left the airfield and took the next train to Amesbury, begging twenty-four hour's compassionate leave. His back ached the entire journey. It was a good day following, and he spent all of it with Kathleen. She responded to his attentions with ardour and he kept her close by his side at all times, not permitting any opportunity for her to look elsewhere.

They didn't speak of the war or the army camp or the soldiers frequenting the inn. Frederick woke from a bad dream in the night, his legs tangled in the bedsheets. Sweating, he waited for his breath to calm against the warmth of her long body against his, and she didn't wake. He couldn't help but appreciate finding himself lying naked with a beautiful woman in a warm room, all the horror of the front lines receding, at least temporarily. Her long, thick hair lay lose on the pillow, her face turned towards him, breathing gently. At times of stress, he still felt the awful itch of the lice, imagining them tracking over his skin and leaving their filth behind. He'd heard that doctors believed those pests were the cause of trench fever. Frederick had seen corpses covered in maggots, the lice literally jumping ship once their hosts were dead. Maybe the doctors were right: cadavers didn't suffer from trench fever. The next day, he returned to the airfield and promised to come and see Kathleen each time he could get a pass. Now that the Allies were making real headway in the war, there would be less need to train pilots. Flight operations had changed from being a division of the army to becoming the brand new Royal Air Force. Frederick loved flying but was glad he didn't have to drop bombs anymore, even on the enemy. He concentrated on his work and not what his wife might be doing in his absence.

The summer passed quickly, and when the Hundred Days Offensive began in August, it marked the beginning of the end of military conflict across Europe. The Allies broke through the Hindenburg line a month later, followed by a peace proposal sent to American President Woodrow Wilson in October. Germany and the Austro-Hungarian Empire had had enough. On November 11, 1918, the war was officially over. In the six-hour time period between the signing of the armistice and the end of hostilities, more than two thousand additional soldiers died. Germany did not swallow the humiliation of defeat easily, and the Treaty of Versailles signed in June 1919 affected the future plans of a young Austrian corporal named Adolf Hitler. Happy celebration ensued early after the armistice, but the world was a topsy-turvy place to be. National identities were forged on a living anvil of bloodied corpses, political and geographical boundaries shifted, and the Ottoman Empire was no more. An influenza epidemic ended the lives of an estimated forty million individuals worldwide, as exhausted soldiers returned home over the next eighteen months, spreading the virus as gleefully as a ticker tape parade. Canadians in uniform were desperate to get back to their families, and the wait became unbearable in short order. War's behemoth of administration took time to wind down. Frederick had not received his release papers yet, transferring him back to the Canadian army and his adopted country. He did receive a military star for his time spent in France during 1915, the same as thousands of other soldiers. His trench fever symptoms continued to improve, and he looked forward to seeing his parents again at last. Frederick spent days at the New Inn, moving his things into Kathleen's room since training had stopped at the airfield. It was only a matter of time before he would be free to cross the Atlantic. Frequent nights were spent with her, and her sisters winked to each other the following mornings. There would be another Christmas spent together in England. On the first Sunday of Advent, as they left the church, Kathleen announced that she was pregnant. Frederick was jubilant, hugging her tightly.

"When is the baby due?" he asked.

"In spring," she replied.

"We'll be back in Canada by then, I'm sure of it."

She went quiet before saying, "I want to have the baby here, with my family."

"The war is finished. We'll return together."

Kathleen raised her head defiantly and said no more. Her

husband was anxious to leave his homeland and start over again, putting the conflict behind him. He'd written to tell his parents that he expected to be back very soon, although he didn't have a date yet. Kathleen was expecting their first child, and he hoped for a boy to name John. He could hardly wait to see the clear skies of Canada, free of shell bursts. A letter came in reply twenty-three days later. John and Mary Dawson were excited for the return of their son and his new family. Words of welcome and hope, confirming that they would all stay together for the first months. When she read the letter, Kathleen refused. "I'm not going to Canada," she told her mother.

Mrs. Corp was a force to be reckoned with. "Oh, no, lovey, you'll go."

"I shouldn't have got married – I don't know what I was thinking."

"You've made your bed and now you must lie in it. Frederick is a good and kind man who did his duty for our country. No one forced you to marry him, and don't think tongues haven't been wagging about you and that army officer."

Her daughter went red. "I never. . ."

"No, I dare say you never," her mother spat. "What were you pretending? That you're Lady Diana Manners? Flitting around London and Paris like a bejeweled butterfly?" She huffed and continued, "We've already got one bastard child in the family, and you can have yours elsewhere, Mrs. High and Mighty, whoever its father might be."

Tears glistened in Kathleen's eyes though she would not give in. "Are you that anxious to be rid of me?"

"It's best you remember where you came from, my dear. We are working stock, not your high society who can do as they please, beyond the rules of the masses. And we still have our dignity."

"Father would have let me stay, I know he would." Kathleen

stamped her foot for emphasis.

"Well, he's gone, rest his soul, and it's left to me to try to send you out with at least some respect. You are married and you will go to Canada just as soon as Frederick is released." Mrs. Corp left the room, her footsteps heavy on the wooden floor. Kathleen sank to her knees, shaking. She did not want this baby and did not want her husband, either, if it all meant that she would be forced to leave home. There was no way out of her predicament.

Two months later, Kathleen disembarked from Southampton on the *S.S. Mauretania*, along with hundreds of Canadian and American troops being repatriated. After a stop in Cherbourg, France, the ship docked in New York on February 27, 1919. Kathleen was six months pregnant and had sailed alone.

Chapter Seven

Toronto, Ontario, 1919

A healthy baby girl was born to Kathleen Dawson in May 1919, at Leaside, Ontario (now Toronto, the provincial capital). The infant was welcomed by her grandparents, John and Mary, and a studio photograph was taken of the child at a few months of age, where she was chubby and smiling. Mother and baby were living with Frederick's parents at the time. Kathleen had endured a difficult journey after crossing the Atlantic, traveling on the Grand Trunk Railway in winter afterwards. She spoke to no one unless necessary, holding her sorrow and homesickness close as the train crossed the border from the United States of America into Canada. Her parents-in-law were happy to host her and made every effort to ensure her comfort. The young mother appeared morose after the birth. John and Mary didn't pressure her to accept her new circumstances and encouraged her to write to her family back in England. They were confident that once Frederick arrived, all would be well.

He didn't return until some months after Kathleen's arrival. The Dawson home became crowded with three extra people but no one complained openly. John and Mary had lived in much more cramped conditions when their own children were young. After coming home, Frederick was restless and ill at ease at times, going for long walks as he used to do before the war. He still tinkered with automobiles, now having trouble concentrating and settling into a routine. One evening, sitting outside while the others were in bed, John gave his son a glass of beer, the day's heat dissipating in a starry sky.

"It's good to have you home again. We missed you."

"Thanks, Da, I'm glad to be here."

His father hesitated before asking, "Was it very bad for you?"

Frederick went quiet, taking a swallow before answering. "I managed, that's all any of us did."

John remarked, "Many were killed from this area. The telegrams seemed to come daily, and we prayed there wouldn't be one for you."

"It's all right. I'm here now." Frederick closed down that part of the conversation. His father began again. "Have you thought about what you might do?"

"No, not really."

"Airplanes?"

"There's talk of them carrying passengers and freight in the coming years, but I think I'd rather stay in one place for the time being. We moved around a lot in the war."

"Were you ever afraid?"

"No, not flying airplanes. But in France. . ." He let the thought dangle.

John said, "One of the fellows at work was talking about something called the Soldier Settlement Act. The government hands out land grants and loans for making a go of farming. That might be something to consider."

Frederick grinned. "We're no longer farmers, Da, not since the potato famine."

"Yes, but it's different here; different land, different time."

"I need to think about everything."

"What about Kathleen? What does she want?"

"Mainly to go back home to her mother, from what she tells me."

"Give the girl a chance, she just got here. And a new baby, too."

"Aye, she'll get used to it."

John chuckled. "Aye? You haven't lost your ma's words, I hear."

Frederick took a long draw on his beer. "No, and I wanted to visit Scotland but never got the opportunity."

"You were at a hospital in the north somewhere, weren't you?"

"Aye, recuperating from trench fever."

"And you're better?"

"It's all gone now, Da."

"Good, that's good, son." John patted his knee and yawned.

The days shortened as autumn came to the land, blazing maples against deepening skies, a hard edge of winter on the horizon. Frederick had applied to the program for soldiers to farm and received a reply by Christmas. He felt better although was still affected by the war, needing to be away from people for increasing stretches of time. Kathleen was against moving anywhere out of the city but was also tired of living with John and Mary. Helpful as they were, she wanted to be on her own. Once her husband came to his senses, they could sell the farm and move somewhere proper. She hadn't given up on returning to England. God knew why she ever agreed to emigrate. Husband and wife had little private time inside the house, and Kathleen did only what was necessary for the baby. Mary spent much of her days with the infant, cooing and cuddling, playing and singing lullabies to her granddaughter. Secretly, Kathleen was grateful for the unpaid nurse, as she viewed her mother-in-law.

Frederick's application for settlement land was approved within months, and by the time baby Margaret was one year old, the family had moved forty miles west of Toronto, to Nassagaweya Township. This area contained a hamlet called Haltonville, intended as a social hub for pioneering families in an effort to bring stability and success to the Dominion, not to mention encouraging settlers to support themselves from the land and therefore require minimal government assistance. The average land parcel size that each person could hold title to under the program was approximately ninety-nine acres, at a cost of forty dollars per acre. Other Canadian provinces held different rules for parcel sizes and costs. And so the young Dawson family moved to their new location in the summer of 1920. What followed was close to a decade of hard physical work, more than either Frederick or Kathleen had bargained for. After large areas of southern Ontario had been cleared of trees in the previous century, erosion had become a problem in some areas. Enormous stumps were left as evidence to record the almost impossible labour required by pioneers, their toil invisible short years after they left the land, dead or broken or bitter, perhaps in search of a future that didn't require so much from them. The challenges of full-time farming in rural Canada would strain the marriages of many couples. At first, Frederick reveled in the solitude of working the earth while he recovered from the war, planting potatoes as his grandparents had done in Ireland. Some days there was nary a sound in the world other than a gentle breeze or song of the wood thrush. Flash of red wings on the male scarlet tanager catching his eye, sending him back to France and the ubiquitous colour of blood, how it looked on a limb hanging from a tree, droplets congealing on the woody trunk where they slowed and stopped. Brownish stains on wet wool uniforms, lending a distinctive sheen to the material. There were no crows seen near the farm; Mórrígan was gone, left behind in Europe. More than once, Frederick was moved to tears, letting them fall without embarrassment since there was no one to see anyway. Kathleen tended their child close to the farmhouse. On the most beautiful days, her husband occasionally sat down in the turned soil and cried, heaving great sobs with his head in his hands, minutes later returning to normal. Frederick thought of Da with his own tears, and Ma, her stoicism and good humour. Although they weren't far away, he missed them more now than he ever had during the war. One hot morning, he returned to the well for a drink of water, priming the hand pump and overhearing Kathleen's angry voice.

"Get out of my way, or I'll send you to the orphanage." She towered over the toddler, who cringed in a corner.

Frederick's footsteps sounded on the threshold. "What's going on? What's wrong?"

"What's wrong? You mean, what's right?"

He pursed his lips, blowing out through his nose. "Has something broken?"

"I'll tell you about broken," she hissed. "Broken is living in this godforsaken place, away from everyone and everything. That's what broken is."

"I thought you'd be glad to move to our own place, away from my parents. I know the house was small for all of us."

"I don't care about them. I want to go home."

Frederick moved towards her. "You know that's not possible. The country is still recovering from the war. We're better off here."

"Maybe you are. I'm not going to live like a bloody peasant for the rest of my days." She huffed out of the room, leaving Margaret behind, her tiny chin quivering. Frederick picked up the child. "Come outside with me, I'll make it better." The little girl clung to him.

Days stretched into weeks, into months, into years. Frederick's younger brother Walter joined them regularly to work, since he wasn't married yet. Constant tilling of the soil with the plow and draft horses, picking stones, planting crops, waiting anxiously through summer storms, clearing out impossible winter snowdrifts, keeping cows and pigs healthy enough for market – there was no time for socializing with neighbours, no reason to dress to impress anyone. Frederick's military uniform hung in the closet at his parents' home in Leaside. He'd lost weight through hard work, his muscles tanned and firm. Kathleen was unhappy with her role as a farmer's wife. At least at her mother's inn, she could look forward to admiration from uniformed military men who passed through, and she could dress as she pleased. She'd married too quickly, and to the wrong man, thinking he would bring her the social status she craved: wife of a handsome young pilot in the flying corps. A chance to show up her sisters, to remind them that she was bound for greatness, and they were not. If her blessed papa hadn't died, she might already be there, she was his favourite, after all. Kathleen's thoughts strayed occasionally to the army officer from the camp and the one walk they shared when she dared to imagine a different life, just in case her new husband didn't return from the war. Airplane crashes were spectacular and often deadly. All that was not here, not this. Definitely not this. Up to her elbows in manure and biting insects, enduring the hellish heat of summer, scorching all in its path. Seasons of wind and rain and snow, not the gentle misty damp of her England. And worst of all, being forced to wear trousers for the dirtiest jobs. It was unthinkable. Exhausted, she fell into bed at night, not caring whether Frederick was with her or not; they'd stopped making love months before. The one time she found a few moments to leave off the mantle of drudgery, she'd gone outside, seeing him in the field at a distance. Moving closer from behind, Kathleen realized he was crying. A grown man, crying like a baby. She turned around and left. And that girl! Her daughter, a needy child, following her around every minute of the day, unable to keep herself occupied. What Kathleen wouldn't give for a few days by herself, completely alone, in a city, anywhere but on this cursed farm. Slipping into depression, she was becoming what she most feared, a churl. There were no letters from England.

A handful of years later, the farm slowly began to prosper, benefiting from Frederick's skill with machinery and livestock, along with a fortuitous run of good weather. Crops were bountiful and enough money could be raised to hire another worker, once Walter was away on his own pursuits. At last there was limited leisure time, enough to leave the property for a few hours at a stretch. The Dawsons traveled back to Leaside, leaving Margaret with her grandparents, while they took the motor car into Toronto. Frederick loved driving and he was relaxed and interested, following the streets to the King Edward Hotel for afternoon tea. Kathleen was giddy with excitement, finally getting away from her prison and wearing clean clothes all day. As they walked down the city street, Frederick enjoyed a cigarette with his wife on his arm, something they weren't used to doing anymore. She was happy and animated, excited for once.

"Look at everything here! I feel as if I've come alive again," she said.

"Oh, it's nice all right, but the farm isn't that bad, is it?"

"Are you joking? You know I don't belong on a farm."

"Yes, but you're doing such a good job of it," he teased.

"I want to go home for a visit soon. I haven't seen my family in over five years."

"That's why people write letters."

"Easy for you to say. You have your family right here."

"Kathleen, you knew when we married that we'd live in Canada."

"And live in backwoods and swill. What kind of a place is that to bring up our daughter?"

"You're a stubborn one, I'll grant you that."

"Can't we move back to Toronto? Even Leaside? You're a good mechanic, you could get a job."

Frederick sighed, tossing his cigarette butt to the ground. "Some things you have to accept, that's all."

"I'll never accept being a farmer's wife. I'd rather be a spinster."

"Aren't you lucky I saved you from that?"

Just then, two men passed them on the sidewalk, going in the opposite direction. Both looked at Frederick momentarily before resting their eyes on Kathleen. Again he sensed her response to them, the same he'd witnessed at the New Inn. An unspoken signal, a desire to be noticed, something that left him frustrated. Wasn't he enough? Didn't he measure up? The men tipped their hats and carried on past the couple without speaking. He took her arm tightly in his and continued walking. That night, together back at the farm, Frederick's insecurity got the better of him. Margaret hadn't wanted to leave her grandparents and cried mightily as they left, Kathleen half wanting to leave her there for the foreseeable future but saying nothing.

Frederick unbuttoned his shirt, facing her directly as she brushed her hair, long and thick. "I saw you giving attention to those two men today."

"What men?" she asked innocently, a small smile on her lips.

"You know who I mean, don't pretend."

Now she returned his gaze, hinting at defiance. "What's wrong with a man or men noticing me? Are you ashamed of me?"

"You're my wife. You do not look at other men. Lower your eyes if they watch you."

"Oh, pffff!" She laughed, "I'm not your chattel."

He took a step towards her. "I know about the army officer at the New Inn."

Kathleen took only the slightest pause. "And what of it? How was I to know whether you'd get home from the war? What if you were killed?"

"And you couldn't wait to find out, could you?"

She said, "We didn't do anything, not that it's any of your business."

"It certainly is my business!" He raised his voice.

"Sshhh, you'll wake the child."

"She has a name. She is not *the child*. Why don't you play with her sometimes? Any mother plays with her children."

"As if I have time for that. Do you have any idea what I do during the day? Lost in this god-forsaken wilderness." Her face went red, tears threatened.

Frederick turned to the side, loosening his trousers. "You know, my mother had time for all of us. You've seen how good she is with Margaret."

"Yes, well, I'm not your mother, am I?"

"Why d'you have to be so argumentative all the time? Is that why your mother was anxious to be rid of you?"

"Shut up!" she hissed. "You loathsome man. I don't know why I chose you when I had many to choose from."

"Oh, so that's it? I was the leftovers, the safe bet." He shook his head angrily.

Her thoughts stalled suddenly, acknowledging the lack of options available to her now. She had no money of her own and no way to return home to England. Switching to a conciliatory tone, Kathleen replied, "Don't worry, you were what I was looking for."

"What, not who. You've made yourself perfectly clear." Frederick's expression changed again as he asked softly, "How I do even know I'm Margaret's father?"

Kathleen stood to her full height, her fists clenched. "You disgust me."

They slept apart that night.

Frederick spent long days in the fields with the hired man, working in silence more often than not. Memories of the war were always present, although he could manage them better. Remembering friends, the ones he dared to believe would survive, both in France and in England. Some had died but others had said they would stay in touch, as people do when parting. There was no time for writing, and he wouldn't know what to say: that constant physical work helped him cope with his trauma? That his wife was becoming an opponent rather than a helpmeet? On his unhappier days, he began to wonder if his daughter was actually his, and this left him feeling worse than ever. The specter of doubt had taken hold. Had Kathleen played him for a fool? She could have lain with another man within days of seeing her husband when he was at Chattis Hill. The very thought of it crushed him. Frederick could barely admit to himself that he missed the camaraderie of the military, as hellish as war was. He didn't know what to do with his future, or with his family's future.

Autumn 1925 brought pleasant warm days with little rain. The sky turned a softer blue, waiting for cold that hadn't arrived yet. A truce held at the farm, a new understanding of sorts. Kathleen and Frederick were cordial with one another, and she had taught Margaret how to sew. The girl had a creative streak that her mother didn't share. Kathleen had played piano competently in her youth, however, Margaret had no musical ability, couldn't even hold a note, unlike either of her parents. She was a child unto herself, a nascent beauty with her mother's dark hair and eyes. The family attended the Royal Agricultural Winter Fair in Toronto that year, staying over a few days while the hired man ran the farm in their absence. Acrimony had died down between the couple and they enjoyed themselves. Perhaps the worst was behind them, Frederick wanted to believe. He didn't want to live his life alone. The new year arrived bright and cold with little snow. As the days lengthened, still the land received no precipitation, and farmers began to worry about drought in the coming months. By the time of the spring equinox, the sun's rays massaged waiting buds with warmth, and birds began to return for nesting. Whistling as he came in for lunch one day, Frederick caught a glimpse of Kathleen standing in front of the cheval mirror of their bedroom, one luxury he'd allowed in the house. She stood in profile in a loose dress, her pregnancy unmistakable. Frederick stopped on seeing her, grinning at the sudden knowledge. This baby was his, no doubt about it. He entered the room and hugged his wife.

A healthy son was born in late October, Philip James. Kathleen slipped into depression once again, and the entente between the baby's parents was strained close to breaking. Margaret lived on the periphery of ugly looks and silent meals. She had no playmates save her infant brother, and she took to him early on. At seven years his senior, she was capable of most of his care, and her mother was only too happy to ignore the both of them when it suited her. Frederick could no longer pretend that he wanted to stay at the farm in the long term. With an unhappy family and little emotional support from his wife, it was no longer worth it. Stumbling in exhausted at night to a home colder than winter, nary a word nor touch nor smile waiting for him. The price of wheat was dropping, making any profit thin indeed. Once when he visited the nearby hardware store on horseback, the middle-aged clerk smiled warmly and asked after his family. Frederick nearly broke down at her kindness, something he rarely experienced at home. He was going to leave but he didn't know how and didn't know when. Working the land had driven much of his war trauma out of him, yet it was no way to make a living over a lifetime, and he understood why his ancestors had given up farming altogether. As happens occasionally, a shift in circumstances occurred as the result of two things: first, as soon as young James turned two years old, Kathleen took herself off to England, alone, for over a month. She made no provisions for either of her children, who went to stay at Leaside with their grandparents. Second, taking advantage of being on his own in a quiet house, Frederick went to Toronto for a day. He'd read earlier in the newspaper about the forest protection service being tendered by the Ontario government in 1924, to conduct aerial surveys and provide reconnaissance for fire patrols in the bush, preserving valuable timber assets for the Lands and Forests department. One aircraft mentioned was the Curtiss H2SL flying boat. A drawing of the biplane accompanied the article, dwarfing the pilot standing next to it. The new provincial air fleet was headed by Roy Maxwell, a seasoned bush pilot himself. Further, the article detailed the first successful air observation in 1921 that had prevented a major fire in the Sioux Lookout region of the northwest. Mention was made of pilot Reg Johnson, who had called in the fire report. He was formerly of the Royal Flying Corps, and as soon as Frederick read this, he was lost to happy imagination. Flying again, in peace time, for a good cause and not war. Oh, how his life might change! While Kathleen was overseas, he applied to the program, to undergo flight training at Camp Borden and join the Ontario Provincial Air Service as a qualified pilot. For the first time in years, Frederick was genuinely elated. He could fly and be away from Kathleen for weeks at a time. There was no question of divorce, and the potential of a more peaceful life left him giddy with relief. He didn't have to be present daily in a loveless marriage and could still provide for his family without leaving any of them. It was a perfect solution. With his previous flight experience and unblemished record in the war, Frederick had no trouble being accepted, with training to begin in a few months. He'd worn his military uniform to the interview, remembering another interview more than ten years earlier, when he'd first got into flight training in England. So much had changed, it seemed a lifetime ago now. The trenches of France no longer haunted his nights.

Chapter Eight

Sault Ste. Marie, Ontario, 1929

Frederick entered one of the happiest phases of his life as soon as he joined the OPAS in 1928. He was posted to the operating base in Sault Ste. Marie, Ontario, at the junction of Great Lakes Superior, Michigan, and Huron. It was a busy hub in those days, with pilots, supplies, mechanics, and all manner of activity in the provincial government's forestry air arm. Frederick flew one of the H-boats, the same aircraft that he'd read about in the newspaper. The ungainly machine stood over seven feet tall and measured thirty-eight feet long, with a seventy-four foot wingspan. Although it was standard procedure for an aircraft engineer to accompany the pilot, Frederick's skill with automobile motors stood him in good stead, and he was in demand during crew selection. He had a knack for knowing the right thing to do with Curtiss's Liberty engine when it became as temperamental as a rutting bull moose. On the base, Frederick fit right in with Roy Maxwell, the man who ran the organization for the provincial Department of Lands and Forests. Frederick was confident without being cocky, not one to take foolish risks, and a man who could be counted on to get the job done. Flying into the wide peace-time sky left him wondering how he had ever stopped flying after the war. A handful of his former military pilot friends barnstormed all over North America. The farm hadn't been a waste of his time; it helped to heal his psychological wounds and now he was ready to break free at last. In the end, he hadn't considered Kathleen's opinion, not that she'd had much choice with two young children. Frederick reveled in the challenges of flying over a wild land with few people, seeing the northern forest's beauty from the air for the first time. Endless waves of green, dotted with lakes large and small, a land ripe for timber harvest and settlement. He never tired of the view. Kathleen and the children had moved with him and they were living in a rented house a few blocks north of the St. Mary's River. She was happy to be off the farm for good, sold with satisfactory profit just before the Great Depression obliterated its value. Perhaps the endless hours of toil had produced a future, after all. A small garden was dug along the south side of the new house and planted with roses, Kathleen's favourite. Once while walking, she chanced upon Salisbury Avenue not far away, and just seeing the name on the street sign left her with a terrible ache and searing homesickness for England. She couldn't leave her marriage and, with dependent children at home, couldn't work for an employer. So she was relegated to following her husband wherever he went, yet knowing every day that he could be killed in one of the airplanes. Still, she felt pride in being a wife of one of the pilots, heroes who were looked up to. A number of the spouses knew each other from their husbands joining the forestry air service at the same time. Young James Dawson had plenty to keep him occupied, forever exploring the natural area and going to the river with his new friends.

Margaret was shy and less outgoing, but she spent time with a few girls in their neighbourhood. Try as she might, Kathleen remained unable to conjure a mother's love for her daughter the more years that passed by. She put away the sting of Frederick's suggestion of an illegitimate child by ignoring the girl herself. Kathleen had wanted to make him understand that she could've married anyone she chose but had settled on him and he was lucky to have her. Her cheeks still flushed at his intimation that she was apparently only too happy to entertain other men during the war *after* their marriage. Her manipulation had failed spectacularly, and father and daughter had little to do with one another. The family fracture was a dormant volcano – not always active but the threat was there. How she wished to turn back the clock and return Margaret to wherever she came from.

Forced landings on lakes happened frequently when aircraft engines malfunctioned, a common occurrence. Needing to communicate back to base was a priority and one that proved problematic before radios were standard equipment in the cockpit. Frederick carried minimal supplies with him: a sandwich or two, flask of coffee, and always his cigarettes. He'd flown to the bases at Sudbury and Sioux Lookout, perfecting his landing skills on water over the course of his first year with the OPAS. Being stranded occasionally was a bonus that he kept to himself as he became more familiar with his new environment. The almost mystical quality of the great northern forest fed his soul and buoyed his spirit like nothing else. He wrote home to his parents, sharing his new experiences as a pilot. Frederick couldn't imagine them living in a place like this. Plane crashes ended in injury and death on rare occasions, and he felt the loss of fellow crews. However, these deaths didn't carry the same evil that he'd endured in the war, men and machines whose sole intention was to kill. He'd sit betimes on a fallen log on a rocky shoreline, alone except for the engineer cursing with his head and hands inside a greasy hot engine. Frederick enjoyed a smoke, inhaling deeply and letting relaxation settle in. They would fly out when they could, that's all. He was untroubled about his wife and family waiting for his return. There were few women in the flying industry in any capacity, and Frederick smiled at the thought of his ma referring to pretty young girls as hens, a Scottish term of endearment. She had never referred to Kathleen as a hen. Frederick didn't frequent beer parlours or flirt with ladies of ill repute, there was little time for that, but once he did see a comely lass in the Soo, her red hair falling loose about her shoulders, light dress swinging just below the knee as she walked down the street on a summer's day. Imagination fluttered as he pictured himself coming home to a warm hug and kiss, kindly words, a loving touch, instead of the cold reality of his marriage. He could not crack the nut of his wife's grudge and eventually gave up trying. More than once, he thought that perhaps she'd seen only his uniform when they'd first met, rather than the man he truly was. After James was born, he'd hoped for a change in both of them but it hadn't happened in the long term. Frederick envied his parents' union, the warmth between them ever visible. He'd heard Da call his wife *grádh* once and asked what it meant. Mary laughed and said, "It means 'my love.' The only Gaelic I need to know." She kissed her husband on his cheek.

    Frederick adapted quickly to the pace and social aspects of his work, so different from the farm. The men in the forestry air arm were congenial, tough, innovative, and practical. Whiners and shirkers were soon gone from the service, leaving behind a corps of dedicated individuals who became legend in the north. Many had previous flying experience in the war, and many had been trained in Canada shortly after the war. Numerous flight schools had been set up to prepare the dominion in case of future conflict, where the advantages of a trained flying force were recognized. There was a definite camaraderie in the OPAS, a willingness to push the boundaries, following safety rules as far as possible but not entirely constrained by them, either. The pilots fed on their own audaciousness in the bush. Without ready help when they were stranded, they improvised whenever and however were necessary. Frederick loved the freedom of his life and what he was doing; it was the first time he'd felt truly happy since childhood. One summer, his family followed him to Longlac (hours away and north of Lake Superior) for months of flying in the H-boat, only returning to the Soo when the children had to attend school in September. Kathleen would not permit them to learn in train cars with traveling teachers as was done in remote communities along the Canadian National Railway. The following winter, Frederick put together a dog team and spent many hours mushing through the forest, crystalline snow wetting his neck as he ducked around trees on the trail. He lived out the wilderness dreams of many boys in England. As often as possible, James would accompany him and they bonded over the painful cold of bare hands tying the dogs' traces. Brittle sun seared the frost on needled branches, making them easy to break off. Breath was hoarded, captured as it left a void in the body for the sharp chill to enter. Bright red spots formed on their cheeks after a run with the dogs. Panting, the animals' tongues lolled as James stroked them, his father smoking a cigarette and grinning. After a snowfall, the world's silence was like nothing else, complete, universal. Frederick was reminded of the different, inner silence he'd felt on the battlefield, surrounded by thousands of men and deafening noise that strapped in his hopes and faith, binding them tightly, put away where they couldn't be touched. In the northern winter, he befriended indigenous trappers and learned some of their ways, such as how to wear snowshoes, how to ice fish, and how to be in the world from their perspective. Many times he was out on the land for a few days, then back at a settlement, being served scalding tea inside a canvas tent. Frederick's observation was that native people couldn't stand being in white men's buildings, save the trader's depot. He saw few children wherever he went and noted a particular sadness among the communities. Communication was difficult as they shared no common language. Frederick ruminated on the expectations he'd had as a youngster, first coming to this rough land so distinct from England. He was glad to return then for the war, not knowing what awaited him. Pride in serving one's country had led to death and dismemberment for so many, when pride no longer mattered, survival was all anyone thought about. And he'd made it back, hadn't he? Where was the glory that he should allow himself for returning with all of his limbs? Out in the bush, he made every effort to concentrate on the beauty and stillness around him, the sense of the great natural world that was unconcerned with human foibles. Frederick had no fear of dying somewhere away from civilization. He gave up his thoughts to the silent woods where they were safe.

By late March, winter's gripped eased, and during warm middays, water dripped everywhere. Spring was Frederick's favourite season. It held the potential of another year of unknowns, but ones that he was happy for, not the ones he'd already lived with in France. He understood that the war would never really leave him. Once in a while, his back would begin to ache, and he'd wonder if it was all in his mind. Perhaps it was only the memory of pain or his imagination of the pain that had laid him flat out for weeks at a time in 1917. By the end of winter, he returned to flight preparations for the following forest fire season. Strategies were formed based on a body of previous years' experience. Roy Maxwell noted Frederick's skill in administration and encouraged his participation in all aspects. The pilot had a good head on his shoulders and was an asset to the department. Frederick also had a beneficent way with the men, getting them to move in a certain direction while making them believe that it was their idea all along. He had an easy grace among the mechanics and liked to tinker with the engines himself, often running them up and taxiing for safety trials. He was well liked by everyone and helped to train the new pilots coming on board. Some were only looking for a meal ticket on their way to commercial flying, expected to be the future of aviation in Canada. It didn't matter to Frederick what he did or was called to do; being a northern bush pilot answered all of his ambitious needs. Ferrying paying passengers around wasn't for him. He wanted the wild places, the risk, every day different. It was the reminder that he still had a life to live.

The Great Depression deepened as the decade wore on. Unemployed men traveled the country on top of rail cars, looking for work that wasn't there. Relief stations were set up and children went hungry. Almost everyone went hungry. Drought in the prairies cut food production, exports of raw materials were halved, and prices dropped to levels previously unseen. Industrial production had fallen by forty percent from only a few years earlier. There were no more pilots barnstorming because there was no one to pay for rides. Governments canceled air mail contracts in a bid to save money, and Frederick was one of a lucky few in his job. Even with the economy in its current state, the forestry department was still considered important to the province. Mining exploration continued, along with the need for air support in remote areas. Forest fires had to be contained before they could do too much damage. Everyone wanted a new gold rush to change the decade's terrible economic trajectory. By the time he turned forty years old, Frederick was more than confident in his role and no longer felt any need to please his wife. They lived like roommates when he was home, ones who shared children. Margaret seemed distant, preferring to be off with her own friends rather than with her family. James stayed with his father whenever he could, following him around and asking questions about flying and everything else. He said that he wanted to be a pilot as well. Ruffling the boy's hair, his dad told him it was entirely possible. At least Kathleen had returned from her overseas trip when James was two; Frederick had wondered whether she would come back at all. He'd grown to love his adopted country and knew that he'd never leave it.

Frederick opened the door to his home in the Soo as a cooling wind funneled down from the north, sending coloured leaves dancing, a fine dust raised everywhere. Kathleen was standing at the kitchen sink peeling potatoes and barely acknowledged his arrival.

"It's almost strange to be around people again," he said, exhaling and setting down his pack.

Now she turned to him. "I'm surprised you remembered us at all."

"Don't be silly, the patrols aren't up to me." He sensed any possible levity quickly dissipating. There was no move for physical contact by either of them.

"And you can't make it back on the days you are here?"

"It's often only overnight, you know that. What's the point of disrupting everyone when I just have to go out again?"

"You're right, what's the point?" She placed the potatoes into a sieve and rinsed cold water over them.

Frederick tried again. "Well, I'm home now. Would you like to go for a walk later?"

Kathleen regarded him as if he'd asked her to attend a public hanging. "No."

"I'm going to take a bath." He left the kitchen and walked into their small bedroom to undress. Purposely leaving his clothes on the floor, he ran water into the claw-foot tub as he soaped his face to shave at the sink. Frederick repeated her phrase *what's the point* inside his head, it becoming a refrain like the chorus of a song. What *was* the point? It's true, he was at the Soo base on a regular basis and could come home for a few hours if he chose to. But he could not fulfill her needs and had given up wanting to. That evening when Frederick took young James down to the river to fish, he marveled at the reality of conceiving the boy with his wife. It seemed fantastic now, the very notion of making love with the woman. The married men he worked with did not discuss their wives and neither did he. Frederick preferred the company of the boreal forest to that of his own family.

A letter arrived in the mail, addressed to Pilot F.J. Dawson. The return address was Toronto, the Deputy Minister's office of the Lands and Forests Department. Frederick was grateful to be home when the postman delivered it because he didn't trust Kathleen. Perhaps she might even have thrown the letter into the stove if she were in one of her moods. He held the envelope in his hands, a bit further away from his face now since his vision had changed in the past year, becoming more far-sighted; he'd told no one about it. The letter was a job offer, for him to run the affairs of the forestry department for the Lakehead region, at the city of Port Arthur. He'd flown over the town a couple of times before, nestled against the northwestern shore of Lake Superior. After reading, he held the letter and sat down, alone in the house. Not expecting this, but an opportunity nonetheless. Had Roy Maxwell put the boys in Toronto up to it? It would mean a steady, increased salary and a lot less flying. Frederick was in his early forties, no longer a young man. He'd miss piloting the Gypsy Moth and the newer Hamilton H-45 all-metal aircraft that were like old friends now. The Vickers Vedette amphibian accounted for few hours in his logbook and he wanted more. It was a lot to think about as he went out for a walk. That evening, he shared the news with Kathleen.

"I've been offered a job at the Lakehead."

"Where?" She stopped what she was doing, listening.

"Port Arthur, at the head of Lake Superior."

"What sort of job?"

"Managing the forests in the region. It would be a desk job mainly."

"Is it still with the government?"

"Aye."

"When does it begin?"

"They've asked for my answer within thirty days."

Kathleen went quiet, ruminating. Frederick watched her, waiting.

"And we'd all move?" she asked.

"Of course. We can buy a house there. Margaret's almost ready for high school. It will be good for her."

Kathleen watched her husband's features, not trusting his motivation. He didn't often speak of his daughter.

"A proper house?"

Now he laughed. "What would you expect? That we live in an airplane hangar? A tent in the woods?"

She allowed a smile. "I'll enjoy getting away from the Italians here. They remind me of bees, always buzzing around, talking with their hands on each other."

Frederick sighed, "Well, there'll be Poles and Finns in the north, I expect. This isn't England."

"More's the pity."

"I'll be implementing the province's forest management policy, coordinating people and programs, making the best use of the resource."

"You sound as though you're running for office."

He ran a hand through his hair. "It's going to be different all right and more money, too."

"Will you still fly sometimes?" She gave him this much.

"Probably not very often, but someone will need to go up at times and it might as well be me."

Kathleen brightened. "This could be a good thing. How soon can we go?"

"I imagine in a few months, perhaps six?"

"Write them back. Tell them *Yes*." Her mind was already made up.

It was as straightforward as that.

Chapter Nine

Port Arthur, Ontario, 1935

By the end of that forest fire air patrol season, the house in Sault Ste. Marie was emptied and rented to another OPAS pilot and his family. The Dawson's belongings were loaded onto a freight car and shipped to the Lakehead by rail, arriving late the following day. Frederick flew one of the forestry planes to Port Arthur, landing at Bishopsfield airport (named for WW-I flying ace, Billy Bishop) on a cloudy evening. The air was still and damp as he set foot on the ground, the same as he'd done so many times before in his flying career. For just the slightest moment, Frederick felt the passage of time moving through his body, and he knew that he would not be flying much longer. Saddened, he removed his pack and walked away from the aircraft. Kathleen and the children had traveled up ahead of him by passenger train. With the security of his new position, the couple purchased a two-storey home on Van Horne Street, on a hill not far from the Lake Superior waterfront. They owned an automobile that only Frederick drove, although he could walk to work if he chose to. Kathleen never learned to drive.

The year 1935 began with cold typical of the region, along with a decided lack of winter snow. There were worries about the severity of the projected forest fire season to come. Frederick's career challenges were significant, as the government had changed hands in the last election and drastic budget cuts were made to the OPAS. For some in Cabinet, it simply wouldn't do, this merry band of renegades flying everywhere on the public purse while under little direct control from the legislature in Toronto. Roy Maxwell's days of being in charge were numbered and he would soon leave the service altogether. He'd run his stable of flyers with charisma and aplomb, leaving the men as tightly knit as any military unit. Now Frederick and others in the department were left to carry on with very limited resources. More than once he wondered whether his former boss had seen the writing on the wall and sent Frederick north as a way to keep him employed, in any capacity. His days were spent in meetings, often deciding where to allocate minimal funds, and he required special permission to take even local flights. Everything was blamed on the Great Depression, yet what was that when the entire future of forestry in the province was at stake? Pulp mills were cutting paper runs, hundreds of piece workers in the bush were laid off, and worry followed men wherever they went. Frederick's biggest concern was the lack of forest fire patrols. Mining was one of the few industries that were buffered in the current hard times, and a forest fire could quickly lay waste to their access roads or at least cut back production temporarily when towns were evacuated. People still talked about the deadly 1916 fire in Matheson (Ontario) and the shocking loss of hundreds of lives. Frederick fired off memo after memo to Toronto and might as well have thrown them out of an airplane for all the response he received. Working indoors most of the time chafed on him and he welcomed any opportunity to get outside. Frequenting the Hoito restaurant below the Finnish Labour Temple downtown, Frederick got to know a number of the older bush workers, sitting quietly in their trademark wool mackinaw pants and checkered flannel shirts, out at the elbows. Now comfortable in his visits, he sat one day at the long counter and ordered coffee, smiling at the man beside him and nodding.

"How are you doing today?"

The man cupped his ear and shook his head, pointing to his neighbour on the next stool. A younger man around Frederick's age smiled, saying, "Old Sulo's lost his hearing. Too much time running a sawmill engine."

"Ah," Frederick replied, adding, "I lost some of my hearing in the war."

His audience looked as if they wanted more. The waitress set down his coffee. He winced after taking a boiling sip. "France and Belgium. Were some of your friends over there?"

"No, sir," said the younger man. "We were living like pioneers; hardly knew there was a war on. Cutting firewood and digging potatoes, that was our life."

Frederick thought back to how much of his younger self had been given to the conflict and how it had changed his future. Occasionally he wondered about that other path – if he'd stayed in Toronto and remained a mechanic, if he'd never been part of the war.

"Where are you from?"

"I was born in Kivikoski, near Lappe. Sulo's from Lauttasaari, it's not far from Helsinki, Finland. Came over as a young boy." He nudged the man playfully. "Tell him how much English you got."

"Goddamned right!" Sulo grinned.

The younger Finn reached across to shake hands. "I'm Heikki. Not born in a sauna like Sulo." He laughed. "My dad emigrated at the turn of the century. People were starving in his village, and he figured it couldn't be much worse here. Worked at the grain elevators."

"Is he retired?" Frederick asked.

"No, he never got that far, died of a heart attack last year."

"Oh, I'm sorry. Is your mother all right?"

"She's well enough. I moved back in with her, y'know, to help her stay in her house."

"You're not married?"

"I know enough to stay away from women." And the two Finns had a good laugh while Frederick drank his coffee and silently agreed with them.

On his lunch hour break, he often left his office and strolled along the industrial waterfront. The city was blessed by the gift of proximity to an enormous inland lake, in turn forming part of a great waterway that stretched all the way to the Atlantic Ocean. Just as he had as a child, Frederick imagined putting together the administrative pieces to create a trading consortium between Canada and the United States using the waterway, embracing commerce and making life better for millions of people. The Welland canal was already in place; what was needed was a complete route all the way along out to the St. Lawrence River, with enough capacity to handle the largest ships from Europe. But for the time being, North America was in the grips of an economic depression that left hope abandoned for many communities. Military veterans who'd believed that they'd endured the worst that could be asked of any human being, were now riding the rails across the country, looking for jobs that didn't exist. Frederick felt keenly for them, many first-generation Canadians whose parents had left the wretchedness of the same war that he'd served in. Now entire families were starving, no wonder there was social and political unrest. He thought of ways to help them as far as he could. Plenty of city residents still heated their homes with wood, and what was needed was a list of suppliers and another of customers, consolidating deliveries to maximize resources. Frederick had knowledge of the Finnish co-operative system that led to a strong sense of fellowship and support for new immigrants. As he'd left the two Finns at the Hoito that day, he determined to start getting names and contact information from some of the men. He was responsible for handing out timber cutting licenses, and if he were able to create a Who's-who in the local industry, that would prove useful. The idea of developing a working system of people and goods appealed to him.

Few single women were visible in the downtown core of the city, other than when they were getting into or out of a streetcar, or occasionally walking with a companion. Frederick never approached any of the unaccompanied ones but did enjoy seeing the married ones' finery at the Prince Arthur, the premier Canadian Pacific Railroad hotel on Cumberland Street, just feet away from the train station. Ladies' hair piled wondrously under impossible hats, waists pinched into dresses of fine fabric and memorable colours. Some of the rich dressed as if it were still the Edwardian era, when more relaxed clothing was the modern fashion. Kathleen wore either navy blue or black at all times by choice, her body completely covered as if she were in mourning. Seeing her like that, occasionally Frederick felt melancholy drift over him as he examined the events of his life. He was currently in a much better financial position than most and didn't need to worry about feeding his family or becoming homeless. Margaret was doing well in high school and James was ever the same, growing quickly towards puberty. A weight of grief burdened him whenever he reflected on the war, strangely enough more often now than when he was younger. It had been twenty years since his time overseas but it still seemed so recent, no more than a few months ago. Why was it that he was allowed to have a life when millions of soldiers in the carnage weren't? Frederick had believed that once he'd readjusted back in Canada, his war would be over for good yet that's not what happened. He wasn't in contact with anyone that he knew during his time in service, even though addresses had been exchanged with a few individuals. It was as if the other men had become ghosts in their absence. He missed his parents very much and wanted them to come and visit the Lakehead, something that Kathleen was dead against. In truth, he couldn't imagine them being in the same house with her for any length of time. Considering how she apparently viewed herself as a tragic *grande dame*, she in fact had poor hostess skills and didn't welcome friendly overtures from anyone. None of her energy was spent on community programs or charity or the local Anglican church. James and Margaret had school companions in their home from time to time, but there were no adult visitors, no dinner parties. Frederick wondered what he might do should any senior government officials from Toronto come to visit Port Arthur; they certainly wouldn't be dining with his family.

One sunny afternoon in September, Frederick left work early with a headache. He knew that he needed glasses and was too vain to see the optometrist as an admission of age. This day, he decided on a whim to visit the waterfront and feel the lake rinsing his mind, listening to the seagulls as they coasted in the onshore breeze. He walked down the hill to the train station, intending to sit on a bench there for a few minutes. As he rounded the corner of the building, he was surprised to see a young girl, perhaps in her mid-twenties, standing at a sketch pad on an easel. She was dressed conservatively, her light-coloured hair tucked up under a hat, skirt well below the knee, and wearing a jacket against the cool wind coming off the lake. Approaching from behind, he slowed his step to see what she was drawing and quickly recognized the local landform known as the Sleeping Giant, out on the bay. She added lines and watercolour paint, from a single brush, using only a somber blue and nothing else. The scene was beautiful in its simplicity. The girl was alone.

"Ahem," he cleared his throat softly.

With the slightest hesitation, her hand was stilled before she set down her brush and turned to her visitor. "Good day, sir," she said.

Frederick tipped his hat. "It's a lovely drawing."

"Thank you," she smiled, not showing her teeth.

He looked around, as if for her chaperone. "Are you. . .?"

"Am I alone? Yes, I am." She stood tall, her chin up, although she was a good bit shorter than he.

Again there was that tiny suggestion of defiance, perhaps better described as confidence, that had attracted him to Kathleen all those years before. Frederick was drawn to the girl but stayed back. He smiled broadly, "Well, be careful, then. You never know whom you can trust." Raising his hat again, he strode the rest of the way to the dock, not looking back. It was enough to know she was there and that he might see her another time. Twenty minutes later when he turned to head back, she was gone, along with his headache. Frederick hummed a tune learned in the British pubs when the armistice was signed, raucous relief across an entire continent. Young men and women cavorting at all hours, literally rolling in the hay on farms, love and lust and sex. His life was not like that.

The summer of 1937 brought Frederick an opportunity to take the train to Toronto for a series of meetings, and he used the occasion to spend a few days with his parents. Seeing them gave him a bit of a jolt after more than a year's absence. John Dawson was stooped and Mary had become forgetful at times. Still, they couldn't hide their pleasure at seeing their son, the bonny one, as his mother always thought of him. He spent hours puttering in the garden and around the house, mainly enjoying their company. For all its ups and downs, they'd come through life intact, and that's all anyone could ask for. They still went to church regularly, something Kathleen and Frederick never did. On a cool, clear night, the trio sat out on the porch, watching fireflies. The rocking chair creaked as Mary pushed up and down, flexing her ankles. She closed her eyes, content.

"Da, have you been keeping up with the news?"

"Yes, and it's not good, I'll tell you that."

"I read a paper on the train saying that Mackenzie King went to visit Chancellor Adolf Hitler," said Frederick.

"Only bad will come of it, mark my words. I would never trust that man. He reminds me of a snake, waiting for the opportunity to strike. Germany wants to take over the world, just wait and see."

"Don't you trust King?"

"Certainly not! For a prime minister, he's a bit strange for my taste. Talking to dead spirits in séances. Well, some of us may do that but we certainly don't broadcast it to the nation. It's unseemly; makes him look like a quack."

Mary chuckled, "That's what comes from not having a wife."

John patted her hand. "And you've kept me from all sorts of things, haven't you, dear?"

The three were silent for a few minutes before John spoke again. "Spain is in civil war now. Some Canadians have gone over to fight for the Republicans. The battalion is called the Mac-Paps."

"What's that?" Frederick asked.

"Mackenzie-Papineau, all volunteers, about fifteen hundred men. Some of them are communists and others signed up thinking anything is better than living on relief. They're tired of having no prospects."

Frederick was quiet, remembering his war.

Mary sighed, "All this talk is so sad. I'd hoped the world

might find a longer peace after what we all went through the first time, and it's not even twenty years yet. What was the point of it, if it just means another war coming?"

John harrumphed. "Indeed, Mary, indeed." He got up from his chair, taking a moment to straighten, wincing in discomfort.

"Da, are you all right?" Frederick asked.

"Yes, quite all right, son. Just the years added onto me. You stay and keep your mother company, and I'll go to bed. I still like an early morning, as the builders say."

"Night, Da."

Mary sighed after he left. "Your da's getting on, no doubt about it."

"Uncle Joe's here, he can help."

"Aye, he comes around often enough, though we don't see much of Walter these days. He has his wife and daughter, Daisy, in Alberta, but Walter seems happier moving around."

"You've been here a long time."

"Aye, and to think that Da built all this with his own hands. Some mornings, he can barely hold a hammer for the arthritis, but he gets around as best he can."

"Are you still going to church?"

"Of course. I'm there almost every day, between Sunday services with Da and charity work during the week. There is so much need now with this Depression. We've been luckier than most."

"Hmmm. It's the same for me. I love the northern forest; everyone calls it "bush" up there, but I miss seeing you whenever I want to. I. . ." He stopped as the final light in the sky dimmed.

In the new darkness, Mary said softly, "I know that you and Kathleen haven't been happy, and I'm sorry for it."

Frederick sighed. "I don't think we were meant for each other. Things were so different during the war, so frightful, if I can say that. No one knew whether any of us would be alive at the end of the day. It's just. . .when I first saw her at the inn, I somehow lost myself. She may have had nothing to do with it." He laughed, "And a good thing you can't see my face right now!"

"Ah, son, you were married before the eyes of God and that's how you must remain. There are many marriages like yours. Just do your best and be thankful for two healthy children. They're a blessing despite any unhappiness."

"I agree."

After another full day with his parents, Frederick took the evening train back to the north shore of Lake Superior. He arrived at the station early the next morning and took a taxi to his home. The day was bright with a hint of cooler temperatures, although it was still early August. He breathed deeply and paused at the top of the steps, turning back towards the lake and its Sleeping Giant landform for a moment. The light was on in the kitchen, Kathleen was up. She barely gave him a glance when he entered the hallway, removing his hat and setting down his suitcase. Frederick was forty-three years old and could not remember the last time he had felt love for his wife – this year would mark their twentieth wedding anniversary. Margaret came down the stairs and smiled at him. She had just turned eighteen.

More meetings, more walks, more coffee at the Hoito restaurant. It was good to sit there, hearing the musical language that he couldn't understand a word of. A faint smell of chainsaw oil and sawdust permeated the rugged clothing on a few of the middle-aged men. Pretty young waitresses fluttered around serving, speaking Finn themselves. Frederick felt at peace as he sat on the stool at the breakfast bar, keeping his back straight. With his own years adding on, aches and pains were becoming normal now, especially when he slouched in fatigue. As required by his employer, he attended a medical examination that pronounced him fit overall, not overweight but needing eyeglasses. His hearing had been affected, he knew that, from the war, and nothing was recommended for it. There was no more flying, something he daydreamed about from time to time. Images of scenes from France in 1917, smoke and death below his airplane, then the great dark green of the boreal forest, spreading out like a carpet unfurled. OPAS pilots did crash land occasionally and were killed, though from the air, the trees looked as if they would provide the softest of landings. Glassy lakes mirroring the sky, scudding clouds and rain showers. An old-timer at the Hoito had invited him to join a moose hunt and Frederick was flattered to be asked, but he knew that he wasn't capable of killing a wild creature, not like that. Moose meat was a staple all over the community, especially in the rural areas. Kathleen wouldn't allow it in the house although he'd been able to enjoy some when he was dining informally with locals.

The new year had barely begun before a frantic phone call came from Leaside with the news that John Dawson had died. *A heart attack, he didn't suffer,* the voice said. It was a neighbour on the line, scratching with static. *Mary? She was all right but in shock, she wasn't alone. You must come.* And Frederick took the train once more, staring out the window of his carriage, reliving the many moments he and Da had shared as father and son. A lump in his throat, a life over. Kathleen stayed in Port Arthur with the children. There were few passengers riding with him, matching his desire for solitude. Years and moments were interchangeable: running after Da when he was a small boy, falling and skinning his knee. Crying as Da picked him up and whispered Gaelic to comfort him. Without warning, tears sprang from Frederick's eyes at the memory and he was grateful to be alone in the carriage. He'd never learned Gaelic and it pained him to think that he would not hear it again. His soul was raw with grief.

Just over one year later, Mary Dawson followed her husband out of the world of the living, leaving Frederick more bereft than ever. Although he was middle-aged, the loss took him back to being a dependent child. For weeks he felt abandoned, orphaned. No longer would he be able to sit with his parents in the simple enjoyment of their company. Later, after the funeral and when he was back home, he took to going out to the bush regularly, on the pretext of inspecting forest cutting practices and ensuring adherence to the terms of licenses. Being with the workers in their tattered clothing and spotty English was one of the few things that gave him reprieve. His boots got muddy and he drank tea from dirty tin cups and it was all good. He wandered off on his own for hours at a time, allowing the scents and sounds of the forest to infuse him. Only there would his unshed tears abate.

War clouds loomed over Europe once again, as Chamberlain's policy of appeasement had only given Hitler more confidence. Austria was annexed to Germany and Great Britain put in place the Munich Agreement to try to stop them there. The effort was derided as a disaster by a political outcast, Winston Churchill. And in early September 1939, Germany invaded Poland. News on the radio in countless homes announced the beginning of the Second World War. That night, Frederick had his first nightmare in years. He woke up sweating and disoriented in the spare room, unable to catch his breath for a few seconds. Kathleen was standing in the doorway, watching him. She left without saying a word.

Canada was called to join Britain's fight without question, just as in World War I. Young men volunteered to join the army, navy, and air forces. There was pride and duty and obligation, all of that, yet Frederick couldn't quell the deep nausea in his very being, knowing what they were heading into. War weapons had advanced, becoming swifter, deadlier, more accurate. Margaret went downtown regularly to watch her classmates from school marching down the streets in their uniforms, while spectators cheered and waved Union Jack flags. It appeared jovial for some, those who didn't know. Mothers of the young men stayed away, along with many veterans. Disabled in mind and body in some cases, they could not stomach the sight of it, not a second time while they were still alive. James was thirteen years old and his eyes shone with excitement and adventure. His father was glad that he was too young to join the others in their kit; he could not imagine his son never coming home. The boy was not allowed to play war games with his friends in the house or around the yard. Frederick had read the newspaper articles of the massive Vimy Ridge memorial opened in France in 1936. Da had talked about it the last time they were together, that and the fact that Armagh was now part of Northern Ireland, splitting up the country. He'd worried at politics like a hound after a badger. John was proud of his son and proud of his adopted country, but all Frederick had been able to feel was loss. He'd said nothing to diminish his father's thoughts, and now that Da was gone, was glad that he hadn't. Young men went to war and died; if they survived, they were broken, all of them. Now that Europe was under threat again, by the same enemy no less, he couldn't quell the sense that he needed to be there, just as he'd felt twenty years earlier. Frederick was middle-aged and had finally agreed to wear glasses, so there was no question of his serving anywhere near the front lines, nor did he want to. He'd have to get permission to take leave from his position with the forestry department. If accepted, he'd be overseas for a period of time, probably years, leaving his family without him. For weeks, he was torn privately between duty to his family and to his homeland, something he didn't discuss with anyone. After a particularly cold exchange with Kathleen in the early spring of 1940, on his lunch break from work the next day, Frederick's footsteps took him to the nearby Armoury. He couldn't help it, and by the time he left, he knew what he was going to do.

Chapter Ten

Scotland, 1941

It had all gone by so quickly, Frederick had to mentally pinch himself at where he'd landed. The process of joining up had been easier than he imagined, not that any problems were anticipated. He passed the fitness test and his eyesight still met regulations. Recognizing Frederick's previous war experience and current work duties, the recruiting officer signed him on with the Canadian Forestry Corps at the rank of Major. During their discussion, Frederick offered to put together a corps of foresters to take overseas, to Scotland. He was keen and had all the connections now, made in the comforting environment of the Hoito restaurant over coffee and pancakes, with the likes of Heikki and Sulo, his first two Finnish friends. From there he'd become part of an informal network, minding the provincial forestry regulations but also supporting the workers and their families. As soon as he spread the word about the corps, men came to his office to hear his plans before they enlisted as well.

Number Five Forestry Company filled its entire ranks on the same day that recruiting began. Of the initial Canadian contingent of twenty forestry companies, over one-third of those from Ontario were already working in the forest industry. Late in the summer of 1940, basic military training took place at Valcartier before the men sailed overseas. Because they were considered combatant troops, soldiers of the forestry corps received weapons training and carried rifles. Frederick had taken the lead in pre-selecting trainers and organizing a buddy system for those men at Port Arthur whose English skills were occasionally limited. His days were purposeful and filled, and he had little difficulty putting his wife and children second. Most of the recruits in the corps had grown up in bush families, where fathers moved around from one winter to the next, hired on as cutters, or teamsters if they were good with horses. After the spring log drives, the men returned home for the summer, many scraping together a meager living from farming. Money was scarce, and once the seasons changed and cold returned, restlessness took hold, just as surely as bears hibernated. These were the people whom Frederick molded into single units of efficiency: Poles, Scandinavians, Italians, Welsh, anyone who was willing to work hard and take orders. Men with previous experience relevant to the forestry corps were taken on at higher ranks: a blacksmith would be a sergeant, as would a sawmill foreman. Millwrights and sawyers were automatically corporals, and so forth. Impossible though it was to ignore why they were there, Frederick hadn't enjoyed himself so much since his flying days with the OPAS. When he recalled his visits to logging crews in the northern Ontario bush, he remembered the smell of sawmill diesel fuel that permeated clothing and everything else. Winter camps full of camaraderie with few fights, all steam and sweat, boiled potatoes and wet wool, folks songs played late into the night by accordion and guitar, and occasional bizarre behaviour by springtime. Men worked for decades like that, until accident or injury sent them out begging or into a grave. Almost every year a greenhorn drowned on the log drive down the Ottawa River; it was not a place for bravado or fools. In forestry's honest toil, Frederick found his home among others who didn't criticize him with a mere look. He never felt better than when he was away from Kathleen.

The Quebec military camp at Valcartier hummed with life twenty-four hours per day. Germany's *blitzkrieg* frightened many, though no one spoke openly of it. Urgency propelled a common goal to get to Europe and stop Hitler in his tracks. There was none of the happy-go-lucky attitude of the recruits in 1914. Frederick had little time to enjoy a cigarette during his days, sometimes standing outside his hut in the cold for a few minutes after dark. He did think of his wife and children intermittently, but the war effort superseded all else. He'd left his home in Port Arthur with little fanfare and no tearful goodbye from Kathleen. Now in Valcartier, the family was irrelevant against the reality of his situation. He might not even return when it came down to it. One couldn't know one's fortunes in war. Frederick turned his thoughts to the immediate future rather than what he was leaving behind. He appreciated the company of other officers and got along equally well with the ranks. Planning down to the last detail, everyone pulling together for a common objective, this is what gave him satisfaction. Frederick's skill at managing people had been put to use from the day he'd re-enlisted. He shook his head at the very notion of another war. And now he was here, in Scotland, billeted first at the Atholl Arms Hotel for a few months before being moved to Dalnacardoch Lodge the following summer. In the beauty of the Cairngorms of northeastern Scotland, Frederick never slept in, worked weekends rather than taking time off, and explored the countryside whenever he did get a chance away. It was so different from his time in the First World War. His inner jangles were quiet now and he could manage whatever came at him, be it people or problems to solve. The first time he heard the bagpipes (or perhaps only imagined that he had) on a nearby hill, his heart clenched with missing dear Ma. Her gentleness and love for Da, for all of them in the family of his birth. Already two years had gone by since her death and it still felt as if it had just happened. Being in her homeland helped his sorrow a little, and he wondered whether he'd have time to visit Girthon in Kirkcudbrightshire, where she'd been born. He would try to go there and see the parish where she had first lived. Closing his eyes, Frederick pictured her as a young girl and his heart ached. He wouldn't be able to get over to Ireland to see Da's people, he knew that already. As the commanding officer of District Four operations, Frederick was responsible for twenty-two staff at Headquarters and seven camps that included Strath Spey, Dall, and Black Island, among others.

The timber being felled grew on private lands owned by wealthy and titled individuals. Lands owned by the state had little wood available, after most of it had already been cut in the First World War. Trees had been replanted but were not sufficiently large and mature enough to be of use so soon afterwards. Britain's War Measures Act decreed that all timber would be made available for the war effort without discussion or delay. The Royal Estate at Balmoral had also been added to the list, resulting in a total of thirty-three camps operated throughout the country. Some of the private estate trees were huge, hundreds of years old, while others were diseased or dying. Prior to that time, the shortage of manpower in terms of the war was appalling. Teenaged school boys and their teachers felled trees on summer break, most with no experience whatsoever. A unit of some two thousand Newfoundland men were hired as civilian loggers in 1939 and 1940 to cut timber in both Scotland and England;

they were housed in a series of thirty camps. By the time France fell in 1940, the situation was becoming dire, and Canadian help was required as quickly as it could be made available. That year in England, the Women's Land Army was created as well as the Women's Timber Corps (known as Lumber Jill's) in an effort to get the work done, since large numbers of men had been sent off to war. Canada formed its newer version of the forestry corps in May 1940 (there had also been one in World War I), at the same time that Frederick joined up in Port Arthur. Timber operations in Great Britain were directed by the U.K. government (decisions about where the wood was sent and locations where Canadians worked), although the men were part of the Canadian military machine as soldiers and therefore subject to the discipline of military life. They were effectively a private army working for an imperial power, but the methodology worked well with few problems. Compared to logging operations in Canada, what equipment met the men was hazardous in a practical sense. Horizontal units called "benches" required logs to be pushed by hand towards the large cutting saws whirring away at top speed. Millwrights made changes to equipment to make it both safer and more efficient, and the Canadians set about assembling a diesel mill to their current standards, capable of sawing up to thirty thousand board feet of lumber in a nine-hour workday. This was up and running two months later. Soon there were nineteen mills operating throughout the five forestry districts in the country, producing railway ties, telephone and telegraph poles, and dimensional lumber for the British Admiralty, as well as pulp wood, firewood, and boards that braced the walls of infantry trenches at the front lines. Untold numbers of pit props were required in British coal mines (collieries) to support the walls of underground tunnels. Wooden decks were laid atop the metal plates of battleships and aircraft carriers because of the damage caused by empty shell casings that slammed onto the deck surface after being fired from the big guns. During naval landings at sea, plane mishaps occasionally scored the metal deck plates, creating hazards for the crew. It was cheaper and faster to replace a wooden deck rather than have the ship in dry dock for repairs. Wood also lessened the chance of sparks or fire being ignited by metal scraping against metal. Timber was constantly required for wired communication poles, replacing those lost to German bombing raids. It was vital that communications, mail, food, and war materiel be kept moving at all times. There was also a great need for wooden shipping crates for ammunition, guns, food, clothing, and explosives. Barracks were required to house troops and to provide mess halls and recreation halls for the men. As cities were bombed, lumber was necessary for reconstruction. The majority species of harvested trees consisted of Scotch pine (*Pinus sylvestris*) and larch (*Larix decidua*). Considerable quantities of beech (*Fagus sylvatica*) and birch (*Betula pendula*) were also cut. Once timbers were ready for shipment, they were sent out of the area by rail and either loaded on coastal steamers for shipment to the Continent or kept in Britain. The amount of time spent in any one harvest area depended upon the size of the stands of trees. Meetings between the officers of each district took place regularly with the Commander in Chief, Brigadier-General John Burton White, who had commanded the same type of forestry work in World War I. In between the wars, he had been a director of the International Paper Company in Canada.

Thousands were part of the CFC (Canadian Forestry Corps) in Scotland, fulfilling many different roles. As District Four commander, Frederick knew that the administrative arm was never without something to be taken care of, and he took it as a personal challenge to operate all parts of the system like a well-oiled machine. Every task, every decision, was to serve the war effort and nothing else. By the summer of 1941, he'd been promoted to Lieutenant-Colonel and reveled in his duty; it was where he felt truly at home in himself. He functioned on very little sleep, and on the rare occasions when he had an hour available, enjoyed walking out in the forests. Always with the pretext for something or other that did matter, he strode along easily, allowing a sense of calm to spread over his thoughts among the trees. Everywhere in the distance was the sound of saws or machinery or trains and not often a human voice. This time during his stroll in the woods, he heard two female voices, and he stopped for a moment, locating them not far away.

"Have ye jus' started then?"

"Aye, only this week."

"D'ye ken your way around, all right?"

"Aye, ah'm gettin' the ways of thin's."

"Good, an' don't be afeart to ask if ye need anythin'."

"Of course. Ah ken there's no suggs 'round these parts."

"Haha, ye'll be ditin' letters home to yer mam about all the hard work."

Frederick rounded a large pine and saw the young women clad in dun field coats and men's trousers. They startled, stopping their actions suddenly and staring at him. One held a tape measure and the other a log book, her hand holding a pencil.

"*Duilich!*" the shorter one said, red with embarrassment. "Ah mean, sorry to ye, sir."

"No matter, girls. I'm just taking a walk." Frederick smiled to put them at ease. His hand that had hovered over his sidearm relaxed as the dark-haired girl blinked nervously.

"Would ye have shot us, then, sir?" Her companion was taller, a braid of reddish hair spiraled about her neck. Lively green eyes.

"Not without finding out who you are first," Frederick replied. "May I have your names?"

"Oh, aye," said the darker one quickly. "Ah'm Aileen and

this here's Ellie." She nodded to her colleague. "We's the timber cruisers, like, we. . ."

Her workmate interrupted, "That's enough, Aileen. I'm sure the officer knows why we're here. We're from the forestry commission." Ellie's lips formed into a companionable smile. She waited, standing her ground, as Aileen practically wrung her hands. Frederick regarded them momentarily before saying, "I heard you from a distance – perhaps you might keep your voices down. Everyone is worried about invasion, and I don't need to tell you about spies."

Aileen's colour rose again. "We's so sorry, sir. We didn' mean nothin' by it. Jus' glad to be outta t'city."

"And you're from?" he asked.

"Glesgae, sir."

Ellie chuckled and dug a friendly elbow into Aileen's ribs. "She means Glasgow, don't ya, dear?" Ellie raised her chin. "An' I'm jus' down the road, in Inverness."

Frederick asked, "Where's your duty roster for today?"

Now Ellie faltered, "Ah, then, it's back at our barrack, sir." She cast her eyes down in submission.

He grimaced. "You must keep your papers with you at all times. Otherwise, how can we know who you are?"

"Ohhh," began Aileen.

Ellie glanced at her sternly. "Yes, sir. Of course, sir."

Frederick took a step forward, to move by the young women. "I'll check for your names as soon as I get back to headquarters."

Aileen whispered as Frederick walked. "Is 'e a general?"

Frederick answered as he passed alongside them, "No, Aileen. I'm Lieutenant-Colonel Dawson, Officer Commanding of District Four. Good day." He strode on without looking back as they watched him leave.

There was so much to do, so much to be done. The camps had been built from nothing: housing for the workers, construction of roads and bridges, setting up power plants. For the most part, the time between first arrival by the Canadians and full operation was just over three months. There were smithies and repair shops for all things mechanical, and millwrights were constantly in demand as the mills were kept running at top production. Each company had one section cutting trees and hauling out logs to yards, and a second section sawing the logs into lumber at the mill. In winter, men of the corps kept roads and rail lines open, and on top of all this, military training continued apace, as the threat of German invasion was pervasive. Frederick seldom slept and was barely out of his uniform, awake up to twenty hours per day, keeping ahead of any problems before they even materialized. Two days after meeting the young lady timber cruisers, his orderly brought him the roster of assignments for the past month. Nearly all such workers were female due the number of men in service; however, the girls (as they were called) were efficient and professional in their jobs. Some stayed in one area generally and others moved around more. A few worked alone but many worked in teams of two, as he'd seen. Since Frederick hadn't asked for their surnames, it was a challenge to find which Aileen and Ellie he was referring to. They were common enough names. He looked over the list as the orderly waited.

"Here's an Aileen in our forest, but there are two of them."

"D'you remember which day you saw them, sir?"

"Yes, oh. . .here she is. Aileen Annie Anderson. That should be easy to recall." He added, "And the other one, Ellie?"

"I haven't found one with that name around here, sir. There's a Helen, but she's over in Rosehall, Invershin. I'm quite sure she hasn't been in this district."

Frederick examined the list. "Correct. Neither of them struck me as spies, especially the younger one, but you never know." He put on his glasses and peered carefully. "What about this one? Esmée Eilidh Ross?"

The orderly reached for the sheet. "May I?" He checked it against another document. "Says she's from Inverness."

"Yes, she did say that. The one, Aileen, was from Glasgow."

"But this Ellie gave you a false name, sir."

"Better get to the bottom of it, just to be sure."

"Right, sir." The orderly looked at the papers again, not moving. "Here we go. Yes, the two women were assigned this forest when you saw them, but it doesn't explain an incorrect name."

Frederick sighed, "There must be a reason. The girl didn't seem addled in any way, so she must've known her own name."

"I'll track her down."

"Thank you. Dismissed. Bring me a cup of tea."

"Sir."

Frederick's tea arrived with the mail from overseas. His handful of letters included one from Kathleen. He opened a few of the others first before slitting open her envelope. No rosewater or delicate flower doodles in the margins from his wife. It was factual more than anything, a bit of news from Port Arthur, war efforts and the like, except he stopped reading near the end. Margaret was planning to become a nurse, a war nurse, so it said. She'd applied to the nursing program at the Royal Victoria Hospital in Montreal and hoped to go overseas after graduation. Frederick slapped his hand down on the words, pinning the letter to his desk. No! He would not allow the girl to do that and especially not to join the war. The next morning he'd dictate a letter to be sent back immediately. As it was, he passed a troubled night of little sleep.

Work continued apace in the forestry corps. Inspections, equipment maintenance, rosters, injuries, production quotas, more inspections. Germany had conducted bombing runs over Aberdeen, Dundee, and Edinburgh, and many lives had been lost during the Clydebank Blitz and in Glasgow. London and the south had borne the brunt of the bombing, and thousands were killed, with some of the evacuated children being sent to Scotland. Worries were voiced over the sawmills being targeted, and enormous piles of sawdust and shavings were left to rot, rather than being burned and therefore providing easy aerial targets for the enemy. Duties of the units included protection of their own camps and cooperation with Britain's Home Guard troops in the district. As well, they were to occupy roadblocks, defend aerodromes and flying fields within their working areas, and lastly, to attack any enemy troops that landed by air (parachutists). There were visits and inspections by high-ranking officers throughout the war years, including a Royal inspection by King George VI and Queen Elizabeth. In September 1941, selected companies of Number Two District (Aberdeenshire) were transported to Balmoral Castle to be reviewed by Their Majesties, along with Princesses Elizabeth and Margaret. Brigadier-General White and Officer Commanding Lt.-Col. Caldwell were invited to lunch at the castle afterward. Frederick knew the workings of military protocol and carried out his duties to the letter, but he never forgot the working men down the chain of command. He grew tired of so much administrative work and welcomed the chance (and change) of visiting various camps in the district. One Saturday Frederick visited a camp recreation hall, where the men played music and danced with local girls. No impropriety would be tolerated, and it was a good opportunity to let off steam and leave some of the stress of war behind. He smoked outside, alone and enjoying the sounds of a guitar and banjo from within the hall. Men from the crews nodded and said hello as they went in or out, acknowledging his presence. Frederick walked further away from the building, the music quieting, when he thought he saw a movement around the rear of the cookhouse. Stepping quietly, he came upon a soldier wiping his face and crying, clutching a letter in his hand.

"Now, then, son, what is it?" Frederick asked.

The young man jolted as he realized he'd been seen. "Oh, sorry, sir. I've had a letter, is all."

"I offer my condolences," Frederick said automatically.

"No. It's not a death, not yet. But my father's family has been taken away..." He sobbed before finishing the sentence.

"Taken away? Where are they?"

The man wiped his face and blew noisily into a handkerchief. In answer, he drew a yarmulke out of his pants pocket, an offering. Understanding dawned and Frederick asked, "What's your name, son?"

"It's Hector Adler, and I was born in Canada. But my ancestors are originally from Austria. When Zaida brought us over before the First World War, he changed our surname. It's Bernstein, or it was."

"And you still have relatives in Europe?"

"Yes, dozens of them." He held up the letter, his hand trembling. "My great aunt says the Germans have rounded up hundreds of Jews and taken them away to work camps. No one will say where they are. There are stories going around, and I'm too afraid to believe what I hear. They've been running ahead of the Nazis and have nowhere else to go." Hector sobbed again, apologizing.

"I'm sorry. I know conditions are bad for many," added Frederick.

"They were there, some of them. At Danzig's *Kristallnacht*. They watched the businesses being burned that took a lifetime to build up. They saw the synagogue in flames while they were trying to get away. My family!"

Frederick didn't know what to say and hadn't considered that some of the enlisted men in his company might be Jewish. All he could do was repeat, "I'm sorry." He left the soldier in tears and walked back to the rec hall.

On a cloudy, humid evening in September, Frederick took the truck from Blair Atholl and drove to the camp at Loch Rannoch. The mountains were broody and quiet, matching his mood. Few were about and he stood by the water for some time, thinking about everything and nothing. Cutting had gone well at this location, in contrast to some of the other camps. Everyone was doing his best, and the war couldn't last forever. Frederick hadn't had a letter from home in months, and he'd written only two himself in the past year. He was approaching the point where he couldn't pretend anymore that he wanted to go back to Kathleen and pick up that life, whatever it was. The idea of spending the rest of his days with her made him shudder. He turned and walked into a nearby stand of trees. Shade from the towering limbs darkened the light considerably but it was a comfort, like being held by a parent. His footsteps confident, he headed up the hill, where the scent of cigarette smoke came to him suddenly. Frederick stopped, half expecting a spy, or at least someone who shouldn't be there. He could see no one in the dim light and crept carefully forward, towards the aroma; it was pleasant, the same brand of tobacco that he enjoyed. And there, sitting on a naturally fallen log, was the timber cruiser girl from months before. Frederick recognized her though couldn't remember her given name, only that she was from Inverness. She turned her head and smiled. The same dimples, same long hair in a loose braid down her back.

"Sir," she said.

"Ah, yes, Miss. . .?"

"Miss Ross, sir. Ellie."

"May I join you for a smoke?"

"Of course." And she offered him a cigarette before he got out his own. He lit it, inhaling deeply, before saying, "Your name isn't Ellie. We checked." Frederick sat down a few feet away on the same log.

"Ye've got me there, then." A hint of mirth about her and she smiled.

"I'm sorry, but I can't recall your proper names."

"It's Esmée Eilidh, sir."

"Ah, now I recall. The orderly found you."

"So he did, an' I didn' even ken." She took a long drag before resting her arm on her leg, completely relaxed. "It's peaceful here, in't it?"

And Frederick delighted in her ease with him, ignoring his rank, ignoring all the protocols of war and of life, here, in this place and time. They were two people sharing a smoke, nothing more.

"That it is." He stretched out his legs, flexing his quadriceps. Frederick's leather military boots were wearing so quickly that they felt like well-used slippers. After a few minutes' silence, he asked, "Where did the name Esmée Eilidh come from?"

"Ah, well, my parents were romantics, y'see. Daddy loved the French and so he wanted the name Esmée for me. It means beloved in their language. Mam insisted on something Gaelic and so she chose Eilidh, which means from the island."

"That's a good choice," Frederick admitted.

"Aye, but they fought for weeks over which order to put the names!" she laughed.

"And you're from Inverness?"

"Bit of a nosy one, ahn't you, sir?" Ellie winked as he began to protest.

"Before ye ask, I use Ellie just so's it's easier and I don' have t'explain to each new person. There's been a lot o' them in this war. And aye, I was born in Inverness."

"Are your parents still there?"

"Aye, but y'ken, my real daddy died when I was wee." She stopped suddenly, coughing. A catch in her throat, a sob, before she spat impressively as if to rid herself of long-ago grief.

"I'm sorry." Frederick felt as if he said that phrase often.

"Aye, thank ye." Ellie took another long drag on her cigarette. "Daddy was part of the Gamecock Fleet. Dunno if ye've heard of it? He was crew on a herring ship that was sunk in 1916 by a German submarine."

"That's awful. How terrible for your mother."

"Aye, she had a hard time of it, with me still a toddler. But some years later, Mam found a good man and remarried; Douglas is his name. He's a fine sort, treats me well."

"That's good."

"I have a half-brother, Donal. He's with the 2nd Battalion, Argyll & Sutherland Regiment. I know he's grown up already, but I still see him as a bairn, I cannae help it. He just turned twenty-one."

"Where is he now?"

"In a place called Malay. I don' even ken where that is." Ellie shuddered, holding her arms together. "It's hard for Mam to have both of us gone, but I'm not far away, am I?"

"No, and I'm sure your parents appreciate seeing you all the more."

"Aye." Ellie was quiet, her cigarette burned near to its end. Another smile, then, "My turn for a question. Is this yer first time in Scotland?"

"Aye, but my mother was born in Kirkcudbrightshire."

"Ah, yer practically a native an' ye talk like us wit' yer *aye*. Where's your dada from?"

"Ireland. County Armagh."

"Hmmm. Were ye in the first war?"

"In France."

"What did ye do there?"

"I don't want to talk about it."

Ellie finished her cigarette, sighed, and stood up. Frederick didn't move, thinking that he could spend his remaining days on earth in this very spot. She shouldered her kit bag. "Per'aps we'll meet again if this war keeps goin'."

"I'd like that."

"War took my daddy away and now it's taken my little brother. God*damn* those evil men who start it!" She wiped away an angry tear, her good mood vanished. "I'm young, I shouldn't have t' be thinkin' of death all the time. I want a normal life! Ye ken, there's a new film out, *Northwest Mounted Police* with Gary Cooper. All the girls love him. I want that in my life, not this." She gestured up at the sky and trees in the near dark. "I want a life, not a war." Ellie tramped down the hill without looking back and without saying good-bye.

Frederick remained sitting on the log until well after dark. Without a torch light, he wasn't worried about finding his way back – the sound of gentle waves in the loch was behind him. Lighting his own cigarette now, he wasn't upset by the girl's talk or her outburst at the end. She's right, he thought, she doesn't deserve to have to live like this, wondering when death will come to those she loves. He sighed, knowing the loss of so many lives and hearing rumours of concentration camps in Europe, where Jews were killed by the thousands. The Blitz he knew was real, but he couldn't believe in death camps. No one could be that depraved, not even Hitler. Reflections strayed back to the first war, the one that would end all wars, and here they were again, barely a generation later. Frederick was glad that James was too young to join up, as the boy probably would do just that. Irritation crept in with Margaret's plan to become a military nurse. He would not allow that and had told Kathleen as much.

Frederick closed his eyes, finishing his smoke. Remembering Kathleen in the New Inn as a young woman, her dark beauty that had beguiled him so. Running headlong into a disastrous future with her, ending up lonelier than he'd ever been, even on the front lines. Ellie was young enough to be his daughter.

He could no longer imagine being married to a loving woman who would support him in all things, whose love was never in doubt. Ellie deserved to find a husband who would care for her above all else, and he hoped she'd find one who would do just that. Stamping out his cigarette, Frederick stood stiffly and went back to his vehicle. The engine grumbled on starting and he drove slowly back on the road, its gravel base softened by yesterday's rain. On the last incline, the truck's power faltered and then the engine stalled. Frederick waited a few moments before cranking the starter again. It was dead, probably the magneto, he thought. Too dark to repair it and not a long walk from here, so he disembarked and strolled along under a cloudy night, the partial moon winking in and out. By the time he returned to his room, he was more awake than asleep. He undressed slowly, hanging up his dirty uniform for the orderly to take the next morning. Always a new one ready, pressed and impressive, all he had to do was to put it on. Just for a moment, Frederick felt himself drawn into a different reality, the one where Da was birthed, the green fields of Ireland. He could picture his father as a youngster and imagined him in the years until he left the island, nursing a sorrow that never truly left. Frederick put on his pajamas and sat up with a drink of whiskey, his emotions a shudder. He watched his own life spool out, thinking of Ellie's comment on how the war had changed everything, and it had. Why hadn't he been shot down in France in 1917? How could the company of an illiterate Finnlander in the northern bush be preferable to him over anyone else so many social rungs above that? There were no answers, there were none. He fell asleep in his chair.

Chapter Eleven

Scotland, 1942

America joined the war after the bombing of Pearl Harbour (Hawaii) by the Japanese in December 1941. It was a relief for England's Churchill, a bit of breathing space. The cost was already enormous and now there was a better chance of winning for the Allies. Britain had requested another ten companies of the forestry corps to support the ever-increasing demand for lumber. The local roads of northern Scotland were in deplorable condition from constant use by overloaded lorries. Most of the wood had been shipped previously by train, to the point of holding up other necessary shipments to local communities. Railroads could no longer handle the volume using them, and so loads of wood were sent to Aberdeen where they could be shipped by sea down the east coast. Late January 1942 brought a tremendous snowstorm, completely blocking all thoroughfares, including the one that led to the port in Aberdeen. New tracks built to access timber were nothing but muck and mudslides for days on end; forestry crews spent much time repairing them in heavy rain. In some of the camps, drainage ditches were dug and duckboards lain down in order to provide any means at all of walking from place to place. Rivers could not be used for moving logs as was done in Canada, since preserving habitat for salmon stocks was a priority in Scotland. Snow removal presented a different challenge because motorized plow trucks were not available to the foresters, only the caterpillar tractor, which was inefficient compared to what was used back home. And in all that, the crews kept working around the clock. In the woods, a trio felled and limbed the trees using eight-foot crosscut saws and axes only. Injuries by tired men were not uncommon, although few were serious. When they weren't in use clearing snow, the caterpillar tractor teams (another trio) dragged the evergreens to roadside landings, hauling them with chains. Once there, the trees were cut to different lengths, usually sixteen to eighteen feet. The British Navy required twenty-four to twenty-six foot lengths and these were cut as well. Frederick was proud of the entire corps and especially of his own companies in District Four, hosting visiting estate owners and newspaper reporters who couldn't seem to get enough of these hard-working Canadians. Reports were glowing on the progress (in terms of war) and camaraderie of the bush workers. Men were permitted to invite their girlfriends and wives to come and see what camp operations looked like. Frederick tramped and drove around the district like a school inspector, always moving, always assessing, always thinking. He preferred it this way, rather than give in to the broodiness that struck him on occasion. Treasuring the smoke break that he and Ellie had taken at Loch Rannoch the previous autumn, Frederick rewound their conversation on many occasions when he was alone. He'd seen her only a handful of times since, and then from a distance. Even though he knew her proper name, he thought of her as Ellie, the same as everyone else. What was it about her? Frederick felt drawn to her in a way that he couldn't easily define, and he imagined having dinner with such a lovely young girl, someone who wanted nothing from him in return. With his wife, Kathleen, he knew he'd never measure up to whatever criteria she set out for him. Why couldn't that imperious bitch (he shocked himself on thinking these words for the first time) simply be happy to be his wife, to be anyone's wife? Instead of deferring to him as she should have, the woman seemed intent on taunting him with her self-aggrandizing thoughts of being a magnet for men. He had lost all trust in her, and the die had been cast. Frederick would never be certain of Margaret's parentage. It wasn't the girl's fault, yet he felt unable to warm up to her. It was different with James – the boy was definitely his son. Ellie's demeanour demonstrated her personality in stark contrast to Kathleen's. Here was a girl who reached out of herself in giving. Everyone loved her in the camps as she roved around the forests, sometimes alone and sometimes training a new girl. Ellie was kind and funny and positive, and Frederick believed that her outburst that night with him was one of the few times that her armour had cracked around anyone else. She was only human, and this is what drew him to her. He would never approach her or seek her out, and their infrequent meetings were nothing more than chance. She was somehow real in a way that Kathleen was not.

Work in the forest was preferable to all else for Frederick, save good dinners with other officers in whatever castle they were billeted to. He was getting used to Scottish food which wasn't bad in general, except for the appalling haggis, that and the lack of fresh meat due to rationing. Still, the men were fed well, given the energy they needed for their jobs. They were a good bunch of lads. A blind eye was turned on village poachers who kept them supplied with rabbits, but nobody fooled the cook with tales of chicken.

"Sir?" The orderly stood just inside the door to his office, in the early dark of winter.

"What is it?" Frederick asked.

"One of the sawyers at Insh has cut off his thumb. He's been taken to hospital at Inverness for treatment."

"Is there a replacement for him?"

"Not yet, sir. They're trying to get a man from Torwood over, but the roads haven't been cleared yet."

"Blasted snow. We'll need sled dogs out here soon enough."

"Sir."

"Let me know when the sawyer's back."

"Sir."

Frederick sighed, a half-glass of malt whiskey in his hand. A missing thumb, just in time for regular Saturday military drills, the last thing anyone needed at the moment. Still, the war came first. It had been a difficult week with equipment breakdowns and another man injured by a falling tree, and his own first report still wasn't done yet. He emptied his tumbler and sat down at the typewriter, lighting a cigarette.

February fourteenth landed on a Saturday that year. A Valentine's Day dance was scheduled for Inverness and scores of men were looking forward to it. Frederick attended as many social events as practicable, and he'd missed some because of other duties or inclement weather. He wasn't far away at Kingussie and so made the trip with a few other officers and men. Never one to sit behind a desk when he could be outside, Frederick was popular with his get-it-done attitude, seldom losing his decorum in any situation and treating others with respect and good humour. He acknowledged his rank but didn't let that get in the way of letting the men know that he was always available to them. This night the snow had mercifully abated and the roads were bare if somewhat slippery in sections. They arrived as the band warmed up, the hall already full. He nodded to another officer, doffing his cap.

"Nice enough evening for it, eh?"

The officer smiled. "You sound like a Canadian with your *eh* all the time. But I heard you're Scottish?"

Frederick grinned. "We understand each other. And my mother was Scottish. I was born in England."

Young couples took to the dance floor, moving energetically, preferring local musicians to the military orchestra that often played. Frederick looked at the door briefly and then the far corner, half-expecting to see Ellie. She wasn't there. They hadn't crossed paths for months.

"Your work clearing the local roads has been much appreciated," added the officer, "although all the wet must make your job harder."

"It does," answered Frederick. "I think the boys prefer our Canadian winters. At least the ground freezes hard for a few months. The constant rain and mud here present a challenge, but we're up for it."

"Well, everyone's impressed, from the locals to the brass to the Royals. At the rate you're cutting, pretty soon there won't be any trees left."

"Don't worry, there's plenty more to do."

Two camp men passed closely by, speaking French between them, each with a girl on his arm.

The officer nodded with pleasure. "Nice to see everyone fitting in here. I don't think some of the villagers ever heard French spoken before now."

Frederick chuckled. "And it hasn't held them up with the ladies!"

Hours passed by in fellowship for all present, a few couples heading outside to kiss in private. Dozens of marriages had taken place in the forestry corps since their arrival. If one could forget there was a war on, it was a happy time to be alive. Some made a point of avoiding the news and concentrating on their work. A few of the men had lost their fathers in the first war and needed no reminding. Frederick enjoyed himself, having a drink of beer and dancing with a girl or two (and feeling like a chaperone instead of a dance partner, he noted with chagrin). He missed seeing Ellie, he admitted to himself. Maybe he did want her but pushed the thought from his mind. The drive back to camp was uneventful, other than being stopped by a military picket. Frederick spoke with the guards briefly before carrying on. He'd decided to go and see the sawyer with the missing thumb in a few days, hoping that the man could get back to work soon. Missing fingers were the mark of most who worked in sawmills, it was a fact of life, and they'd had few injuries so far. The worst thing for any soldier was a feeling of being useless; Frederick got enough of that in his marriage, and he determined to do everything he could to keep the injured man working.

The Wednesday was bright and sunny, below freezing. On the way to Inverness, Frederick stopped at Phoineas House for a meeting with Brigadier-General White that lasted just under an hour. He arrived at the hospital before noon, happy to see the sawyer doing well and wanting to return to work. The injury was not as bad as feared, only missing the end of the digit to the first knuckle, and the man would stay on strength once his hand was better. Buoyed by the soldier's cheerful spirit and eagerness, Frederick left and stood outside the hospital, lighting a cigarette.

"Ah, sir," a voice called from nearby.

He'd know it anywhere. "Ellie! What a pleasure to see you." The words stalled before he'd finished his sentence. Ellie's eyes brimmed with tears.

"My dear," Frederick said, "Come and sit down. Tell me what's wrong." He squashed his smoke under his boot and guided her to the bench beside the main doors.

Ellie allowed him near but brushed away his proffered arm.

They sat close together, not touching. He waited for her to compose herself.

"Ohhh," she moaned. "I can barely say the words."

"I'm here, I'm listening." People came and went all around them yet the world had suddenly become very small.

"It's Donal," she said on a sob.

Oh, no, he thought. *He's been killed.*

Frederick took her hand gently and this time she let him. "Tell me what happened, Ellie." His voice was soft, encouraging.

"I've just come from Mam and Douglas. They got a telegram. Donal's regiment surrendered at Singapore. They say my brother is a prisoner of war." Her words were jerky. "Mam's in shock, we all are." She hiccoughed.

Frederick let go of her hand. "I'm so sorry, Ellie."

She cried, "My little brother, wee Donal. It cannae be true!"

He gave her his handkerchief and she wiped her eyes and nose. He'd heard the news already about the surrender but didn't realize that's where Donal was. A prisoner of the Japanese. Frederick's heart stilled.

That night, back in his room, and for nights afterward, he couldn't sleep. Tossed and turned, got up and smoked. Headache, back ache, stomach ache. If he were lucky, he'd drop into a fitful doze an hour before dawn when the orderly's wretched cheeriness would wake him. Ghosts of the first war haunted behind his sight, their gruesome bodies come alive. It was one thing to know that men were killed on paper but quite another to see it close up or to know one personally. Suddenly the scene came to him, remembered after he'd first got to the front in France, when the young soldier shot himself a few feet away. Japan hadn't been in the war long and was already known for its savagery, the "yellow peril." They'd just bombed Darwin, Australia, killing hundreds. Frederick couldn't imagine Ellie's brother surviving a prisoners' camp. Nelson and *England expects* and suddenly he couldn't do it anymore, smothering a sob in the darkened, claustrophobic room. How he hated what had taken the light out of dear Ellie's eyes. Nursing a tumbler of whiskey, he remembered Ma's words from long ago, whispering of Da's Irish heart, where love and sorrow were twinned tight, and the two could not be unhooked one from the other. For the first time, Frederick understood his father's loss, a piece of his soul excised forever in the famine. *Oh, Da*, he moaned. Now with his drink, he felt completely emptied out and there were mere hours before he dressed again as Officer Commanding, put on his military bearing and carried on. Another day and another after that. It had to be done.

With America's entry into the war, Germany had a field day with their U-boats in the Atlantic, sinking merchant ships; they called it the turkey shoot. Great Britain was desperate for goods from North America in the form of weapons, food, raw materials, and fuel. It added up to more than a million metric tonnes per week. Convoys left Halifax, Nova Scotia, escorted by the Royal Canadian Navy and, perhaps by nothing more than ill luck, they were intercepted twice as often as ships of the British Navy. During the entire course of the war, over thirty thousand merchant navy seamen lost their lives. Civilian deaths also occurred, with the sinking of the vessel *The City of Benares* by torpedo, off the coast of Ireland in 1940. Children were being transported from Great Britain to Canada for safety, and as a result of this deliberate hostile act by Germany, the program of evacuees being sent across the ocean was discontinued. At times, if it weren't for Churchill's rousing speeches, hope would have soon turned to despair. Everyone dreaded the individual telegrams that brought news of death. The forestry corps kept working at top speed despite the weather that only men from Vancouver were used to, and Fort William received more than nine inches of rain that summer. Timber shipments left from

Inverness and Aberdeen, Cromarty and Burghead, carrying every last tree from Scotland it seemed. There were no more century-old conifers left to cut. Exhausted by the weekend, camp crews still donned their uniforms for Saturday drill, but they were recompensed by entertainment courtesy of the Scottish military band on a regular basis. The first time Frederick stood at attention during parade to hear "A' Dol Dhachaigh" on the bagpipes, he felt the worst pain in his sternum and imagined dear Ma listening to the same when she was a little girl with her own da. Another time the corps men watched a display of traditional Highland dancing at Inverness. After living and working in mud for much of the past two years, the men were spellbound by the bright tartans and brighter smiles of the performing youngsters. No one wolf-whistled at the girls and a few held unshed tears as they thought their faraway thoughts of children left behind in their own homes.

A loaded lorry went off the road in heavy rains once and overturned, throwing the driver part-way out of the cab. His injuries were severe and a rescue team took him to Darnaway Castle (converted to a military hospital) where he died. Friends of the soldier hung their heads low as they mourned at the service of remembrance in his camp. Frederick gave a short eulogy, extolling the deceased's qualities of kindness, a sense of fun and hard work; no words could lessen their collective pain. The body would be returned to Canada for burial. That evening, Frederick wrote a letter to the man's parents, describing the son they hadn't seen in over two years. All their future promise gone. At least the soldier wasn't married yet, meaning one less heart to break. By the end of the week, full production in the corps had resumed and the following month, everyone enjoyed a sports day. Different camps forded teams to compete at horseshoes, football, tug of war, and baseball, a game that the Scots could make neither heads nor tails of. The Canadians had given up on hockey the first winter, since no ice rink was suitable for the game and all it did was rain. However, they did teach the locals log-rolling skills in the lochs, always a popular event. Wives and girlfriends rounded out the group, on a glorious summer day with remarkably little cloud. Brigadier-General White toured Frederick's camp at Strath Spey for an informal review.

"We've accomplished a lot," the senior officer said.

"Aye, sir, that we have."

"If I hadn't been here in the first war, I'd never believe how much it rains."

Frederick squinted at the sun. "Nice to have good weather today."

White nodded. "How have you found working with the French Canadians?"

"They're a good lot, no different from the others. The locals love them, apparently."

"In what way d'you mean?"

"At the dances. They never have any trouble picking up Scottish girls."

"It's a good thing, what with the conscription debate. I can't call it a crisis yet. Quebec won't have it, and the sooner McKenzie King realizes that, the better off we'll be."

"Sir."

"I doubt they'll get enough volunteers willing to come overseas. We're not in the same position as in World War I. Borden paid the price for that."

"Sir."

White adjusted his cap. "Well, I'm off to the next camp. Good job, Dawson, you're doing fine."

"Thank you, sir."

Frederick watched the games for a few more minutes before heading to his room for a whiskey with his feet up. Even he earned a break now and then. Eleven requests for forty-eight-hour leave passes waited on his desk for approval. Leaning back in his chair, his boots off, Frederick wondered about Ellie. He'd meant to write a letter home the previous month but had left it, and there had been no contact from Kathleen. Enjoying the warmth of his drink, he mused at how those two women always appeared together in his mind, when neither knew of the other's existence. Try as he might, he could not accurately define the quality in Ellie that so attracted him. She was stubborn and strong, the same as his wife, but somehow the girl had no edges. Frederick remembered back to his time in France, when he was still in the service corps. It was almost a dream now, this much later, as if he'd only imagined it all without actually being there. The horses they had to shoot or were shot by Germans, the dumped wagonloads of desperately needed supplies, infantry soldiers toughened and ending their lives in gore, calling for their mothers. When he met Kathleen, he'd been at the edge of collapse, believing he too would soon shoot himself if only to escape the world as he knew it. She represented strength and beauty and something about never giving in, like a life-ring thrown to a drowning man. And yet, could he admit now that he didn't want her, he wanted what she represented instead, a type of military faith, if there was such a thing? The sense of rightness, an unwavering belief in the supremacy of Britain's victory in war, tied to this woman who was the counter-balance to his weakness; that was how he saw it then, subconsciously. He wanted to be wedded to her, to draw on that strength as he needed it, whenever he needed it. But she wasn't that strength, she was her own person whom he hadn't seen as an individual in his own immaturity. After their marriage and especially after the birth of Margaret, he saw Kathleen as herself for the first time, what her wants and needs were, and they were not the same as his own. Some of the officers, married ones, did take lovers while serving and they were the souls of discretion. There was no question of divorce, of not returning home to the wives and children they already had. In truth, he hadn't been tempted until now. So much work to be done in the forestry corps, and he genuinely loved what he was doing. He experienced no homesickness whatsoever. Meeting Ellie had jolted his sensibilities, knowing that she was caught up in war in the same way that he had been affected twenty years earlier. She felt the worst of it, swam in it, where it engulfed her. Frederick had been where she was now, and he wanted to comfort her and tell her she would be all right. There was simply no way for them to be together, other than random meetings which were fewer now as time went by. He wanted to write a personal letter to her, but there was no means for him to reach her without drawing attention to himself. It was inappropriate from all directions. He wished he could lie down with her and stroke her hair. Instead of drawing on her strength as he had with Kathleen in 1917, he would give Ellie his own, something he'd never done with anyone. It was giddy, silly old man talk. This is what he told himself.

Lighting a cigarette, Frederick recalled his childhood war games with his friends, not understanding then what war actually was: the snuffing out of humanity. Yes, there was right and wrong, but in the end, they were all just human flesh, blood the same from one as another. When a man dies, does it really matter which side he is on? Frederick was no longer sure. He sighed, set down his glass and put on his boots for another round outside. Nothing lasted forever, not even war. And not Ellie, nor him. He couldn't help thinking of Da's utter devotion to Ma, all of their long lives together. Da would not approve of his son's want for Ellie. And Da was gone, too.

By June of that year, the moors actually became dry, and camp men assisted in firefighting with the local civilians. Luckily the fires were small due to the *muirburns* (controlled burning of heather) carried out the previous autumn. Given the nearly constant rain in Scotland, it was almost surprising that anything would catch alight. There was lowered risk in the forest for the simple reason of so many of the trees being cut down and the ground rucked up by tractors, making it difficult for fires to attain purchase. The look of the landscape had changed, noted by the men in remote camps who hiked or went cycling when they were too far away from village halls and dances to attend on their time off. Hills were denuded and stark, giving long and wide horizon views. At one of the camp concerts, a local guest complained that soon there wouldn't be a single tree left standing anywhere in the country. Thirty-four German bombing raids were made over Aberdeen over the early part of the war, leaving almost two hundred civilians dead and almost three times that many injured. Despite not burning their slab and sawdust piles to avoid detection of the camps, bombs were dropping close enough to make the men keep one eye on the sky at all times. Allied planes crashed in accidents from time to time, causing disruption in forestry operations though not for long. All five districts continued going full bore, a well-oiled Canadian production machine. Occasionally, men of the corps helped to build new airfields and repair existing ones that had been damaged by bombs. The Royal family remained an inspiration to all in the United Kingdom, with young Princess Elizabeth making her first public radio broadcast with her sister, Princess Margaret, in October 1940. Later, Elizabeth carried out her first public engagement by inspecting the Grenadier Guards as their honorary colonel. She also joined the Auxiliary Territorial Service, where she trained to repair and drive lorries. The steadfast refusal of the King and Queen and their daughters to bow to fear and despair gave the country hope and determination to keep going. As with Prime Minister Churchill, they would never leave, never surrender. Only once, Frederick thought of staying on after the war, in England or Scotland, instead of going back to his family.

Soon after the rains returned later that summer, news of the Allied failure to establish a beachhead at Dieppe hung heavy on everyone's minds. Despite much planning and intent at achieving success on a beachhead, Canadian casualties counted more than three thousand, with almost two thousand more taken prisoner. One of the CFC men was given two days' leave to attend the funeral of his cousin in Suffolk. He returned grim, cutting down trees in fury until his rage was spent. District officers discussed war matters informally because, after all, what could be done? The following weeks ushered in more dances, dinners, and a sheep dog trial that was well attended. In mid-September, a chartered bus of Women's Land Army members came to visit, in order to learn how to measure, cut, and load trees. The girls were earnest and hard-working, and after a few days' instruction, returned to all-female camps in England, Scotland, and Wales. Numerous were the plaintive good-byes of the men, appreciating the presence of females in trousers, some of whom wore lipstick. One sawyer from Calgary swore he'd find his chosen girl after the war, marry her, and take her back to Canada.

Wet snow fell in early December, inciting the annual holiday fervor in the highlands – it was the one time of year when residents felt able to celebrate. Camp men used the workshop and scrap wood to make toys for local children, or they fixed items free of charge. Families with enough money purchased firewood from the camps, and some wood ended up free in the yards of the poor, having fallen off the lorry with a wink and a nudge. Christmas was memorable and Frederick enjoyed military dinners where he and other officers and NCOs served the ranks. Truly, they'd become one large family in their struggle to carry out their duty. King George VI delivered his annual speech on the BBC, and Brigadier-General White required that printed copies of the text be made available at the camps. Santa Claus was busy visiting recreation halls, where children received gifts of toffee, chocolate, and perhaps a small book. The men treated the civilians as they would their own, and a few fought tears thinking of their wives and families celebrating so far away. When the men saw the worry on the faces of local wives whose husbands were serving soldiers, they could only imagine what their own wives were feeling. The Battle of the Atlantic was not over, and who could say whether any of them would make it home safely?

On Christmas Day night, quite late, Frederick poured himself a brandy, his uniform crumpled on the chair in his room, cigar smoldering on the table beside his bed. He lay half-sitting, rereading the brief letter from Kathleen. Of all the things she could've written, she chose to list the young men from Port Arthur who were either killed or missing, presumed dead. Was it some kind of black joke? He wouldn't put it past her. They were much too far apart to miss each other's company, but still. Meeting someone like Ellie had led to a change in him, he could feel it. Frederick couldn't see divorce as an option; if he chose that, he would be a disgraced officer, something he'd never allow. And Ellie would never have him as a husband, he was sure of that. She needed a young man, one full of love and adventure like she was, not a father figure. He sighed, thinking that only death would separate Kathleen from him. How he wished that he'd seen into the future in that bleak winter of 1917, when he'd returned to London from France. As he finished his cigar and drink, he set Kathleen's letter aside and remembered his last Christmas alone. It had been in Popperinghe, twenty-six years earlier, as he lay sick with trench fever, yearning to get back to England. Frederick wished somehow that he could access a time tunnel, and find Ellie when she was his age instead of hers. How happy he might've been with her.

Chapter Twelve

Scotland, 1943

As winter 1942 slid into early 1943, Nazi Germany's fortunes were turning in the tides of war, and not to their benefit. During February, the Reich's Sixth Army surrendered at Stalingrad. The Eastern Front counted over two million casualties from both sides in the months-long battle, the greatest military campaign loss of life in world history. By the end of the war in 1945, that number had risen to thirty million, including civilian deaths. The Axis loss in the Soviet Union marked the tipping point of Hitler's tyranny, and there were many more contests to fight. Churchill called it the end of the beginning, and he was correct. Montgomery's Eighth Army was victorious at El Alamein; the Wehrmacht proved no longer unstoppable. It was bittersweet success for the Allies following the failures of Dunkirk and Dieppe, a leveling of sorts. British and American bombing of cities deep inside Germany forced Hitler to defend his home territory, pulling needed resources away from other campaign fronts. The Soviets went all out against their enemy, and an ocean of Aryan blood could not assuage their thirst for revenge. Dunrobin Castle at Golspie, Scotland, had lain under a hush the previous summer when it received the Duke of Kent's body following his fatal air crash on a hillside near Dunbeath. As brother of the King, no one was untouched by war, including Prince George, who had died in the accident. But even that, the first death of a serving royal in four hundred and fifty years, could not dampen the sense of hope that one day peace would prevail.

Around the clock the forestry corps continued their duty, cutting and hauling trees from further and further distances from the camps. Frederick contemplated how many millions of seedlings would need to be planted in order to restore the forests that had been sacrificed. The foresters were unseen, unheard in a sense, when compared to the more visible men and women in uniform fighting across Europe, but the camp men were well known and loved by the Scottish people who saw them daily. Local businesses washed laundry from the barracks, and corps men purchased goods and services in the towns and villages, keeping employment levels stable. The many marriages that had already taken place testified to the good relations between the Scots and Canadians. Approximately twenty-five percent of all Canucks who went to Scotland married local girls whom they took back to Canada with them after the war. Besides planned children, there were illegitimate ones sprinkled among the lot, the result of fevered liaisons. A number of Canadians of Scottish ancestry who had previously loosed ties with their homeland found family bonds restored. It was a busy time as Frederick attended a meeting at Phoineas House, to discuss how quickly the forest stands had been depleted in the previous two and one-half years. For all that was on his mind, as he entered the meeting, all Frederick could think of was his brief conversation with Ellie about her brother, Donal.

Brigadier-General White welcomed the district commanders with pleasantries before sitting them down to discuss the future of the forestry corps. Windows were open in the hall due to unseasonal spring warmth.

"Gentlemen," he began, "There are reasons for hope now in this war. We've won the Battle of the Atlantic, and U-boats are no longer a threat to shipping. The Canadians are just now gaining a foothold in Sicily. Things are changing, and it's about time. If I had my way, we'd see no more of our boys lost anywhere, but I'm not so naïve as that. And I don't need to tell you how valuable the work of the forestry corps has been to the outcome of the war. The Brits are more than pleased with our performance, the men in Whitehall have told me more than once. By God, the people here won't soon forget us."

"Here, here," said Frederick, and the others joined in agreement.

White continued, "You know yourselves how much wood we've harvested, and it's true, some areas are pretty well denuded of trees. A massive effort will be made to replant, but that's not a discussion for today. At peak strength, we number close to seven thousand, of all ranks. I've gathered you here to report that sometime later this year, several hundred from the corps will be assigned other duties in other places. In short, it means that your camps will be broken up."

There was momentary silence. "Any specifics yet, sir?" one of the district commanders asked.

"No, but I imagine it could be more than a few companies, perhaps as many as seven or eight. Decisions are made elsewhere in this, as you know."

Frederick looked out the window. Before speaking, he thought of his first airplane solo. He said, "It's going to be hard for everyone. They've worked together and formed allegiances."

"You don't need to remind me, Dawson. I know that," replied White.

Another man sighed. "We've accomplished a lot here, haven't we?"

White continued, "It's because of how much we've done that we're in this position. I expect that some men will be sent to the Continent, France or Germany, as foresters. Others will join armoured or infantry regiments. I don't know yet, I can't say. There aren't enough trees left anymore to keep the camps running as they have been. The need is still there, but mills will be set up in other locations. It's inevitable." He stood and the officers straightened in their chairs. "Let's go out and enjoy the sunshine for a change."

They rose as one and put on their forage caps, striding for the door and a smoke. A few words with White before he left them, followed by a few minutes to talk among themselves.

"It's not that I want the war to go on, but in some ways, this has been the best time of my life."

"By God, I don't want to have to tell the men."

"Yeah, but they aren't stupid. They know we can't keep it going forever."

"Have your junior officer do the dirty work for you," one said, laughing.

"No. We need to maintain respect and authority. When the time comes, each of us will do it for his district."

"I need a drink."

"Well, no point shitting over it now. Wait for the word. It's been good here, none of us in much personal danger from Jerry. Not like the poor buggers at the front."

"What about you, Dawson? What d'you say?"

Frederick blew out a long stream of smoke, squinting towards the sun. "I say I like it here."

"Don't look, but White's watching. We'd better go."

Cigarettes were stamped underfoot as they climbed into their vehicles.

At the end of his regular duties that day, Frederick brooded, walking alone through the denuded landscape near the loch, staying near the last stand of trees. The tall green sentinels made him feel protected. He recalled what had gone right for the corps in Scotland: no camps had been bombed, either deliberately or accidentally; only a handful of deaths and serious injuries had occurred; morale was good, bolstered by the presence of the Royal family nearby at Balmoral. His colleague after the meeting was correct with his comment that they had it so much better than other soldiers. Honest physical work in all weathers, enjoying friendships and good rapport with the locals, weddings and babies and company dinners. The prospect of leaving it all behind was not a happy one, necessary though it might be. Frederick coughed as he inhaled from his cigarette, a small shock of recognition that soon he would no longer see Ellie nor any of the forestry commission people. How well they had all worked together, a perfect fit in the jigsaw of war efforts. Coughing more, he threw down the butt, crossed his arms and leaned against a tree. It was silent, darkness coming quickly. *Oh, Ellie.* Was he in love with her? No, not that. He'd seen her just six or eight times in total since he'd arrived in 1940. They were nothing more than two people sharing a common piece of history. Frederick began walking again, feeling worse. Leaving Scotland meant the end of the war was at last on the horizon. And later? He would return to Canada and Kathleen, something that filled him with dread. There was not even an imagination that led him to believe she would welcome him as a wife should. No matter how he turned the matter over in his mind, Frederick could not find the place to set Ellie down and watch her there, wanting nothing from her. He fantasized over her sometimes, when he woke in the morning, other times when he least expected it. Her warmth and good humour and fiery temper just below the surface. The girl was like a spark, not like the many thousands of people who went through life as a herd of sheep: go here, be there, do that. Ellie was different, and he wanted to be around that thing in her, whatever it was. Next year he would turn fifty, half a century old. His parents had emigrated at that age, such a change for older folk. But they did it, they worked hard and stayed in the new land, stayed together in love and died within the same year. Frederick loosened his collar and tie, swallowing. How he wanted to be loved! He wiped his eyes on his sleeve and started walking while the forest listened to his heart. He knew what to do for his district, pass the word along to have a few celebratory events before the corps broke up. Invite the forestry commission people as well, the timber cruisers. Ellie.

With the cooperation of the Royal Navy and Royal Air Force, the Canadians and Americans reached their objectives by landing virtually unopposed on two beaches in Sicily during Operation Husky in July 1943. What followed were months of tough fighting, a grind from the heel to the top of Italy's boot. In May of that year, Churchill had met with President Roosevelt at the Trident conference in Washington, D.C., where an overall view of the war's future was discussed. An invasion of France was to take place in 1944, code-named Overlord, and Italy needed to be forced out of the war. In this scenario, the Allies would secure the port of Naples and the Foggia airfields across the peninsula. It looked easy on paper. In reality, desperate battles occurred with German counterattacks, and the armies of Britain, Canada, and the United States fought their way north with determination through the dry hills and valleys of the south. Salerno, Monte Cassino, Ortona: these became part of Allied lexicon by the end of the year. Churchill's prize was the capture of Rome, where Mussolini was arrested. In August, the Quebec Conference hosted Roosevelt and Churchill once again, hosted by Canadian Prime Minister Mackenzie King. What the Allies wanted was to tie up as many German divisions as possible in the south, leaving a much thinner mass of them available in France, where the 1944 invasion was planned. The strategy worked, as Hitler commanded his troops to continue fighting in Italy, and this action helped to ensure the success of the Allied landings in Normandy, by their not facing the full strength of the German army. After Hitler's loss on the Eastern Front and now another one in Italy, the Allies had a much better chance of success on D-Day.

Not knowing what the future held required a faith in outcomes that was easier for some than others. The war deaths continued, entwined with hope. A Royal Navy aircraft carrier, *HMS Dasher*, was accidentally destroyed in an internal explosion on the Firth of Clyde, with the loss of over seventy percent of her crew. The most intense bombing of Aberdeen took place, and actor Leslie Howard was killed when the passenger plane he was flying in was shot down by Germans in the Bay of Biscay. Against those losses, the Dambuster raids breached dams in the Ruhr valley, disrupting Germany's war industry production. Over one thousand people were killed by catastrophic flooding, and two hydro-electric stations were destroyed. In hindsight, the results were perhaps less of a contributing factor to the war's end, although they gave a tremendous morale boost to Britain, in a truly remarkable feat of engineering and planning.

Frederick followed the war news regularly this time, unlike during his first war. Then, he didn't think he'd survive, and he thought only of the next few hours at the front lines or his next flight later on. Now he saw his future in front of him and wondered where it might lead. Things were moving quickly, without the long stalemates at the European fronts that had occurred in the conflict decades earlier. He was amazed by the technological progress in aviation and the machines built for killing men. To think that he'd flown in a wooden and fabric aircraft, a delicate thing like a child's toy, and now youngsters who hadn't even been born at that time were flying the new P51 Mustang and the Spitfire. He shook his head to realize the change in supremacy; no wonder the Allies had won the air war. It was only a matter of time until everyone was being sent home. However, the war in the Pacific was not on the same trajectory as that in Europe. Stories abounded of Japanese brutality towards prisoners and those they regarded as enemies. The country had not ratified the 1929 Geneva Convention. Ellie's brother, Donal, was now subject to such uncommon brutality, it didn't bear thinking about. Within the week following their meeting with White, the forestry district commanders had arranged a series of dances and dinners, as the inevitable ending of their operations loomed. News spread among the ranks of their camps winding down, and most waited for an extension of some sort. Rumours were the worst, growing and changing direction with each iteration. Frederick was asked more than once what would happen, and he couldn't give a clear answer because he didn't know himself. They would all find out together, it seemed. On a clear August evening, a dance at the Huntly Arms Hotel in Aboyne was well attended. Men from CFC Districts Two, Three, and Four attended, bringing their guests.

"Dawson," a jovial voice declared, patting Frederick's shoulder from behind. "A good turnout tonight."

Frederick turned to find his orderly of all people, lubricated by a few drinks. He smiled, letting the disrespect go. "Aye, it is."

The man grinned, swaying almost imperceptibly. "I wish, I wish sometimes this weren't all ending." He covered his hand briefly over his face, and Frederick understood what he meant exactly. Taking the man's arm gently, he led him to the door. "Let's go out for a smoke." No point in starting anything he might regret later. They stood together in the warm light, nodding to others who entered the hall.

"I might be a little drunk, sir. I'm sorry." Fresh air had altered his demeanour.

"That's all right. We've done a lot here, a lot to be proud of."

"I know, and it's been good. That's the trouble, almost too good. I've heard that some of us may have to join infantry units."

"Don't get ahead of yourself. We don't know yet, and it's not our decision anyway. You know that."

"Yes, sir, but I don't have to like it." They watched the piper playing a short distance away.

"Correct. Just try to enjoy yourself tonight and stick to tea or ginger beer. Your career is too valuable to take a chance with. I have great respect for you, and the war's not over yet."

The man blushed, faltering. "Oh, now I've made a fool of myself. I'm sorry, sir."

Frederick offered, "Take my advice and you won't go wrong."

"Thank you, sir." The orderly strode away unsteadily as Frederick re-entered the hall. He moved slowly along the wall of guests, following the sound of a boisterous crowd of forestry commission people, as dozens more mingled drinks and laughter. It occurred to Frederick that the sound was not unlike a wedding reception. And then he saw her. As if a loose thread between them were drawn tight, Ellie raised her chin, cocked her eyebrow and gave him a big grin, her face opening up like a flower. In the split second before someone else in the group followed the direction of her gaze, she was his, as if she were expecting him. And in a moment of madness, he forgot who he was and where he was and the entire world around them. Time stopped.

"Sir. Sir!" An annoying tug on his sleeve, insistent.

"What is it?" he grumbled, not looking to see who was at him.

"Time to sit down. District commanders must open the

event." A little man in formal dress left him just as he heard his name called. Damn. And so the night began with congratulations and speeches of appreciation and thanks, highlighting the bonds between civilians and the military, going over what they all knew and had lived. Frederick and the other commanders flanked Brigadier-General White at the head table, who'd arrived late and stayed barely an hour, his face grim but courteous. The officers could only guess at what news he had that he wouldn't share. A night's revelry didn't gather him into its arms like it did the others. After White left, the party got going in earnest. Dishes and glasses clinked as they were raised and removed after dinner. The air was thick with cigar and cigarette smoke. Table napkins fell to the floor as patrons got up to walk outside. A small band was warming up in preparation for the dance to begin in the adjacent room. Frederick could absolutely not help himself; it was a thing away from his conscious mind. His eyes followed her everywhere, beautiful red hair upswept, gown of sea green with one shoulder daringly bare, as only she could carry off. Men both in uniform and out flitted around her, wanting some of her light to fall on them, but Ellie held herself away, not promising a moment to anyone, not even him. It was enough to watch her, to imagine what she was and what she might be. Frederick felt no jealousy at the attention by other men – he was confident in his Ellie. His Ellie. She was his, for this moment. He chatted with others, talking about nothing, enjoying a whiskey, but his heart was on something else. As darkness fell, she caught his eye, and he knew she wished to meet him outside. The air in the hall was stifling and hot; a trickle of sweat traveled down the back of his collar, and a few strands of damp hair hung down the side of Ellie's neck. They exited close together.

"Ah, what lovely cool air there is out here," she murmured, a stole over her arm. Frederick loosened his collar and tie just a little. He offered her his arm, asking, "Shall we?"

"We shall," she replied, smiling and placing her hand inside his elbow.

"You look lovely tonight. Your dress."

"Aye, thank ye. Mam and I remade it from an old one of my auntie's."

"You have many talents."

"Ah, go on with ye, sir."

"Ellie, please call me Frederick. I am not your superior officer, not here and not anywhere."

She blushed. "I'll try then, since ye've asked."

They walked slowly down the street to the River Dee, the sounds from the hall growing fainter. Frederick stopped, his heart pounding. He'd heard something spoken when no one was there.

"What is it? Are ye all right, then?" Ellie looked up to his face.

"My dear, I don't think you'll believe me."

"Oh, come on, now. Ye know me. I won't laugh, promise."

"My da has been gone since before the war. He spoke Gaelic growing up, though not later in his life. I just heard the words now: *bean óg álainn*. It's as if he's here with us."

"What do they mean?"

"That's the odd thing. It's like Da is telling me that I'm with a beautiful young woman. But I don't speak Gaelic, never have."

"So that's two of us. I was driven half mad by Aileen with her Gaelic and superstitions."

"I'm sorry. I shouldn't embarrass you," he added.

"It's no trouble. I think it's sweet."

"How is Aileen? D'you still work with her?"

"Ah, no, not anymore. She got herself pregnant from one of the camp men and has a wee bairn now."

"Oh."

"Aye, oh. But she's not a fallen woman, rest assured. Her

parents had a small and quiet ceremony a few months ago, so the child wasn't born in shame."

"I'm glad to hear that."

"Aye, me, too!"

"So she's no longer working?"

"Poor Aileen, she didn't have a head for numbers, not in the least. When we were out together, I had to spend hours afterward correcting her calculations."

"We've always found the timber estimates to be very accurate."

"Well, then, that's the main thing, in't it? Aileen will be a good mother, I'm sure."

They came to a wooden bench on the river bank. "Let's sit," Frederick suggested.

"Glad to," she answered, pushing off her shoes. "I'm more used to work boots, now. My feet are achin'."

Momentary dizziness overtook him and he pushed it away. She was not his and never would be. The river flowed past as if speaking, rushing words away, words he could not say.

"I know ye're married, if that's what ye want me to ken," she said softly.

"Ellie, no. I don't. . ."

She interrupted, "Nay, let's at least be honest. Ye're a good man, Frederick, and I'd be lyin' if I said I never t'ought of ye."

He sat silent for half a minute. "Before I met my wife, we went walking just like this, by the River Avon at Amesbury in Wiltshire. It was during the first war where the training was done on Salisbury Plain."

"Tell me about her, will ye?"

"I'm not sure I can. D'you mind if I smoke?"

"Nay, go ahead."

He lit a cigarette, taking a long inhale and holding it before blowing the smoke away from her.

Ellie watched the river. "It's all right if ye don't want to tell."

"I've never said this to anyone before. We don't love each other."

She flashed a startled look. "Please, sir, I mean, Frederick. Don't say that."

"It's true; I won't lie to you," he said on a sigh.

"I'm sorry, very sorry."

"Don't be. It happens."

"Now don't ye laugh at me, but I've never been truly in love. Not like I want to be."

"Ellie, you're the best girl I've ever met. I wish I were twenty years younger. Sometimes I wish. . ."

She interrupted, "That's very kind of ye, but I doubt I'm the marrying type, somehow. I don't ken exactly, it's just a feelin' I have."

"You'll find someone. You most of all, Ellie."

"Sometimes I'm afeart of life passin' me by. I think of dear Donal, in that prisoners' camp in the jungle, and I try t'send my t'oughts to him. D'ye think we can do that, as people? Can we send our t'oughts to others?"

"Aye, I do."

"So every day he's there, he's losin' a day of his life, y'ken? Days are taken away from him that he cannae get back." Ellie gulped and wiped a tear from her cheek.

"Here, now, it's all right. Donal will be fine. You're right, he's losing days now but when he comes home, he'll make up for them, I promise you."

"May I have a cigarette?"

"Of course. I should've given you one."

He lit it for her and she took one long drag to begin, her fingers slightly trembling.

"I wonder what our lives would be like if there was no war?" she asked.

"I wouldn't be in Scotland and we wouldn't have met each other."

"It's like my daddy. He died because there was a war, and it changed everything for Mam and for all of us. Nana is old now an' she still cries over her lost boy."

"I didn't think I would live to see the end of the war."

"What did ye do? Please tell me."

"I started in the army service corps and brought supplies to the front lines in France for two years. After that I got into the Royal Flying Corps as a pilot."

"That's excitin'."

"Aye, but I was sick for much of it. Trench fever."

"If ye were in the RFC, how could ye join from Canada?"

"There was an agreement between the two countries at the time. It wasn't difficult. I was born in England, you know."

"Really? Where?"

"Enfield. North of London."

"Aye, I ken where t'is. Ye've no accent that I can hear."

"My family emigrated when I was nine."

"What a life, and I've barely been out of Inverness."

"I'm sure you'll see a lot of the world, Ellie. You have time yet."

"Aye, I s'pose." She looked at him sadly. "On Armistice Day, me an' Mammy used to go an' watch the soldiers paradin', to remind us of Daddy, not that we'd ever forget him. Mammy an' I gave our grief to each other, back and forth. I wished to take it all from her, she was that low. Ye ken how I get angry at the war now? Back then, I believed that Mammy would die of her broken heart, an' it seemed that way. But then she met Douglas an' she felt better. I didn' feel guilty about Daddy, I was happy for her. Does that make sense?"

"Absolutely. What was it that Churchill said, *Never give up, never despair?*"

"Sometimes it's near impossible to keep faith."

Frederick stood up. "Let's walk some more. D'you have to get back to anyone?"

Ellie grinned mischievously. "Nay, I've forgot who I came with," she said with a laugh.

"It was a good dinner, and I've been to a lot of them."

"Aye, I'm glad there's still plenty to eat for thin's like this."

They stopped at the end of the well-trodden path, and he turned to her. "You'll think I'm a silly old man, but seeing you from time to time has made my stay here that much better."

"Aye, an' by the sounds of thin's, we'll be wrappin' up this forestry work soon enough."

"That's true. The men are nervous; they've become like family now and don't want to be separated."

"If I think really hard, I can picture the end of the war. It's got to end sometime."

"When I was sick in the first war, I couldn't see it ending. When it did, I felt nothing but surprise. It was as if that's all the world would ever know."

"How old were ye?"

"I was twenty-four when it ended."

"Almost my age now."

"Don't remind me," Frederick said ruefully.

"I'm not pokin' fun. I meant the age of anyone at a time like that."

"The funny thing is, now we're twenty years later and then some, yet it feels like such a short interval."

"Ye've been wearin' a uniform forever, sir!" Ellie laughed.

"Y'know, I think you're right."

"What plans have ye got, then?"

"It's a little too early for plans. I'll have to wait and see where Headquarters want to place me. Once logging is finished here, we may be going to the Continent to carry on the same there, or at least some of us."

"Will ye have to go an' fight?"

"No, dear girl, I'm too old for that. They'll find me a desk with a comfortable chair somewhere, I imagine."

Ellie sighed. "So many changes an' we ahn't in control of any of them."

"That's true," Frederick mused.

The air became misty, more humid, as stars dimmed in the southern part of the sky. Standing still, the pair looked at the far horizon. Faintly, the drone of an airplane sounded but they weren't worried about bombers. She spoke softly. "What's it like to be in an airplane?"

"It's like being a bird, truly. When you aren't afraid, it's the best feeling in the world. Like floating in a way. You're above everything and what's on the ground is no longer important."

"I'd like to try that one day. As a passenger."

He looked at her. "No reason you can't be a pilot, Ellie. You've heard of Amy Johnson, Mary Ellis? There are many women pilots, flying as well or better than men."

"Honestly? I don't think I've got the guts, but I want to give it a go, as they say."

"You should, I mean it."

"Were you ever afraid? I mean, in the RFC?"

"Constantly. Every time I went up over France or Belgium, I expected to be sent home in a coffin."

"Did it ever change?"

"Aye. They had me training new pilots in 1918. I wasn't afraid then."

She shivered, pulling her stole over her shoulders. A chill of air passed between them and he leaned towards her just enough to be dangerous before she said, "We'd best get back. Don't want anyone talkin', eh?"

It was almost completely dark, their faces in shadow. Frederick whispered, "Ellie, I won't ever forget you."

"Oh, sure, ye will. When ye get back to Canada, ye'll forget all about me," she joked.

"No, I won't."

She moved towards him. "Tell me yer wife's name."

"It's Kathleen."

"A good Irish name."

"She's not Irish."

"D'ye have children?"

"Aye."

"Tell me about them."

"Margaret is a few years older than you. She's training to be a nurse."

"Really? That's excitin'."

"She's in Montreal and wants to come overseas with the Red Cross. I won't allow it."

"Oh, won't ye? Margaret may have other ideas. Who's next?"

"My son, James, is sixteen, still in school."

"An' that's all?"

"Aye, just the two."

Frederick touched her arm, goosebumps on her flesh. Without warning, she raised her face and kissed his cheek, blushing furiously. He stopped breathing.

"There now, I've kissed a married man. Ye're the first." She smiled. "An' now we'll go back."

At the hotel grounds, few were about any longer. He ached for the night to end differently and couldn't tell her. "I hope I'll see you again," was all he managed to say.

"Perhaps you will." And with that, she turned and was gone. He moved into the spot where her feet had just been, to claim the piece of earth that had held her. It felt as if they'd been together no more than twenty minutes, when in reality over three hours had passed. Frederick stayed overnight at the hotel, looking out the window and not sleeping.

Chapter Thirteen

France, 1944

The Italian campaign was going well for the Allies, and Churchill's trap for Hitler had worked a treat. German divisions were held up in Italy while Allied plans were discussed in secret for the great invasion of France, initially scheduled for May 1944. The military operation called D-Day represented the largest land, sea, and air assault on a foreign enemy known to that time, and it began in the earliest hours of June 6, 1944. Beach heads were established and ground troops began the arduous crawl from the Normandy coast inland towards Germany. Every battle led to exhaustion and death, victory and so much loss, yet an inexorable move was being made that would end only when Hitler acknowledged that his thousand year *reich* had lasted less than a decade. Men from the forestry camps in Scotland had begun serving with infantry and artillery units, wherever they were needed to replace heavy casualties in Europe: Belgium, France, Italy. Some soldiers had little notice of where they were going, and many were killed in the final years of the war. They were fighting against German teenagers barely old enough to shave, their lives lost along with their childhoods. Camp men had been part of the D-Day invasion as well, leaving their bloodied bodies on the beaches of France when only months earlier, they'd breathed the misty air of Scottish forests. Although war events had progressed in due course, Frederick's mind could hardly keep up with it all. His love for Ellie had opened up something inside him, an aspect that he'd never shared with Kathleen, not even when he'd loved his wife. A feeling of vulnerability dogged him privately, and he was determined to retain the authority of his military role with duty above all else. In October, just weeks after the dinner at the Huntly Arms, District One headquarters and ten companies of foresters were unceremoniously returned to Canada. Dislocations occurred when men were severed from the groups they had served with ever since joining up; feelings of dismay and anxiety ran high. Working together for nearly three years in a goal-driven environment had drawn the men together, some viewing their colleagues as closer than their own families back home. Those who weren't going back overseas were sent to other units, while some remained with their companies in Scotland. It was a parody on the worst type of ragtag adoption and no one was happy – all sense of geographic or cultural togetherness was lost overnight. The ten remaining companies in Scotland could see the writing on the wall, and they knew that it was only a matter of time before all of them were gone. One or two officers appealed to higher authority but for naught, as everyone was ground together in the war machine of unexplained decisions. For whatever reason, Frederick's orderly was one of the first to leave. He'd rarely thought of the man outside of a normal acceptance and couldn't say that he actually liked him. Yet now his absence was keenly felt and Frederick was frustrated by having to do the menial tasks that previously had been done for him. In fact, he only then realized how much easier the fellow had made his daily life. Frederick was not assigned a new orderly.

A few months earlier, in March, a handful of officers and sixty other ranks went to Southampton for the purpose of building rafts to float lumber across the English Channel to France. Along with more of the same constructed at Cornwall, one hundred and thirty rafts in total were towed successfully across the channel by tug boats. Frederick had wanted to go on this venture but was denied. Now that he knew his time in Scotland was limited, he felt an urge to leave, to get it over with and not brood. By supreme effort he'd kept Ellie at bay, yet she was never far from his thoughts. At nights, he had an unbearable urge to contact her and sat up late many times with his whiskey, willing himself to let her go. Instead, he thought of his children. Margaret had her mother's dark looks and thankfully little of Kathleen's temperament. The girl was stubborn and fearful at the same time but without the cruelty of her mother. Frederick regretted his distance from her. She likely was his daughter, and if it weren't for Kathleen's damnable ways, they could be much closer. He was proud of her decision to become a nurse although he hadn't told her; he'd written no letters specifically to his children since leaving Port Arthur. Margaret was nearly finished her studies, or would be by now, he wasn't exactly sure when. Whatever his feelings, he was glad that she wasn't coming overseas. Frederick wondered what France was like in peace time, since whenever he was near it, the country had been at war. *You're getting old*, he told himself. Wanting slippers and a warm fire to sit by instead of life's many excitements, growing tired of his uniform at last. It surprised him, how much he still missed his parents. When he'd drunk enough, he had conversations with them, as if they were still alive. Dear Ma and beloved Da. Da never spoke of the famine that had occurred a century before in his home country, yet Frederick knew of it. He tried to imagine the fear and despair among the population, hatred for the British, and the stark choice to either leave Ireland or die. Da had been older than Frederick was now when their family got on the ship for Canada. How did they take such an enormous leap of faith and start over? More than once, he'd calmed himself from an irresistible desire to go and find Ellie and ask her to be with him, whatever that meant. Followed just as quickly by ridiculing his idea for what it was: silly old man talk. He would not bring disgrace on himself or his wife or their marriage, not even for the girl he loved. Still, sorrow lived in him like a benign tumor and he could not excise it.

Kathleen's last letter had said that James had got a summer job clearing trees for a prisoner of war camp at Neys, backed by deep forest on the north shore of Lake Superior. Her words left Frederick cold, the thought of his dear boy being in the company of hardened German soldiers. He'd heard of the SS officer Kurt Meyer being interred at Neys, suspected of ordering the murder of Allied prisoners at Normandy. Now in his later years, Frederick realized the futility of war, no matter the reasons. Time and again in the current state of political and military flux, he'd remember camping trips with James. The lad's excitement and curiosity reminding Frederick of his own many years earlier. He wondered at the changes he'd see when they were together again, as there surely would be some. His son was almost eighteen. Momentum for the war's end was everywhere, in the atmosphere and the smoke and stench of death, in the singing of a single bird after an artillery barrage. It was coming, they all knew, they just didn't know exactly when. Western powers were discussing how Europe's new boundaries would realign once Germany was subjugated once and for all. That country alone was the cause of so much suffering, and now it would pay dearly. Time sped up as lasting solutions were sought in rearranging a new world order. Roosevelt's health had suffered during the war, as had Churchill's, from exhaustion more than anything else. Frederick felt mistrust for Stalin, though his absolute power was not in dispute. The Soviet ruler had formed an allegiance with the west only when it became the logical course available to him, and he would not ignore or forgive the Fuhrer's betrayal. As well, the west had Stalin to thank for bearing the brunt of Hitler's attack with the invasion of the USSR in 1941. Had Germany concentrated its army elsewhere, it might have been a very different world indeed. In the Pacific, America and its allies were beating back the Japanese, island by island. Sickness and heroism, death and torture, brutality previously unknown in warfare hugged its opposite, love, in the jungles and on the beaches of the tropics. The souls of men were nothing more than grains of sand falling like stars on the battlefields with their comrades. Frederick did not permit himself to think of Donal.

Affairs of the European war sometimes shifted by the hour, and Frederick understood that his orders could change quickly. Starting out with administrative work in Scotland as forestry camps were decommissioned, he was then sent to France for weeks as sawmill operations were set up, before being returned briefly to Great Britain and feeling every bit a pawn of the military. It reminded him of the time when he'd recovered enough from trench fever to work, yet the powers that be apparently couldn't decide where to place him. He'd waited for months, having no idea of where he might go. In this case, he was willing to wait it out. Truth be told, he wasn't overly anxious to be released back to Canada, like many of the younger men were happy to be. He couldn't blame them, with girlfriends, wives, and children longing to welcome them home. Every time Frederick imagined reuniting with Kathleen, he felt only sorrow and disappointment. Now that he'd known Ellie, he wasn't at all sure about taking up his marriage again, and the thought cornered him. There was no answer and he threw himself into his duties as he'd always done. A number of the camps in Scotland were shutting down, and five companies (including Frederick's) were mobilized as Number One Canadian Forestry Group in May 1944. A further five forestry companies joined this first group for enhanced military training before they all landed together on the beaches of Normandy between late July and early August of that year. The remaining ten forestry companies of the original thirty stayed in Scotland until near the end of hostilities in Europe in 1945. During one of his journeys through London, Frederick witnessed a V1 rocket, known as a buzz bomb, that had been fired from a launch site near Pas de Calais, on the north coast of France. He watched it for a moment before heading to an underground shelter. After securing Normandy, the First Canadian Army's next task was to destroy the rocket launch site, after more than two thousand buzz bombs had struck London's metropolitan area. Within months, the Allies were fighting in the Netherlands' polders, deliberately flooded by the defending Germans. Losses remained high for Canadian infantry battalions, underestimated by their commanders, and the unpopular topic of conscription was again raised. If only the war would end, if only the collective will of millions could make it stop. Frederick missed the simple duties of cutting and milling trees in Scotland. There was more to it, of course, but compared to his almost daily disruptions at present, it seemed idyllic in hindsight. He knew everyone in the camps by name, and genuine friendships had formed. During parties and events, it was almost possible to imagine that there was no war and they were just a group of working men doing a job together. Already word had got around of some of the men who'd been killed where they were reassigned. Yes, they'd volunteered to serve their country and to carry out whatever tasks they were ordered to, but it seemed an inhumane way to end their time overseas. Frederick no longer wrote letters home to anguished parents, that was someone else's job now. On days when he was out of sorts, he thought of Ellie most of all, realizing that she was the panacea for his rumination. He wasn't going to have her, that was a fact, but it didn't stop his wishing it. In this war, he spent much time contemplating what he would do after being released back to civilian life, something that never occurred to him in the first war. Now he knew that he was going to survive and that life would carry on. There had been no correspondence with the Lands and Forests Department, his employer, and there was no need for it, either. It was accepted that he would return to his previous job in Port Arthur. He missed James most of all in his family, followed by Margaret, and lastly, Kathleen. Perhaps he was to blame for her unhappiness? She hadn't done any volunteer war work at the Lakehead as some women had, especially those who'd been widowed. At the Canada Car factory in Fort William, just a few miles from Port Arthur, women were building the Hawker Hurricane fighter plane, the only location where it was manufactured outside of Great Britain. The chief engineer was a woman, Elsie MacGill. There were opportunities for women, they weren't forced to stay home. Frederick couldn't imagine Kathleen in such situations as those, but surely there was something she could do? He tried hard to remember a time when they were close, nothing more than a distant and ever receding memory now. How was he supposed to travel back home across the ocean to her and pretend that everything was all right?

Tossing and turning at night, Frederick hadn't slept well since the news came of the first company being repatriated to Canada almost a year earlier. There so was little timber left in Scotland, all of the cruisers were gone, and he made no move to contact Ellie. What could he possibly say to her? Their walk the night of the dinner at the Huntly Arms would be their one time together, one that would have to last him the rest of his life. Her kiss on his cheek. Frederick grew angry with himself. He had little fear in facing anything the military set before him. Chain smoking and drinking far more than advisable, he could not find the courage to face his own wife whom he hadn't seen in almost four years. The only answer was that the war itself had transformed him. Had he only looked upon Kathleen at first as a trophy for a man of his stature? What was it about her that had so attracted him? He honestly couldn't remember anymore. Fantasies dogged his waking hours, forcing him to concentrate on his duties in a way that he'd never had to before. He would be going over reports when suddenly his imagination took him to the fields of Ireland that he'd never seen, showing Ellie where Da's people had come from. Or standing on rock cliffs of the Isle of Lewis, looking out to sea with her beside him. Miserable, Frederick could not determine the moment when his love for Ellie had touched his soul. Was it the time he'd found her sweating and cursing when training a particularly inept understudy? She'd looked up to see him, anger flashing in her eyes and warning him away – it was not the situation for a joke or even a friendly comment. Or perhaps the time when she said privately that she viewed the big trees as her spirit guardians? Or just viewing her from a distance, the characteristic red braid cast loosely around her neck like a fashionable scarf? How he ached for her, now that everything was over. There was no reason for either of them to ever meet again. The thought left him in despair. Frederick went for walks at night, wherever he was, striding away his unhappiness. He'd never felt such loneliness in his entire life.

After the heady event of the successful D-Day landings, the end of the war in Europe began to feel further away for some. Infantry on the Allied side were expected to attack, occupy, and hold small patches of ground, similar to what was required in World War I. Men at the front lines made up fifteen percent of the total army numbers but suffered seventy percent of the casualties. Some companies were fighting at no more than half strength. There was dire need to fill the ranks, and these men were provided by soldiers from artillery, engineering, and service corps, along with those from the forestry corps. What is today called Post Traumatic Stress Disorder (then known as battle fatigue or shell shock) was rampant among the troops and was becoming as serious a problem as it was in the first war. There were few volunteers in Canada willing to travel to Europe when there was a strong possibility that they might not return, and so conscription was called into play. By November, Prime Minister Mackenzie King announced that troops trained for home guard would be sent overseas to fight. It was considered a betrayal, since after the fall of France in 1940, the National Resources Mobilization Act called for conscripts to do home defense duties only. Another problem was the return of U-boats. In response, the Allies changed tactics and hunted German submarines instead of trying to sink or evade them in convoys. A new cypher known as Ultra had been developed by the British Admiralty, and U-boat movements could now be followed in real time. As a result, Germany lost twenty-eight of their undersea vessels when they tried to interfere with the D-Day landings. However, they had more success in lurking off the east coast of Canada, targeting ships in or near Halifax harbor.

Frederick moved around frequently, between Scottish camps being shut down and serving to keep hastily setup sawmills running at capacity in France, then later in Belgium and Germany. Wherever there were trees, the forestry corps wasn't far behind. There was little time to relax in the momentum of war. On a cool windy day in autumn, he found himself sharing a cigarette with a warrant officer near Amiens, France. The man squinted momentarily through his own smoke.

"How long are you here for?" he asked Frederick.

"The end of the week, I'm told."

"I know things are changing fast, but I can't tell my arse from my elbow half the time."

"I only think about the day I'm in, nothing else."

"You're a lucky one, then. Wish I could do that."

They smoked in silence. The warrant officer threw down his unfinished cigarette and lit another one. "God, I wish I were home in Alberta right now."

Frederick eyed him without saying anything. The man looked down, then continued, "It's been over three and a half years since I last saw my Nel. Came over in March 1941."

Frederick was silent and the warrant officer prodded. "How 'bout you?"

"I left Port Arthur at Christmas 1940."

The man whistled. "Even longer than me." He was halfway through his second cigarette. He added, "Now that there's an end in sight, I worry that I won't get home."

Frederick was irritated by the remark. "What makes you think that?"

"I might get killed first."

"We're a damn few miles behind enemy lines, in case you hadn't noticed." He hated cowardice, which was his opinion of the man's comment.

"No, you're right. Sorry. I just want to go back, that's all. I've had enough over here."

"What was your life before?"

"I'm a cattle rancher with my sons. Boys were just teenagers when I left. They've had to grow up fast, and I wish I could be there with them. I don't know what came over me in joining up, I must've been crazy."

"Did any of them join?"

"God, no! I wouldn't let them. They were too young and it's a reserved occupation anyway."

Frederick finished his cigarette and butted it out under his boot. "Well, that's something," he said.

"Have you got kids?" the man asked.

"A couple. Too young to join." He didn't want to talk about them.

A spatter of rain started. Before they went back inside, the warrant officer remarked, "I just want to see my family again."

Frederick wished he could say the same. By the end of that day, he was thinking about the Allied invasion of France on D-Day. The week before that was the final time he'd seen the last of his men from Number Five Company. They'd all gone on a route march on June Second, up into the mountains near Insh camp. After splitting up, part of the group had got lost and returned to the camp and safety. Now a number of those same men were dead. Frederick could understand what the warrant officer meant. At the beginning, a good portion of the forestry corps believed they'd be cutting wood in relative security throughout the war. Leaving Scotland was clearly dangerous business. He acknowledged that it was only his age and rank that kept him from the front lines now. On his bad days, Frederick hardly cared anymore. Again he agreed with his smoking companion: one got tired of it eventually, wanting to return to whatever had been before. Paris had been liberated, the end of the war was in sight, yet it also brought a sense of anxiety, of needing reassurance that could not be given. Frequently Frederick was unable to relax or sleep, and he socialized less wherever he was. The good times (as he thought of them) in Scotland were quickly receding, like a train leaving the station. In France, he met a country man and his wife who'd been part of the *résistance*, their stories of courage no less impressive than those of military campaigns. Hiding downed pilots in barns and cellars, moving them constantly, some caught, some killed, some reaching their own side again at last. When Frederick thanked the two in his non-existent French, the man only smiled and shrugged, as if to say, anyone would do the same. Frederick knew this wasn't true. His own effort and the contribution of the forestry corps were important but so was this. He'd never heard the sound of SS jackboots striding over the floor above him, never stared down the barrel of a gun before being shot, never lived the humiliation of the Jews. In his first war, he'd thought mostly of himself, of surviving, because he didn't think it possible. The experience had marked him, left him damaged, and he hadn't forgotten the days afterward, of digging potatoes on the farmstead in 1920, reliving the nightmares of the front lines for hours at a time, to where he no longer knew where he was or what year he was in. Kathleen watched from a distance, never reaching for him in his distress. No wonder he didn't love her, nor she him. The wall between them could not be scaled. Without thinking, he'd slowly gravitated to those who had been crushed yet still endured. Frederick recognized that these people were his tribe now, the survivors whom he'd met in Canada. By the time the second world war had begun, he was most comfortable with the loners in the bush, trappers and loggers, those who had stepped out (or stayed out) of society. Finns who came to Canada for a better life and didn't find it, becoming injured during forestry operations and spending their days begging outside the Hoito restaurant, gnarled hands grasping a cup of coffee given by a stranger. For the first time, Frederick realized this about himself, and about why he preferred the people he did, and the boreal forest that made him feel safe. In his loneliness, he'd found a kindred spirit in Ellie, sensing a similar quality in her, despite the difference in their ages. Speaking of her daddy as if he'd died only months before and not twenty-five years earlier. And her restlessness, a type of itch beneath her skin that she couldn't reach. He would contact her again; he would find her before having to return to Canada once the war ended. Frederick forced himself to think of James, his son, the boy who was waiting for him, waiting to reconnect. Frederick would give that to him, it was the thing he could get right. Sometimes he smoked incessantly, coughing hard every morning, throwing up once.

As the cold winds of winter 1944 approached, he spent his last rotation day in northern France doing paperwork and preparing the wood operation to move again, this time to Belgium. In twenty-four hours he'd be back in Shorncliffe for perhaps one day before returning to Scotland or the Continent, who knew? As he'd told the warrant officer a month earlier, he focused on the day he was in, no further than that. One afternoon, Frederick strolled along a laneway behind a few damaged houses. The Americans had liberated the area and not many of the locals had returned yet. It was difficult to see where the proper road had run through the hamlet, with mud everywhere, broken down military and farm equipment, and shell holes full of water. He picked his way along, humming tunelessly, when an old woman approached suddenly like a ghost, frightening him. She grasped at his arm, her skin dirty, grey hair a mess under a kerchief.

"*Monsieur, viens avec moi,*" she implored.

He stopped, thinking her injured. The woman looked into his face, pleading. "*J'ai du café. Viens boire avec moi.*"

She pulled at his sleeve, her other hand making the motion of drinking. He smelled no alcohol on her fetid breath. Frederick allowed her to lead him to a nearby house with most of its roof missing. Stepping over rubble, she picked her way carefully into what was once a kitchen. A shovel with dried manure flecks stood against one wall, having been used to clear away a small area of earthen floor. On this tiny spot stood a table missing one leg, balanced with rubble to hold it steady. She motioned to it, saying "*Les Américains ont fait ça pour moi.*" From behind a cluster of broken wood, the woman carefully withdrew a tiny metal tin, opening the lid as she smiled, holding its contents towards him. Fresh coffee. He looked into her eyes, at once seeing her pride and desire to share such rare treasure.

"*Mais je n'ai pas de bonne eau.*" She allowed a sad smile, turning her cracked drinking cup over, nothing running out of it.

At last Frederick comprehended, remembering the warning for Allied troops not to drink the local water, as the Germans had contaminated rural wells with human waste and dead livestock. This old woman wanted to share her coffee and had no safe water to drink. He knew no French to communicate with her but pointed at his chest, saying, "Frederick."

"*Ah, Frédéric.*" She smiled, nodding. "*Je m'appelle Eliane. Eliane Marie.*"

By the rarest of circumstances, he'd brought along his canteen; usually his walks were not more than fifteen or twenty minutes. With a flourish, he unscrewed the cap and raised it to her, holding out his hand to take the cup. She gave it to him almost shyly, her fingers brushing his. Frederick filled it one-third full, up to the crack before giving it back. Eliane Marie shook a few grains of coffee into the water, swirling the mixture with her finger. Then she held the cup under her nose inhaling with the fervor of an opium addict, until she took a tiny sip. A smile spread across her face, lightening her brow and making her appear a decade younger. She held the cup out to him and he took it and drank. The water was clean and yes, it was fine coffee, even if unheated. They both sighed and regarded their surroundings. Eliane Marie gestured out the window opening. "*Ils ont tué mon bétail.*" With her hands she motioned the shape of a chicken and a cow. "*Je n'ai rien maintenant.*" The farm animals were gone, killed.

Frederick turned to leave as the woman held out her hands towards him. "*Merci, monsieur. Merci.*" She let him go first before coming up a step behind, chatting under her breath.

He held out his hand to thank her, basking in her generosity. Turning back to join his men nearby, he remembered the dinner at the Huntly Arms one year earlier, when the tables were laden with more food than could be eaten at one sitting. Eliane Marie had nothing to eat, her bare legs like spindles beneath her ragged dress.

Chapter Fourteen

Scotland, 1945

At the end of March 1945, the Allies began Operation Plunder, their first objective being to cross the Rhine River into the very heart of Germany. The country had been previously softened by a four-month campaign of bombing that left cities in ruins, particularly Dresden, where a fearful firestorm resulted in some twenty-five thousand deaths. Bomber Command sought to break the spirit of civilians as it targeted the industrial economy, transportation links, and supply centres that fueled Hitler's war efforts. Stuttgart, Leipzig, Chemnitz, Berlin: they were all blasted into submission with heavy casualties. Churchill finally ordered the bombing to stop as he noted that the Allies did not wish to take control of completely destroyed land and infrastructure. After years of struggle, the Soviets surrounded and took Berlin in late April. The Red Army was merciless with her vanquished.

Frederick was in the middle of closing the last of the CFC

camps in Scotland when news of Hitler's suicide arrived. Many postulated that they would've been happy to pull the trigger on that monster, even if it meant their own death in the process. The war in Europe was finally over. That night, Frederick sat alone and considered the tree harvest numbers of his corps. An estimated two hundred and thirty thousand acres of forest had been clear cut, and close to four hundred million board feet of sawn lumber had been produced. The figures were almost mind-boggling, and they didn't include what had been cut on the Continent since 1944. Barely four and one-half years had passed since he'd left Port Arthur and now the war was finished. Not in the Pacific yet, but still. He knew that he should be jubilant yet felt numb. Patiently Frederick reviewed the percentages attributed to each of the five forestry districts. His own, Number Four, had come in third in terms of total production, right in the middle. It was all necessary, he knew, yet he missed the large dark forests, now nothing more than bare earth left open to the sky. As he had done more than once, he wondered if he could stay on when others were demobbed. Scotland needed a serious plan of reforestation; perhaps he could start the program? But no, he missed his adopted country and realized that he was only putting off the inevitable. He had no idea what he might do once he returned, and it wouldn't be long now, surely within the next few months. His job with the Lands and Forests Department awaited him, but after serving in uniform for the second time, he wasn't sure that he wanted to return to it. Frederick felt himself an old man, suddenly, not liking what he saw. Soon after Hitler's death, the full horror of the Nazi concentration camps became widespread news around the world. No more rumours and wordplay surrounded the evil that became known by the place names of Sobibor, Auschwitz, Bergen-Belsen, Treblinka, Dachau, Buchenwald, and others. It was unbelievable, beyond all reasoning. Frederick remembered the young Jewish soldier he'd met outside the recreation hall, the one whose family had changed its name from Bernstein to Adler. The boy had been crying as he held a letter saying that his father's people had been taken away. Now Frederick could not make his mind go to a place of imagination where innocent human beings were corralled into gas chambers to die. He shivered as he wondered where the young soldier was today. Perhaps he was already dead, as well as his family.

The forestry camps were closing down systematically with some buildings repurposed and others dismantled. In a few years, all sign of their operations would be gone, vanished like the morning mist on the hills. Frederick considered how each of the companies comprised some two hundred men of all ranks, which included three to five officers, all under the command of a major. And now here he was with a mere handful of workers, tearing down what they had built in such a hurry as the war got underway. He was deeply grateful for coming to do his part and had no regrets about leaving his family, they'd all been fine without him. Margaret had graduated as a nurse but too late for the Red Cross to accept any more of them in France, where she'd wanted to go. She'd taken a job in an office somewhere, he wasn't sure which one. For a moment he imagined his daughter and Ellie as friends. James was working as a logger. Frederick would have to get the boy into a trade, he thought, and talk to him about his future plans. And Kathleen? Well, there was Kathleen.

After the years of privation in Britain, millions of deaths around the world, horror and bravery and unending sorrow, somehow the day had come. Victory in Europe celebrations went wild in London's Trafalgar Square and everywhere else on May 8, 1945. Frederick spent most of that day by himself, walking around Loch Rannoch and the remains of Dall camp. He was glad and relieved, of course he was, but a sense of unease pervaded his mind. Nightmares from the first war had returned a few times and he didn't know what to do about it. Whiskey was too easy to come by, too easy to dilute his sadness with, and so he avoided it now. The misery left him feeling more real, as if he had to do his penance before returning home. One week hence, he had two days' leave, and without hesitation Frederick traveled to Inverness to calm his thoughts once and for all about Ellie. They hadn't been in contact, and he hoped that she had found a young fellow to love her as she deserved. It was raining as ever in Scotland when he discovered the street where she'd said she lived. Festivities were still going on in a more orderly fashion – groups singing together, the pubs busy, smiles and laughter everywhere. Frederick walked until he saw Lochalsh Road and turned down it. The homes were unpretentious, just as Ellie had described. He didn't know the house number and slowed his step, thinking that perhaps he wouldn't find it, or her, for that matter. And what would he say anyway? He stopped.

"Are ye lost, then?" A man's deep voice off to one side, down low as if he were squatting.

"Ah. . ." Frederick began, swallowing.

"Ye lookin' for someone?"

Clearing his throat, he said, "Ellie. Miss Ellie Ross."

The man's face clouded over, his eyes mistrustful. "An' why d'ye want t'lass, then?" He stood up and walked to within a few feet of Frederick, challenging him.

Gaining confidence, Frederick offered, "I wish to say goodbye to her. We used to work together in the forestry camps."

Now the man relaxed slightly, his frown eased. "From the camps, ye say?"

"I'm Frederick Dawson, Officer Commanding of District Four. Or I was. The camps are being shut down now."

"Aye, I would think so. There's no trees left in Scotland."

The man paused, and the two faced each other for moments before Frederick asked, "D'you know Ellie?"

"Ye could say. I'm Douglas, her step-da." He held out his hand.

Frederick grasped it warmly, smiling. "Ellie told me a lot about you and her mother. May I see her?"

"Ellie?"

"Aye, Ellie."

Douglas lowered his eyes. "Nay, ye cannae. She's not here."

Frederick hadn't considered this. "Is she married and moved away?"

"Nay, t'lass is'nae married, but she's gone."

"Where?" A chill came over him.

"London, I think. She's been gone months now."

"Is she working? What is. . ."

Douglas regarded Frederick critically. "Ye asks lots of questions, there."

Frederick felt exposed, his temper rising as he sought to remain calm. It was none of this man's business; he and Ellie were both adults. "We became friends in the camps and helped each other through, you might say."

"Oh, aye? Helped?"

"I have no intentions for her. I'm married and returning to Canada soon. I came to say good-bye." His trip to Inverness had been a waste of time. "I won't trouble you further. Good day."

Turning to walk back, Frederick squared his shoulders. A few steps away, he heard, "Nay, there. It's all right. T'war's changed us all. Come with me."

Feeling suddenly tired, Frederick followed Douglas to the next house down before the man stopped outside the gate, saying, "'Tis been a bad year for Ellie's mam. Donal died in the prisoner camp and she's nae t'same anymore."

Frederick stumbled, steadying himself by gripping the gate. "Oh, God," he whispered, "the thing she was most afraid of." Speaking up, he added, "I'm so sorry, for all of you."

"Thank ye. Come an' say hello to Morag."

They entered a tiny parlour where a woman with white hair sat motionless beside the fire grate. Douglas kneeled down, taking her hands in his. "Morag, this man has come t'see Ellie. Let's make him a cuppa tea, how's that?"

She didn't respond as Douglas went to the kitchen to put on the kettle. Without being asked, Frederick sat on the opposite side of the room. He spoke softly. "I'm Frederick Dawson, and I was Ellie's friend in the forestry camps. We worked together."

Now she raised blue eyes, bright with tears, and Frederick saw where Ellie had inherited her beauty. Morag almost sighed out her question. "Ye're Frederick?"

"Aye, Frederick Dawson. I was in charge of District Four in the Highlands."

A tear rolled down her cheek. Struggling to find the muscles to smile, Morag said, a bit louder, "Ellie spoke about ye all the time. She said she was'nae afraid around ye."

The admission startled Frederick, making him blush. Douglas stood at the doorway. "Will ye take milk in yer tea?"

"Ah, thank you."

"Mother?"

"Aye, Douglas. Why don' ye make us some lovely tea?" She sat up straighter, placing her hands together in her lap.

Douglas nodded, a slow smile creeping across his face.

Morag regarded their visitor carefully. "Are ye takin' care of our Ellie?"

Frederick answered, "I haven't seen her in over a year. . ." Before he finished the sentence, Douglas came in with a plate of store biscuits, setting them down near him, interrupting. "We were jus' talkin' t'other day, were we not, dear?" He turned to his wife. "Ellie's all done the forestry work now, love. She's away a little while, is all."

Morag's face clouded over. "But she'll be home tomorrow, I'm sure."

Frederick smiled and murmured, "I'm sure she will."

"An' Donal, he'll be back soon, too. We got a letter from him. . ." Her voice trailed off as Douglas shut his eyes in pain. Frederick remembered that Donal was *his* son, and he imagined how he would feel if James died. His shirt collar felt too tight, and sweat trickled under his arms in the closed room.

"Ellie loved the trees, y'ken." Morag spoke louder again. "She said she imagined being a wee bird at the top, lookin' over all t'world."

The men sipped their tea in silence, the clock ticking on the mantelpiece. Morag closed her eyes and Frederick wondered if she'd dozed off. After a decent interval, he cleared his throat and said to the both of them, "Thank you for the tea and biscuits. I'm glad to have met you." He stood up, ghost pain spreading through his lower back; it always came at times of stress.

Morag startled at the movement and opened her eyes. Staring at their guest, she asked, "Have ye brought Ellie home with ye?"

Frederick looked down. "No, I came to see if she were here."

"If ye'll open yer eyes, ye'll see she's not," was Morag's angry response. She looked to her husband. "Who's this then? Some tosser from t'street?"

Embarrassed, Douglas placed himself between his wife and Frederick, saying quietly, "Come on then, I'll see you out." Louder, he turned to Morag. "I'll be back in a moment, dear."

"Takin' all an' sundry from anywhere's, I don' ken what we're comin' to."

With two steps the men exited the house. "I'm sorry," Douglas offered. "Her mind's been turned since the news of Donal. She believes he's comin' home, but t'lad was buried out there somewhere in t'jungle." He waved his hand in the air, his voice breaking on the last words.

Frederick placed a hand on the man's shoulder. "I'm very sorry for your pain. I have a son, too."

"Is he servin?"

"No, he's too young."

"Thank God for that."

Reaching a hand into his tunic pocket, Frederick asked, "D'you mind if I smoke?"

"Nay."

Pulling out his cigarettes, he offered one to Douglas, who said, "Thanks, I'm grateful. I cannae smoke in the house no more, makes her cough."

Inhaling a long draw, Frederick said, "Tell me about Ellie growing up."

Douglas's face brightened. "Oh, she were a champion lass, that one. Never settled for second best, always had to be the smartest, fastest, ye name it." He chuckled quietly, flicking ash off the cigarette.

"She told me that her dad's ship was torpedoed when she was just little."

Douglas nodded his head as he agreed. "Aye, that were a bad business, very bad." He looked at Frederick, assessing. "Ye might think this daft, but I'm glad that I could come an' rescue the two, so t' speak."

"How's that?"

"Well, they had no money a'tall, jus' livin' on charity. Poor wee bairn had no shoes the first winter, I heard."

"Where did you meet Morag?"

"I was in t'roomin' house, my first job on the fishin' boats mysel', though I didn' ken her daddy; this were a few years after he died. Anywa', I'd needed mendin' done on my overcoat, and the landlady said that Morag took in washin' and such. I went over there one day, an' the rest was history, as they say."

"I'm glad you were able to help. Ellie told me how much you meant to her and her mum."

Douglas scuffed his shoe. "Aw, it were me who got t'treasure."

He coughed. "But now ye sees Morag. Hearin' about Donal has broke her mind. I dinna ken whether she'll ever improve. Nothin' can be done." He sniffed.

"Does Ellie know? How long has she been gone?"

"Oh, aye, Ellie kens. She were here when t'telegram arrived. Poor girl fell down when she read it. Tried to hide it from us but I got it out o' her hand. She stayed about a week after that an' then left, said she needed some time away. But y'ken, we need her, too." Douglas's eyes were red rimmed and wet.

"You've been holding things together for your family."

"Aye, that's t'size of it an' all."

Before he could edit his thoughts, Frederick blurted, "D'you want me to try to find her?"

Douglas smiled sadly. "Nay. I don' think she wants t' be found, t'truth of it. She'll come home when she's ready an' not before."

Frederick crushed his cigarette butt under his boot. He held out his hand and Douglas shook it. Douglas said, "'Tis kind of ye to come like this. Even if Morag don' ken, I do."

"It's my pleasure."

"Ye're from Canada?"

"Aye, but I was born in England, and my mother was Scottish."

"No wonder ye talks a bit like us, then."

Frederick blushed. "I used to say *yes* until my ma died and then just started saying *aye* instead. Can't explain it. It was her word, all her life."

"Bless yer parents for havin' such a good son."

Douglas turned away and reentered the house. Frederick watched until the door closed before leaving. He felt as if he'd been given something fragile, like a china teacup or an egg, and that it would take everything he had not to break it. He walked away stiffly, his back aching.

By August, the last CFC units had been disbanded in

Scotland. Cleaning up was still being done on the Continent and it was only a matter of time before that ended as well. Canadians were being sent home in greater numbers, returning as civilians as the country counted its great cost of war. Now the time was beginning for the rebuilding of Europe, the political jockeying, the new world order. Frederick was also preparing to leave when news came of Japan's surrender, after the Americans had dropped two atomic bombs on the island country. Grainy television pictures and radio broadcasts described the devastation and loss of life. Frederick wondered if the killing ever ended. Man's inhumanity to man, Da would say.

The world war was at last over, everywhere. It was left to others to pick up the pieces and start again. Frederick was awarded an OBE (Officer of the Most Excellent Order of the British Empire) for his war service before being sent home. The voyage back to North America was uneventful – no German U-boats patrolling, weather in a quiet mood, a sense of relief among the passengers. Dozens of English and Scottish war brides were travelling with babies and toddlers, making some areas of the ship sound like an infants' nursery more than anything else. Frederick spent most of his time walking around the deck, unable to concentrate on any one emotion and none of them positive. He felt anxious, tired, sad, and completely uncertain as to what he wanted to do next in terms of work. He'd probably return to the Lands and Forests Department, at least for the short term. They were holding his job for him and the thought didn't fill him with joy. His life was changed now, not the least of which were his thoughts of Ellie, as much as he tried to set his memories of her aside. Every nautical mile west that took him further away from her increased his gloom. Frederick's sailing orders had come on short notice and he hadn't sent Kathleen a telegram. He couldn't even imagine what it would be like, standing on the steps of his home in Port Arthur after five years of separation. Seeing her, speaking to her. Was Margaret still at home? She was in her midtwenties and he wondered if she had a gentleman friend now. It was surprising how quickly the children had grown up, as if it were all done behind his back. He hadn't received or written a letter to James since the previous year. Would his progeny be that interested in him anymore? The thought chilled him.

After a peaceful crossing, Frederick's vessel docked at Pier Twenty-one in Halifax as winter began in earnest. From there he boarded a train for the Lakehead, arriving to his home exactly eighty-four days after seeing Douglas and Morag in Inverness. He had no idea why he'd kept count of the days, but there it was. There were no familiar faces on the train, and he'd changed into his civilian clothes before boarding, appearing no different from any other passenger.

Chapter Fifteen
Port Arthur, 1946-1947

As he walked up the hill to Van Horne Street, Frederick's footsteps were heavy. He carried his suitcase in one hand, five years of the war contained therein, and his overcoat in the other. A forgotten memory reared its head, threatening him. It was his first week supplying materiel to the front lines in France during World War I. The constant rain had rotted away the sole of his left boot and when the corporal noticed, sent him to the company cobbler. Frederick hadn't realized such a person was available to the men, but of course it made sense. The young private sat on the hitch bar of a wagon, smoking for all he was worth. The cobbler worked swiftly, a middle-aged fellow taken out of his trade in London. He squinted good-naturedly through his own cigarette cloud, safe this far behind the lines.

"Eh, lad, you're new then?"

Frederick mumbled, "Only a week."

The cobbler smiled. "Don't look so grim, you'll never

get through."

Frederick took another drag, holding the smoke in his lungs.

"Where're you from?" the man asked.

"Canada. What about you?"

"The old country, son, as you might guess from me accent."

Frederick didn't want to talk. He watched the cobbler work. Another few minutes and his boot would be good as new.

"Have you heard from your folks yet?" the man asked.

That just about did him in. The very thought of a letter from Da and the impossibility of answering it, trying to explain his constant terror and diarrhea, his fear of panic, his certainty that sooner or later, a bullet was going to catch him. It wasn't only the infantry being shot. Going to war was nothing like he'd imagined. Was he the only coward? Those new recruits like him, boys as they were referred to, was their bravado all an act? Frederick couldn't see how he would be able to hide his anxiety for the duration. At night when he couldn't sleep (he never slept), he tried to recall Ma's stories about the great Scottish warriors and battles, where heroism was *de rigeur*. No chance of turning tail, not for those men. He wished he'd known his grandfather, who had died by the time Frederick was interested enough to ask about him. Ma said the man loved nothing more than to tell tales of Highland bravery, it was the very air that he breathed. All the way back to Roman times when they kept the invaders out. Hah, the Homeric cowards built Hadrian's Wall in their defeat, knowing they would never trounce the clans. Giving up was easier than merciless slaughter by madmen. But the childhood memories didn't help Frederick. He decided that he wouldn't disgrace either his family or the army, yet he hadn't found a way to get through his life right now. At times boredom at the front was almost as dangerous as snipers. Groups of men had taken to playing cards and gambling, and some created entertainment among themselves with musical instruments or impromptu performances in the trenches. Letters and magazines provided reading material, and on breaks lasting a few hours, soldiers could attend variety shows in nearby towns. He'd heard that traveling vaudeville troupes from America were coming to keep the men in good cheer although he hadn't seen any yet. Maybe they would remind him that there was a different world where he came from, maybe that would help.

The cobbler held up his repaired boot, spitting off to the side. "There lad, she's good as new."

Frederick pulled up his sock, took the boot and put it on, immediately comfortable. He looked up, the man's kind eyes understanding his plight. In a softer voice he added, "Just do as you're told, son, an' you'll be all right. Try not to worry. And change your socks every day!" He winked and Frederick smiled weakly. Humming to himself, the cobbler picked up another damaged boot and got back to work.

Now, a lifetime later, Frederick trudged the last few feet to his own home. No one was outside; he'd sent a cable from Halifax the week previous. Up the steps, one, two, three, four. After a moment's pause, he tried the door – it was unlocked. Into the vestibule, he put his suitcase down, his hand strangely lost without it, and there she was. Kathleen stood at the hall entrance, her face a mixture of emotions: relief, interest, pity, resentment, gladness. Frederick watched her carefully, not moving, just as she remained still. A thought whisked through his mind of Ellie and how he would rush to her and she to him, hugging, kissing, crying with joy after a separation of war. There was none of that here. Kathleen spoke first.

"How was the train?" Her voice was low, measured.

Frederick cleared his throat. "Fine. It was fine."

"You look. . ." the sentence unfinished.

He turned to the side and removed his hat, hanging it on its usual hook by the door. Bending to undo his shoelaces, his back in minor spasm, he pushed the footwear to the side and walked close by his wife, thinking that she was as dangerous as the Hun, perhaps even more so. Stopping inches away, he looked into her eyes and saw their familiar hardness. Nothing had changed. He'd returned to the same world he'd left half a decade earlier. What had any of it mattered? And in that moment, Frederick understood that it was only a question of time until they formally separated. He didn't know when or how, but he couldn't spend the rest of his life like this. Not much later in the day, there was a happy reunion with James, the boy grown impossibly tall, his voice changed, a man now. He was full of stories of what he'd done and seen on adventures, peppered frequently with observations about his work clearing the forest in preparation for the German POW camp at Neys. Frederick shuddered inwardly and listened, happy at least that his son had no direct experience of war. The lad seemed to think that German soldiers were a fine lot in general. In the early evening, Margaret came to the house, smiling shyly, as if seeking her father's approval. He was startled momentarily by seeing her, the baby fat gone from her face, her features as beautiful as Kathleen's had been in 1917. Frederick asked about her nursing training, and she answered with disappointment about not getting over to France. As with James, he was happy that she had not been part of the war.

That night, his first back in the Lakehead, he slept in the spare room. The dream about the rat dogged him as it had many times before. He was at the front, working as a stretcher bearer on a cold, windy day in November 1915. Rain had fallen all day, changing to a frosted mist with the temperature just above freezing. There seemed to be no end to the wounded, it was like a conveyor of misery, and so very much blood. Most patients were quiet or groaning, but a few called out, one for his mother, another for his dog, a third crying something in French. Each was transported the same way, placed as carefully onto the stretcher as possible, legs and arms in, head aligned. With a nod, the bearers rose from their knees. The patient's shared weight wasn't much but the mucky, pock-marked ground provided a challenge. Frederick tried not to look at the wounds, tried not to catch the eye (sometimes missing) of the felled soldier, tried to be brave and do his duty. One of the front men stumbled and they almost all went down as their feet slipped, the one in the rear instinctively putting out his hands to stop the patient from falling off. The front man cursed and stood up again, flexing his arm. It was then that Frederick saw it: a rat, eating the face of a soldier who lay nearby, not quite dead, his mouth gulping air. His legs were missing and parts of his intestines were flowing out of him, like sausage casings flecked with dirt. All Frederick could wonder was why the rat chose the face; why not eat the open wounds instead? He stared and started retching, losing his breath. The stretcher bearer beside him knocked his elbow purposely, shaking his head. Don't look, mate, just keep going. Next time they went back for another wounded, the rat and the soldier were both gone, and Frederick was sure that he'd conjured the entire scene. It couldn't be real, it couldn't. He'd had the same dream for years.

After a few days puttering around the house, feeling lost and doing nothing, he reported for work at the Lands and Forests Department office downtown. Some of the staff had changed since he'd left although the supervisor remained the same, welcoming him heartily. An older man nearing retirement, he made reference to his brother fighting in the Boer War in 1901. Its relevance was lost on Frederick. By noon of that day, it was as if nothing at all were different, other than the experiences that Frederick had brought back with him, and he felt as if he were in a foreign country. But no, there was the quiet ache for Ellie and the sense of doom over his inevitable short-term future with Kathleen. He wanted to see a lawyer to discuss legal separation, knowing the news would be all around town by the end of the week. A spokesman for the mayor had already asked him about participating in a fête to celebrate both the end of the war and the local heroes, as he'd called them. Some hero. Frederick didn't see himself that way. Try as he might, he could not feel elated. Relieved that the war was over, certainly, and not much outside of that. It was hard to recall how to acclimate to civilian life again – that part had blanked from his memory in 1919. There was Margaret's birth and the farm, then apparently nothing until he joined the OPAS as a pilot. These last weeks on his return to Canada, he'd felt old and used up, something to do with visiting Ellie's parents and knowing she was gone, unaccounted for, and on purpose. As a married man, Frederick felt little shame at how often he thought of Ellie, blaming it on Kathleen's coldness. They still hadn't touched one another's body in any way, and he'd been back for almost a week. No hug or kiss, no caress. The least encouragement from her would make it so much easier for him to try to be her husband, but it wasn't there. For a crazy moment he thought of leaving again, going to another city where he could become someone else. His life seemed as though he'd stepped out of it and was watching the stranger who was really himself. Frederick took to drinking one or two whiskeys in the evening to help him relax. Sometimes he walked or sat in the backyard of his home, gazing at the stars and reciting the names of the men he'd known in the forestry camps. Brigadier-General White had died the previous year in a Montreal hospital. The man was in his seventies and so his death was not unexpected, but still. Newspapers were full of White's accomplishments and his role in Canada's forest industry. Frederick kept his OBE medal in his desk drawer, safe in its box. That was a proud moment when he received it, he kept reminding himself. His uniform hung silently in the closet, gathering dust. A ghost of his previous life.

Finally sick of his own gloom, he asked James to join him for a walk in the bush. The young man was ecstatic and impressed his father by driving the family car like a professional. On the outskirts of the city, they travelled as far north as possible on roads before borrowing the tractor and wagon of one of Jim's friends to continue a mile or two further along. Before bogging down on the rutted track, they left their conveyance and continued on foot. Frederick took deep breaths of boreal air, finally feeling better for the first time since his return. They moved in silence, vegetation brushing their pant legs. James's strides were long, longer than his father's. After a few minutes, he asked, "Was it awful, Dad? I mean, as bad as the first war?"

Frederick had expected the question. "No. It was different."

"Were you in Scotland the whole time?"

"Mostly, but as the war was ending, I went to France and then Belgium, but not for long."

"Did you meet anyone there?"

The question threw him. Surely the boy had no idea about Ellie; he'd never spoken a word about her, ever. "How d'you mean? In the military?"

"Sure. You know, a friend, someone you'll stay in touch with?"

Without meaning to, James had cut him to the quick. Of all the things he could bring up. "No, not really. We in the camps were split up in 1943, assigned to other units. Some were killed in action later."

"Oh, that's too bad. My friends and I wanted to write to the German soldiers from Neys when they were sent back, but the Canadian guards said no. They refused to give us any information."

Frederick coughed. "Well, you can hardly blame them, can you?"

"No, I guess not."

"James, war is a bad thing, something I hope you'll never experience."

"Sure, Dad. And please call me Jim, everyone else does."

"I bet your mother doesn't."

The lad laughed. "No, not her."

They walked on, the woods getting thicker. He forced himself to look around at the trees and insects, the life in the forest. His troubles would wait another day. During the week, Frederick had taken to walks along the industrial shore of Lake Superior on his lunch breaks from work. He stared out at the water, at nothing, reliving memories that crowded his thoughts together. There was no reason for it, the return of hurts and frights and the tumbling days of World War I, ones that he believed he'd let go of years before. Kathleen moved around him like a phantom in the house, never touching him, never reaching out. The woman reminded him of a porcupine, moving along its own path and not wanting to be bothered by anything. Or anyone. Their marriage was a catalyst for his depression more than anything else. And every night there was Ellie, tormenting his dreams. He realized far too late the trap that he'd led himself into, willingly. The girl would never be his. It was clear to her and should've been to him, but he'd slipped somewhere, letting her into his heart where she now lived. The more he tried to turn away from it, the more intense his feelings grew, and he worried about becoming unstable. At night he drank. Every cigarette became the one that he'd shared with Ellie at Loch Rannoch. How he wished he'd taken her in his arms, just that one time, just to be utterly loved for an instant. He could no longer remember that with Kathleen.

So much had changed with the war. There were jet airplanes now, something unimaginable when Frederick was flying. He missed being a pilot but didn't seriously consider going back to that as a career. Now in his mid-fifties, he was beset by the inevitable aches and pains of age, exacerbated by stress. Although both of his parents were life-long church goers, Frederick didn't look to the Divine for answers. He'd seen too much, done too much to believe whole-heartedly anymore. Where was God in the horror of the trenches? Even if the question was unfair, it's what he thought. Months into his return to the Lands and Forests department, the work no longer satisfied him in the same way that it had before. Many of the young men he'd known had joined up, with just as many killed or maimed for life. The Finnish old-timers were dying off, some alone in their bush cabins, mummified corpses found in spring after a long winter. James had found one while traveling on his new trapline and came to tell his father about it. Frederick called the police and when conditions were optimal, an RCMP patrol went up by dogsled, to haul the body back on a toboggan. Frederick wondered later whether the deceased might've preferred to be left where he was, slowly returning to the forest. He spent as much time as possible outdoors and it was more difficult than before. Occasionally he became short of breath, dogged by bouts of coughing. On cold mornings his joints were stiff, and his trench fever decades earlier had left behind endocarditis, an infection that had weakened his heart valves. One of the doctors at Furness Hospital in Harrogate where Frederick had been sent to recuperate had described his patient's heartbeat as "soft" in his report, possibly indicating fluid around the heart muscle's lining. Trench fever was not adequately understood until 1918, and Frederick had been suffering from it for over a year at that point. Bedrest was the only treatment for him and anyone else afflicted. In all, the man was uncomfortable in his own skin, unhappy and having no idea how to change his mood or circumstances. He was considered too old for the military and endured feelings of uselessness as part of that. A few short years ago, he and others had been at the forefront of desperately important war work in the forests of Scotland, every day a challenge. He was often tired, yes, but was also appreciated, the efforts of the entire corps recognized for its value. The only time Frederick unwrapped his OBE medal in Port Arthur, the sight of it almost brought him to tears. He couldn't live on memories, he needed to feel productive now. And in his worst moments? Ellie. God, how that girl had affected him. She'd got under his skin and was just as impossible to get rid of as the lice in his uniform in 1915. More than once Frederick considered leaving Kathleen and returning to Scotland to locate his great love, consequences be damned. Waking up with another morning's headache and silent breakfast with his wife, he put such thoughts away. *Foolish old man.*

"Oh, it's you." She turned around part-way, starting at his unexpected appearance on the walkway.

"Aye, it's me."

Kathleen was on her knees in a working smock, weeding the front flower bed. Her hands in gloves held a dandelion by its stem. "Is everything all right?" The question was almost strange, coming from her.

"I took the afternoon off – nothing going on."

"Does Mr. Carpenter know?"

For a brief second, Frederick laughed heartily before the sound stilled in his throat. He coughed. As if he needed the boss's permission at this point in his life.

"He knows."

She resumed her task, her back to her husband. Later on, months and years later, he came to thank her for this moment, because it provided the catalyst, the turning point where his life changed again. It was the image of her turning her back on him, her indifference. No longer could (or would) he stay in a loveless marriage. Loneliness was preferable. He had thought nothing out beforehand, but that didn't stop him from going into his home, packing the same suitcase that he'd brought back from the war. Less than one half-hour after their exchange, he passed her again on his way out.

"I'm leaving," he said. Not stopping, not waiting to explain. His feet moved confidently to the sidewalk before turning right. Walking downtown to take accommodations at the rooming house near his work, one month paid in advance. The following day, Kathleen appeared at his desk at the Lands and Forests department. Her eyes were pleading, another thing he hadn't seen before. "Won't you come home?" she asked.

Frederick shut the door of his office behind her, corralling them both inside. "No."

"I know it's been hard, with the war."

"You don't know the half of it."

She sat silently, weighing her options. "Is there someone else?" A tiny quiver in her jaw.

And he nearly said yes, wanting to tell her what it was like to meet and to know and to love Ellie. To find someone he was happy with and would never forget. To be all the things that Kathleen wasn't. "No," he answered.

"You can't leave me. We're married."

"In name only. What we have is not a marriage. I don't love you."

Kathleen faltered, hearing that. Anger flashed in her eyes. "If it weren't for me..."

He cut her off. "If it weren't for you, I might've known what it is to be loved and supported, to be missed."

"Wait a few months, or a year. Things can get better."

"No. I'm finished with you."

Kathleen caught her breath and stood up. "What about James and Margaret?"

"What about them?"

"What are you going to tell them?"

"Nothing. You can tell them whatever you wish. I'm sure you've told them enough already."

At that, the telephone on his desk rang. He picked it up. "Hello? Yes, I'll be right in."

Standing as well, Frederick said, "You'd best leave. I'm needed." He walked out of his office, leaving her alone with the door open.

That night, he slept a dreamless sleep, an unusual and welcome occurrence.

"Dad, are you and Mom getting a divorce?"

A week had passed, and Jim sat with his father in the coffee shop around the corner on Cumberland Street. He'd just returned from one of his adventures, his features rugged and tanned, a spruce needle almost ready to fall from his hair the second a breeze caught it.

"No. Or not now."

"I'm not sure what to think."

"You don't need to think anything. I'm not going to live at home anymore."

"Are you staying here? I mean, in Port Arthur?"

"I don't know, haven't decided yet. Probably"

"Well, it's your decision." And that was all. Jim finished his coffee and pie, leaving a nickel's tip behind on the counter. He strode away as his father watched, proud of his son. Their meeting had been brief and Frederick felt lighter, as if he'd set down a weight that he'd been carrying. The boy went fur trapping all winter and had just started a job timber cruising for the local pulp and paper company, a good position for him. Frederick wanted to tell him about Ellie, about that part of his life but didn't. There was no discussion with Margaret.

Within a year, Frederick was troubled by frequent episodes of coughing and bronchitis that lingered for weeks every winter. He'd almost given up his walks and was regularly short of breath. Other than bed rest and plenty of fluids, his doctor advised him to cut back on the number of cigarettes he smoked each day. By the summer of 1948, he began waking up at night, wheezing for air. Another visit to the doctor. Stripped to the waist, Frederick sat on the examining table, trying to breathe through his nose as instructed and unable to do so. Holding a stethoscope to the patient's left side, his doctor said, "I don't like the sound of your heart."

"Am I going to have a heart attack?"

"Well, you could," the doctor replied.

"And there's nothing you can do?"

"No, but you had trench fever during the war, didn't you?"

"I was hospitalized in England for two months."

"That can cause long-term damage." He scratched his head. "There's a new hospital just opened in Toronto, called Sunnybrook; it's for war veterans specifically. Would you be willing to go there for treatment? They might have specialized care that could make things better."

"It sounds as though I haven't got much choice."

"You don't have to go, of course, but there isn't anything else I can do. The shortness of breath will continue and will likely get worse over time. How are you sleeping?"

"All right, but I don't sleep through the night and haven't for a couple of years now."

"My advice is to go to Sunnybrook and see if they can help."

Frederick got off the table and put on his shirt. The doctor wrote in his notes before asking, "Are you still working?"

"For now."

"And you're fifty-four years old. Too young to retire."

Frederick tucked in his shirt tails without answering.

"You might want to start thinking about working less, if your health worsens," the physician said, adding, "If trench fever contributed to your condition today, you could apply for veteran's pension. I don't know that much about it, but the folks at

Sunnybrook probably do."

Frederick nodded and left the doctor's office. He worked another six weeks before a second bout of illness laid him low for close to a month. A windy day in October found him on the train to Toronto, admitted to Sunnybrook. Although there was no one else there that he knew, he easily recognized the memory of war on the men's faces: resignation and trauma rolled into one. After a restless night, his turn came to be examined. In Frederick's blood serum there was no trace of trench fever bacterium from the First World War, yet symptoms very similar to it plagued him still: fevers on occasion, pain in his shins, headaches, and skin rashes. The lower back ache that he thought had ended earlier returned with a vengeance. Being in a hospital left him depressed and longing for the days when he'd felt useful. He was given a course of antibiotics which did help his constitution. After a few days' rest and quiet walks, Frederick was ready for a change. The doctors agreed that he was well enough to travel, and he returned to the Lakehead. On the train journey back north, he fell asleep dreaming of Ellie and frightened himself next morning in the washroom car, seeing in the tiny mirror that his hair had gone completely grey. He could barely stand still to shave properly with the train's motion. The day after arriving home, Margaret came to visit at his apartment.

"Hello, Father," she said formally.

"It's been a while since we last spoke," he tried. There was awkward silence. "How's your job going?"

"I like it, actually. Mr. Woods is a nice boss, and the office is busy. And I like living in Marathon."

"That's good."

She smiled. "We're all still in the forestry business, one way or another."

"Aye, that's correct."

Frederick couldn't find much familiarity to create warmth

with his daughter but they spent thirty minutes together before she left. Neither discussed Kathleen, who had finally agreed to move out of the family home and find another place to live in Port Arthur. She and Frederick had sold their home after being separated for three years, and he gave her half of the proceeds of sale. Once he was alone again after Margaret's visit, Frederick was seized by a violent fit of coughing. He spat into the bathroom sink, sputum flecked with pale pink froth. He'd cut back his smoking, trying to keep to ten cigarettes per day though it was difficult. It would've been good to spend some time with James, except the boy (as he always thought of his son) was away in the district somewhere. That evening Frederick sat with a slow glass of whiskey, looking out the window at the street.

Chapter Sixteen

Toronto, 1950s

The care that Frederick received at Sunnybrook Hospital was exemplary. He made friends of other military veterans after seeing the same broken men for weeks during his own treatment. Antibiotics helped the pneumonia he was prone to every winter. For the first year, he traveled back and forth between Toronto and the Lakehead before deciding that it wasn't worth the effort. The Lands and Forests Department had allowed him to retire early with a reduced pension, and he took an apartment close to the hospital, going back and forth as an outpatient. When he felt most alone, Frederick cast his mind back to the forestry camps in Scotland and how different his life had been then. Constant activity, meetings and directives and production, all for the war effort. And Ellie. He sighed, wondering what had happened to her. It had now been ten years since his visit to Inverness, meeting her mother and stepdad. Both of them could be dead by now. What was dead? How many deaths had he witnessed in France? Frederick understood that the scenes he'd witnessed would continue to return in his thoughts, this long after the war. It was as if there was nothing to push them away anymore, and so they came to live with him, like a painted backdrop to his life. In the service corps in 1915, he'd tried not to get to know many of his comrades well because he was afraid of his reaction should they be killed. Many were killed. Now, however, their names and faces came back, speaking to him at odd times. More than once, he believed that he might be losing his mind. War must be easiest for the ones who die, that's what Frederick assumed. It was only luck or fate that he wasn't among the fallen, not by God's good grace. And then he felt shame, knowing what Da and Ma would say to that. In the middle of a night when he lay awake, he heard the words distinctly, *Ní mór duit a chreidiúint*. You must believe. Frederick didn't speak Gaelic, and he was unnerved by the ghost of his father, if that's what it was. In the trenches of World War I, among the groans of the doomed, he'd experienced a sort of atmospheric miasma of mourning hanging over the front lines, as if the world's grief had been made manifest. All the years since then, he'd had a good life, other than his marriage. He'd counted on the horror of the first war being behind him but instead, now it was back. Frederick wished for his younger self, the one he was happiest with. He wrote a letter to James and the boy answered. They would meet up for a short visit in Barrie, fifty miles north of Toronto. Perhaps seeing his son would calm his mind. Frederick was afraid of dying alone.

Jim fidgeted. "What are they doing to you in the hospital?"

Frederick coughed. "Not a lot they can do."

"What's the matter, other than your cough?"

"Oh, I guess after-effects of trench fever, something about my heart. I had that in the first war." He reached into his jacket pocket for a cigarette and brought it out, but the look on Jim's face stilled his hand. A sheepish smile. "Perhaps I'll have to stop smoking."

Jim looked out the window of the coffee shop. "Lot different here than up north." He shook his head ever so slightly. "Feels like I don't belong here."

"How was your trapping last winter?"

"Really good. Lots of marten and fox, lynx, couple of timber wolves. Prices are up, too."

"That's good. It's a good, healthy activity."

"I don't suppose. . ." Jim paused before finishing his sentence quickly. "You could come out with me once? I mean. . .?" He looked away, knowing the answer.

Frederick coughed, reaching for his glass of water. "No, but I'd like to. I think my days in the bush might be coming to an end."

Jim touched his hand to his forehead, running an index finger down his brow. He frowned, noting his father's loss of weight, his thinner face.

Sounding cheerful, Frederick asked, "So, have you got yourself a girl yet?"

"No, not many of those out in the bush." He grinned.

"I hope you'll settle down someday, have a family."

"Have you told Margaret the same thing?"

"No. I'll leave that to her mother."

"Dad, you know Mom misses you, right?"

Frederick blinked. "I doubt it."

"Are you going to telephone her?"

"I don't see the point."

Jim pursed his lips. "I just. . ." He left the sentence hanging.

"It's all right, son. Some marriages end, that's all."

Draining his coffee cup, Jim set it down. "Did you know that Margaret's found a fellow?"

"Oh? Where?"

"She's got a job as the camp nurse in Caramat. For the lumber company."

"She didn't tell me."

"Yeah, I think she likes it. Comes home every few months for a sauna. Clean some of that bush dirt off," he chuckled.

"So who's the fellow?"

Jim blushed. "Look, I'm sorry to have to tell you this way, but she's married."

"Married?" Frederick couldn't help feeling the emotional pain, like a bee sting in his arm. "When did this happen?"

"Over a year ago. And they have a baby boy now."

His grandson. He was a grandfather. "No one told me."

"And I'm sorry. I'm telling you."

"What d'you know about her husband?"

"Seems okay to me. Speaks French, comes from a big family."

"About as far away from us as you can get, eh?"

Jim grinned. "You might be right about that."

"I don't suppose I'll see him, or them, anytime soon."

"No, maybe not."

"Where did they meet?"

"In the bush camp – he's the company clerk. It's like living in a fish bowl in those places, so it's no wonder that they found each other. No one else around."

Frederick stopped for a moment, thinking, that's exactly how he and Ellie met. Two individuals in a bush camp. He began coughing again, for close to a minute.

"Dad, is that going to get worse?"

Draining his water glass, Frederick took a ragged breath. "Probably. I just have to live with it."

"D'you want me to come and see you more often?"

"No, don't worry about me. We'll get together when you have time."

They stood up to leave, Jim paying. As they moved out

the door, he noted that he was now taller than his father, who seemed shrunken by comparison.

Frederick got to know the men he saw most regularly at Sunnybrook. Many of the oldest were veterans of the first war, barely hanging on. A few had been gassed, and it amazed him how they were still alive, hardly able to breathe. A handful like him had served in both wars, making it through the first and becoming debilitated by the second. There was no staring at absent limbs or nervous conditions that would make mothers cry. Those that could be mobile to some degree were wheeled to the area set up for Remembrance Day services every November. One veteran had visited the new Canadian memorial monument at Vimy Ridge twenty years earlier and shared some creased black and white photographs of the trip with his wife, now deceased. Not all patients at Sunnybrook had visitors. All the war heroes were already dead. Those who survived fought the most challenging battles of all. One rainy afternoon, Frederick sat in the ward's common area, startled by being spoken to by a man he previously thought was mute.

"Me name's Stan. What's yours?" Northern British accent, Yorkshire or Lancashire.

"Frederick."

"Think I've seen ye before." He squinted, pulling himself forward in his wheelchair.

"I doubt it."

Rheumy eyes blinked aggressively.

"Nay, I've definitely seen ye."

Frederick sighed. "Where would that be, then?"

Stan put up his index finger. "Salisbury Plain, 1914."

Coughing, Frederick decided to humour him. "Oh, really? And what division was I in?"

Gumming his absent teeth, Stan replied, "Ye were with the Canadians. Let me think."

Believing his companion had gone to sleep, Frederick resumed looking out the window at the soaked trees. Tap tap went Stan's finger on the wheelchair's arm. "Hah!" he said after a few minutes. "Medical corps."

"No." Frederick wasn't going to tell him until he saw how disappointed Stan was to not guess correctly. "I was in the service corps."

"I knew it! Just couldn't think of t' word, y'know."

"And where were you?"

"Lad, I were one o' t'instructors on the great mud plain of Salisbury that winter."

"Let me guess: drill."

"No!" Stan chortled. "Horses. That were me game."

"It was hard on the beasts."

Stan slapped his hand down. "An' that's why I remember ye. Ye were only a handful o' men that treated t'lovely animals with respect." He shook his head sadly.

"Well, thank you, but I barely remember it now."

Sliding down in his chair with fatigue, Stan called an orderly to take him back to his room, before promising to talk to his new friend again. After they'd gone, Frederick asked the nurse on duty about Stan. "That one's a real lady-killer, keeps the girls on their toes," she said. Curious as to his age, Frederick learned that Stan was six years older than he was. Frederick thought Stan looked to be in his eighties. Ruefully, he wondered how old he himself appeared. When better, stronger days arrived, Frederick always went outside, his memories keeping him company. The ship docking in Halifax in 1946 and the able-bodied men rushing off after the war, no longer caring about military discipline. Fittest first, followed by the lame and wounded, followed last by the basket cases: men who had no limbs and were carried off. What had happened to them? One day he spent hours thinking about Margaret, his daughter. He wanted to regard her in a fatherly way but still found it difficult. The issues that had driven an ever-bigger wedge between himself and Kathleen seemed silly now, irrelevant. The two hadn't seen one another in close to a decade. In all honesty, he admitted that he no longer cared about the woman he was still legally married to. His animosity wasn't fair to Margaret, he saw that now. Frederick wished she had sent him a photo of herself and her husband, one that included his grandson. But there was nothing, leaving a gaping emotional hole that he hadn't counted on. Many times, there was nothing to do but ruminate. He'd given James his address in Barrie; he would keep his house, no matter what happened.

There had been so much sex going on during the wars that it was incredible that he and Ellie had never made love. Certainly the desire was there on his part. He remembered losing his virginity on a cold night outside Amiens in 1916. Staggering under the weight of his trauma until he learned how to let it go before it crushed him. A starving prostitute, maybe, (he never found out whether she was or not) perhaps only an innocent girl, lost in the same way that he was. She was barely dressed and shivering, grabbing at his pants, looking in his pockets for a crust of bread. He had nothing but she shoved him down, straddling him, and in moments it was over, the wet, hard earth digging into his back. This was not how he'd imagined the act his first time. In Scotland twenty-five years later, he wasn't surprised by the sheer numbers of enlisted men, NCOs and officers, who saw nothing wrong with fraternizing with the locals. Wives and girlfriends on the home front was one thing, this was war. One never knew when one would buy it, so better enjoy whatever was available. Frederick was an outlier among his corps; the only girl he'd wanted was Ellie. A handful of ladies had offered themselves to him at dinners and after a few drinks, and he felt a prude, turning them away. Probably thought he was homosexual, and he'd seen that, too, in the ranks. It was a serious offence although he and the other officers turned a blind eye when it happened. As long as the men could work, their private lives were their own business. Care was taken to keep it secret.

With little else to do, Frederick reviewed his earlier life as his health deteriorated, trying to make sense of it and fearful that he could not. It wasn't the past he was afraid of, it was the here and now. He still easily recalled the thrill of his days flying for OPAS, nothing but his machine and the sky and the great green forest below. That was all he'd ever needed and wanted then: the freedom, the utter joy of being alive. Spending nights stranded on lakes while the engineer cursed and sweated over a broken part. He felt as if he could simply disappear into the landscape like a wisp of smoke. It didn't matter what Kathleen thought, and now for the first time, he began to understand that what he hadn't brought to their union was just as important as what he had brought. Perhaps James had been right two years earlier when he'd come down, perhaps she had missed him. It was all too late, all gone now. But how he'd wanted Ellie, almost from the first. That spark about her, as if her life were jumping out of her own body. With his present days beset by coughing, aches, and chest pain, he believed that corresponding with her would have made his life much easier and less lonely after the war. Kathleen couldn't help the way she was, just as Ellie couldn't. He didn't want to think of Ellie being married to someone else, loving another man and having his children. It was always the idea of her that kept him going, a fantasy more than anything. She was the whiskey in his glass, slaking his thirst as she ran unbidden through his mind. *My Ellie.* He often whispered her name when he went to bed, remembering her kiss on his cheek, the only one she gave him. The ending of all things was upsetting as he wished to cling to memories and people whom he'd been fond of, and places of excitement and glory. Frederick could not recall a single political or military event of either of his wars anymore.

What remained were the men, women, and children he'd met, the looks on their faces, the words they'd spoken. Young faces of death on the front lines. All souls, all together, free of sin where war was not. While outside the hospital once on a walk, he'd had to sit down on a bench, out of breath and unable to move. Slashes of anxiety blighted his mind and he believed that he might die right then, until a short time later, two orderlies came and helped him up and inside to safety. Imagine, he thought, having to enter a building to be safe, when his entire life, he'd felt safest outside. Frederick looked up at the clear blue sky before it was replaced by fluorescent lights. His days were filled by occasional conversations with old men, increasingly timid walks, and coughing. And doctors. Much earlier in time, Frederick had somehow pictured spending his later years in the company of a loving wife, enjoying a bit of adventure, and living with the memories of his life's accomplishments. He did not expect to be on an examining table or in bed or hardly able to breathe and alone. Always alone.

Eighteen months later, and as an outpatient at Sunnybrook for a two-week stay, Frederick was nervous about being admitted to their long-term care wing, the place for veterans who would not recover sufficiently to live independently again. On good days, he prowled the ward as much as he was able, weak and breathless if the weather was damp. On bad days, he waited to die. There were activities to keep the patients occupied, board games, and cards. Sometimes invited guests would bring music and song or perform a public reading of poetry. Radios were permitted but few were interested in the news of the outside world any longer. By and large, patients lived in the past of their memories. On a cold day in late 1959, Oliver (Frederick's sometime roommate) sat in the one lounge chair beside the room door, struggling to arrange his newspaper without dropping any of it. Cursing softly, at last he had the desired sheets spread flat across his knees. Frederick was awake, watching him.

"What's the news?" Frederick croaked, his throat raw with a cold virus.

"Let's see: war and commies. Nothing new."

"Eh? What's that?"

Oliver answered, "Fidel Castro's taken over Cuba. You know, the Soviets, commies." He ran his eyes briefly over the column, not reading in detail. A crinkle and the page was turned to its other side. "And here: American troops in Vietnam, wherever that is."

Frederick sighed, then coughed again.

Dropping a page on the floor, Oliver said, "I thought we were done with all that. What the hell did we go to war for?"

"I went to the war," offered Frederick.

"I know, old boy, we all did. That's why we're here now."

After another cough, he added, "I was in Scotland."

Knowing he'd heard it all a dozen times before, Oliver waited patiently for the same few sentences. They came as expected.

"We were in the forestry corps. We cut all the trees from Scotland. Nothing left."

"Must've been a lot of wood."

"I met a girl there, Ellie. Most beautiful girl I ever laid eyes on."

"And you were married, too!" Oliver chuckled.

Frederick ignored him. "She's coming to see me sometime. I'm sure of it."

"Oh, yeah? In here, you mean?"

"I've got an apartment in Barrie. She'll come, just wait and see."

"Could be waitin' a long time then."

Frederick coughed some more and then lay back on his bed. Ellie would come, if he just waited long enough. He hadn't forgot her.

A nurse stopped by the door. "How are you two gents today?"

"We're doin' fine, sister. Old Fred here's livin' out his past again, poor sod."

"I know. Just play along, will you? It's not as if he's the only one."

"Kinda sad when you think about it. Nothin' more in the future, just lookin' back and nowhere else."

She moved her hand to the cushion of Oliver's chair. "Can I make you more comfortable?"

"Oh, yeah, sure!" He laughed. "Come an' sit on my lap, why don't ya?"

"You!" She slapped his arm gently. "Nothing wrong with that part, is there?"

"No, there isn't. Come back anytime." He winked as she left the room. Frederick slept.

In his waking moments, Frederick saw many scenes from both of his wars, at the same time. A Tommy eating out of his mess tin before both he and the tin were blown to bits by a mortar round. Another man that he evacuated from the front lines who'd been shot in the groin, a bloody horror where his penis had been. Ellie in the forest, like a dream. Discovering the cook's help and a boy from the village having sex in the camp store-room late at night. Bottle of good whiskey, gentle cigar in a rare peaceful moment, stink of his uniform in the sweat of summer. One night Frederick awoke terrified, coughing out a scream. It took two orderlies to calm him down, leaving Oliver's nerves in tatters. The next day, Frederick didn't know what his roommate was talking about, all that trouble the night before, until he remembered the rat dream. It wasn't chewing the face of a dying soldier, it was chewing his own face. He'd felt the tickle of whiskers below his nose. That morning, the staff had to search the room and prove that there was no rat present. Only then did Frederick begin to relax. He turned on his side, disconsolate.

January brought a cold snap in the second half of the month with temperatures plunging to minus twenty degrees Celsius. No patients went outside for days, before a handful mutinied when they had visitors and demanded to be given some fresh air. No one came for Frederick, but he was wheeled to a sunny spot near the window most mornings. His eyes were clouded, his breath weak, heart whooshing and skipping every so often. He wasn't in pain, sitting in a trance-like state, rolling over the days of his life, all the places and people he could no longer name. All except Ellie.

Chapter Seventeen

Toronto, 1972

Ellie adjusted her hat against the wind on a damp April morning, pulling it down over her ears. Rain and sun together, the season not knowing yet which weather to settle on. It was her first time in the city, and she was no longer overwhelmed by differences in urban environments, having spent her career traveling internationally. Some things were the same wherever she went. Now that she was retiring, the cities tended to jumble together in her mind: Paris, Washington, Tokyo, Sydney, London. Ah, London, where she'd spent almost three years after Donal's death. On certain nights, at certain times, his loss still stabbed her heart quietly, and Ellie understood the permanence of grief. Mam and Douglas were gone for decades now and she missed them, but it was not the same with Donal's passing. Wee Donal, light of her life. Holding her hat with one hand as it threatened to blow away, she was determined to enjoy this trip, the last of her professional career. The flight from

Heathrow had left her drained, though after a few hours' rest, she took to the open air, memorizing all that she saw; it was unlikely that she'd ever return here. Wind whistled down Jarvis Street, carrying a lingering winter's chill. *The wilds of Canada*, Ellie thought with a smile. She was alone now, but good, a comfortable type of alone. Coming around the edge of a building, she ducked in beside its corner, warm sun on her face and no more wind for a moment. What a difference! Closing her eyes briefly, she remembered Edward, her husband who'd committed suicide eight years earlier. Dear Edward, hiding his demons until they literally killed him. She didn't blame him, felt no animosity for his act, despite how it took place. He was gone and she was alone and that was that. Alone except for Charles, their son. A sensitive man, newly engaged, on the cusp of the great adventure of life that held so many pitfalls along with its promise. Charles and his father had had little in common, the boy was much more like his mother. Now that she was past child-bearing, Ellie wished that there had been more children for her and Edward. Just in case. After the war, after Donal and everything else, she could barely bring herself to even imagine giving life to a child, knowing what was out there, waiting. Yet Ellie had never been a coward and she had no regrets about Charles. Charlie, his American fiancée liked to call him, an abbreviation that made her cringe; at least it wasn't the beastly Chuck. That would never do. However, they seemed to be a couple destined for each other, and a happy union was all anyone could hope for.

Arriving at her destination, Ellie entered the hotel and headed for the meeting room, noting the display in the foyer advertising it. Her name was listed farther down, along with others on the placard. Imagine, little Ellie Ross from Inverness, now a respected foreign correspondent. She still smiled on seeing her name like that, one of hundreds of times. And it had all started from her grief, wandering aimlessly around London when the war ended, trying to find out what had happened to Donal, trying to understand why he'd been there and why he died in a prisoner camp, the military be damned. She was awash in tears, there was no other way to describe it. Ellie knew Mam and Douglas needed her yet even they couldn't bring her back home. It was the *why* she so desperately needed to know. Starting from those earliest days of despair, within a month she was hired by a news service, assigned to travel to the Far East, and she left Great Britain willingly. Looking back now, she realized that she was running away from her grief, seeking an end to it somewhere else, but her plan didn't work. She was back in England before the winter set in, suffering from malaria. Sweating and shivering in bed for weeks, her illness beyond her control, at last she turned the corner and carried on. During convalescence, Ellie often remembered Frederick, wondering where he was by then and what he was doing. The impossible romance was how she thought of their relationship. She'd loved him and told no one. Once she'd recovered enough to be mobile again, Ellie soon met Edward from Hounslow, as he'd introduced himself. Edward worked for a rival news agency and they met at his local when she stopped in for a look around. Like a lost puppy, he teased her later, the first time they slept together. Scottish birdie, he laughed. Within weeks they'd moved into a shared flat and he was gone to the Middle East. Ellie set up house and soon became bored, prowling for stories, going home for a visit at last. Restlessness ate at her without pause until she scored an assignment to America – it felt like winning a prize. Edward came home the day before she left and admitted his envy of her posting. She was gone a month. And so their relationship grew into a sort of one-upmanship of ambition for a time, each trying to outdo the other. Publications, interviews, photo shoots, a whirlwind of activity. She felt unable to commit to anything or anyone, but the moment he proposed marriage, she accepted. And Edward promptly went off to cover the Korean War, leaving her with a ring and a promise to return.

Registering at the conference, Ellie returned to the present, wondering why her early memories of Edward had come to visit in Toronto. Sometimes he seemed more real to her now than he had when alive. He'd been a ghost his last years, she should've seen it coming.

"It's Ellie! Ellie Ross!" That loud voice hadn't changed in years. Ellie turned around.

"Hi, Ruby. How've you been?"

"Oh, you know me, on husband number four I think, or is it five?" She guffawed, almost snorting like a horse. Ellie never quite knew how to take Ruby.

"Good thing you're here then. Take your mind off the domestic situation."

Ruby playfully punched her friend in the arm. "So, have you found anyone new here?"

"No, I've just arrived. D'you mean new as in the trade or new as in a man?"

"That's my girl, always answer a question with another question. Okay, new man, might as well get it over with."

"No to both categories and we can save time."

More seriously, Ruby stated, "I'm sorry you're retiring. Gee, you were the inspiration for so many of us silly school girls. You'll be sorely missed, my dear."

"Thanks, but there's a lot of fresh talent coming in. I only look old now."

"Oh, bosh to that. You're never out of fashion. I wish I had your guts."

"Be careful with the compliments, you might have to take them back," she laughed.

A woman handed Ruby and Ellie each their name tags. Walking away from the table, Ruby tossed hers into a nearby trash can. "If they don't know who I am by now, I might as well go home."

They looked around the room as more people entered. "Ooo, look. Is that Dane?" asked Ruby.

"Who?"

"Dane. Stanfield, Stansted. I can't remember his surname."

"Better think about hubby four or five. Stay out of trouble."

"Noted. But he's not nearly as good looking as Dane."

Ellie sighed. "Let's find our seats."

The day was predictable, with awards and reports, speeches and industry news. Socializing was well underway by late afternoon as clutches of delegates headed to nearby bars. Time to reaffirm connections and collect a full head of gossip. Ellie tagged along as always and stayed just until Ruby left with someone who wasn't Dane. Then she made her own excuses and exited. These days, a soak in the tub and a good book were all the companionship she needed. The city was coming alive for the night, and Ellie was exhausted. She acknowledged that she would turn sixty years old the following year. It seemed incredible. Her old work-mate in the forestry commission in Scotland, Aileen, had kept in touch sporadically over the years, and her recent letters included news and photographs of her grandchildren. Grandchildren! The superstitious girl of long ago was now matriarch to a brood of five grown children, still married to the man who'd got her pregnant during the war. Ellie didn't envy Aileen, didn't regret not taking that path, although she'd certainly had offers, not all of them respectable. Ordering a glass of wine from room service, she sat in her room's Regency chair and looked out the window down six floors to cars and people. That view never changed, no matter which city she was in. She turned on the water to fill the bathtub and didn't hear room service arrive until the second door knock. Grabbing her purse, her mind went blank on how much to tip, so she gave the young man a Canadian five-dollar bill. His eyes widened momentarily before he lowered his head, thanked her, and backed out into the hallway. Just a boy, she realized, barely old enough to shave.

Ten minutes later Ellie slid into the warm, deep water, her whole body sighing with contentment. Pure heaven. Random, airy thoughts roamed through her mind, stopping only a moment before moving on. She paid attention to some and dismissed others, a habit of journalism. This was part of her process of relaxation in the evenings. Saddened, Ellie recalled always telephoning Edward from wherever she was, just to hear his voice, and to let him know that she was safe. She would hear the relief in his words and his need to feel her close to him, no matter where they both were, often on different continents. He worried about her far too much; he was the one going into war zones. Once or twice she'd asked him what it was like, and invariably Edward broke down in tears, unable to continue, especially after the first decade. He should've given up that job, never mind the attention and respect he gained in return. What use was the Press Photographer of the Year award when he was dead? And he wasn't the only one. Sipping her wine, Ellie went back to the time before Edward, when she'd known Frederick. He'd never wanted to talk about his World War I experience, and now she understood why. Opening up that wound could be deadly as she (and Edward) learned. Smiling, she recalled kissing Frederick's cheek that time, as they walked after dinner at the Huntly Arms Hotel. Oh, she knew of his yearning for her, and perhaps she was a tease then, but she couldn't resist. If she were turning sixty, then he would be eighty or so. He hadn't aged at all in her mind and she viewed him as her contemporary now. What was his wife's name? Katherine? No, Kathleen. And his children? Their names were missing entirely from her memory. Visions of Charles as a baby, then a child of eleven, then leaving home for university. Now a settled man, or so she told herself.

She worried about his wanderlust that he worked to keep hidden from her. See if that American wife could tether him, but she doubted it. Perhaps there would be children, perhaps not. A stab of sorrow with remembrance of Donal, starved to death in a Japanese prison camp. He was as young as the room service boy. Ellie put down her wine glass and floated her hands in the water, gently moving it in cupped palms. What would Donal's life have been, had he not died, had there never been a war? Inhaling quickly, she went back to the time in the forest at Loch Rannoch when Frederick had surprised her and they'd shared a cigarette. She was angry then, so angry about the war and what it had caused. In all honesty, she could say today that war had killed Edward, just as surely as if a soldier had shot him. Nothing changed. Suddenly she sat up in the tub, rivulets running from her shoulders. She began to cry in great wracking sobs for all the losses, the families whose loved ones never came home. Hiding the telegram about Donal's death, determined to keep it from Mam until Douglas pried open her fingers, not caring if he hurt her; they had to know. They *had* to. Only to find out that their only son was gone. Reaching for the towel, Ellie stepped out and onto the bath mat, shivering but not from the cold. She needed to leave the conference but didn't want to fly back home when she hadn't yet recovered from coming here. Another day, maybe two. After dressing, she took the elevator down to the lobby. Two people were working at the check-in desk, a man and a woman.

"Good evening, Ms. Ross. Is everything all right?"

"Yes, thank you."

"The room is acceptable?"

"Of course." She waved her hand in dismissal before asking, "I wondered whether there is a small town or place that I could visit? Not too far away, more rural and quiet?"

The man reached behind the counter where she couldn't see

and brought out colourful brochures of suitable tourist sites for visitors. The woman beamed. "You might like Niagara Falls. It's close by and everyone loves it."

"No," Ellie replied. "I mean somewhere where it's very quiet." She emphasized the last word.

The two clerks exchanged a quick glance. "Here, I'll get you a map." The man unfolded a paper map showing the entire province of Ontario, flipping it over to show the southern half only. "You can see how many towns there are to visit, if you want to rent a car?"

"I'm not sure," she answered.

The woman continued, "We have Stratford, Guelph, Peterborough, Barrie. Plenty to choose from."

Something pinged in Ellie's brain at the name Barrie. "How far away is Barrie?"

"About an hour and some, if the traffic is good. It usually is."

"Can I take a bus there?"

"Oh, yes, the Greyhound bus drives north every day."

"That's fine. Can you please book me a ticket for the day after tomorrow?"

"Of course, Ms. Ross, we'd be happy to. Will you be traveling alone?"

"Yes, I will." Early in her career, Ellie had learned to substitute her natural *aye* with *yes*.

She returned to her room and slept soundly all night.

Ellie got through the next day of the conference and enjoyed it. She was presented with a lifetime achievement award, collecting chuckles at her speech when she reminded the audience that she was still alive. It was good to see so many of her colleagues in one place, both current and former, and to have her work recognized for its importance. By the end of the day, she was more than tired. Turning down two dinner invitations before leaving, she walked the short distance to her hotel and was handed the bus ticket by the woman she'd spoken to at the front desk the previous night. It tickled her funny bone to imagine the questions at the conference when she didn't show up the next (and last) morning. Suppositions of why she'd disappeared, nefarious and otherwise. After another good night's sleep, she took a taxi to the bus depot and was on her way just after nine o'clock, grateful to be incognito. The ride out of the city was relaxing, and she loved how easily the landscape turned from urban to rural; within thirty minutes, Ellie saw nothing but farms on either side of the highway. She couldn't help smiling, the scenery was lovely. As promised, the bus arrived in Barrie a little over an hour later. In talking to another woman traveler in the station waiting room, Ellie decided to try staying at a bed and breakfast for the first time, at the woman's recommendation. She wasn't sure what to expect but was in an adventurous mood, having the odd feeling that she was being drawn along a path not entirely of her own will. A short cab ride and she was dropped at the door of a charming old house with a veranda and a wooden sign out front. It read *Lewis House, Sandy & Marjorie Lewis, Prop.* All very formal yet quaint, painted red and white. She stepped up and was just about to knock on the door when it opened to a beaming woman dressed some forty years out of date.

"My dear, I've been expecting you! Please come in, and please, call me Marjorie."

Ellie had the strangest feeling of her life, a frizzle going up her spine. "Oh, but I didn't call ahead, how did you know?"

Marjorie laid a conspiratorial finger aside her nose. "Sandy told me the minute I woke up this morning. Have you got a suitcase with you?" She leaned to the side, looking around Ellie.

"No. Thank you. Just my bag."

Stepping back, Marjorie pushed in the door and touched Ellie's arm. "It's so nice to have you visit. Go right on in. Your room's waiting."

They climbed to the second floor together, her host chatting in the friendliest way. "Here you go." And she opened a door to a small but cozy room, like something out of a fairytale. Ellie moved to the window, looking out to the street, a very different view from that of her hotel room in Toronto.

"I'll let you get settled, then. We lock the front door at eight o'clock sharp, no exceptions. Breakfast is at seven, on the dot."

"Yes, thank you."

"The bathroom is the next door down. Shared, but you're our only guest at the moment. Please try not to linger when there are other guests. Fresh towels are on your bedstand."

"Thank you. I. . ."

"Was there anything else?"

"Well, yes, actually. Your accent. You sound as if you're from Scotland. So am I."

"Of course you are!" Marjorie smiled broadly. "My people come from Fort William, and I met Sandy right after the war. Just think, he was Mr. Lewis from Lewis!" She chuckled with all the satisfaction in the world.

"Is Mr. Lewis here today?"

"Oh, yes, he's here every day. You'll soon see him. And you're from Inverness."

Ellie opened her mouth but something about Marjorie stilled her tongue.

"Well, I'll leave you to it. Take a walk along the lake, it's lovely in spring. And there's an excellent little diner on the way for tea and sandwiches. You could do with fattening up!"

Alone again, Ellie sat on the bed. This was not what she'd been expecting. She unpacked her few things after removing her coat and shoes, then lay back on the quilted cover. It was scrumptious in comparison to many of the places she'd visited in her career. Clean, soft, innocent somehow, as if she'd entered a time tunnel. There was little noise from the street below. Ellie drifted into a light sleep before being wakened not long after by a door slam. She sat up rigidly, her heart pounding. Listening, there was nothing, and she wondered if she had dreamed the noise. The bathroom was spotless with all modern conveniences, decorated in the colour and style from before the war. Funny how that expression was still so common in parlance: before the war, after the war. Perhaps only when all those who had lived it first-hand had died, would the phrase finally disappear. Ellie wished that Mam and Douglas could've stayed in this house, their deaths now more than two decades earlier. And Donal, kept forever a young lad.

She went out and walked along the lake, pulling her coat together against a fresh breeze. Winter ice was newly gone, with slivers of it zig-zagging along the shore in shady places. After ten minutes and just as Marjorie had said, a restaurant diner sat brightly on the corner, its sandwich board of prices on the sidewalk out front. Ellie welcomed a cup of hot coffee and fresh scone with butter, recalling again the shortages of the war. It was good to be here, now, and she was very lucky to have had a good life and career when so many others were denied. Edward would be proud, she was sure. Beautiful view out the window, almost a place for a honeymoon, she smiled to herself. Setting out again forty minutes later, she stopped at a used bookstore and spent almost an hour perusing titles before finding two that she bought. This would be an excellent opportunity to step into another life, just until her return to Toronto. In two days she'd be on her way home for the last time. Given her career, Ellie didn't foresee traveling for pleasure in future. She'd put on enough air miles to last a lifetime and then some.

Returning to Mr. and Mrs. Lewis's, she watched her hostess chatting animatedly with a woman on the street. As soon as she saw Ellie, Marjorie broke into a wide smile and waved. Ellie waved back and entered the house. Setting down her bag and books on the bed, a devilish thought took hold quickly. She pushed away any guilt; she was a journalist after all. Tip-toeing needlessly, she peeked through the window and saw Marjorie showing no signs of re-entering the house. Ellie went into the next vacant bedroom and peeped around. It was decorated much like hers, with the window facing the side of the neighbouring house rather than the street. That was all she planned to do, she promised herself, but instead, she kept going down the hall, entering the room marked Private, which was the bedroom of her hosts. Ellie held her breath, feeling entirely awful and giddy at the same time. A larger room, but again, much like the other two. Framed photo of the couple when they were young, Mr. Lewis wearing his military uniform at their wedding. She turned to leave when something caught her eye. It was a memorial card from a funeral service. Picking it up, Ellie read a prayer with Bible reference on one side. Turning it over, there was Sandy Lewis's photo and his dates: Alexander Duncan Lewis – June 3, 1909 to May 20, 1968. What? She read the dates again. Sandy Lewis had died almost four years earlier. Was Marjorie out of her mind? No sooner had she blinked when the bedroom door slammed, shutting her inside and giving her a terrible fright. Ellie wrenched at the knob unnecessarily and the door whooshed open, almost hitting the side of the wardrobe. She dropped the card and hurried back to her own room, lying down on the bed to calm her breathing.

    A gentle tap on the door woke her over an hour later. Marjorie stood at the threshold, smiling.

    "Have you met Sandy then?"

    Ellie sat up, groggy, rubbing her eyes. "Is he haunting the house?"

    "Oh, goodness, no!" Marjorie said. "Sandy would never do that."

    "But he's here."

"That he is. He always comes to comfort those who've lost a loved one, like you."

"How did you know. . .?" Ellie dropped the question as another frisson ran up her spine, causing her to tremble.

"It's in your face, dear. Never mind, no need to avoid Sandy. He won't go away, you know, he told me."

Wondering what she'd let herself in for, Ellie concentrated on what was only in front of her, the best coping skill she'd learned over a lifetime. Clearing her throat, she asked, "Can you recommend somewhere for dinner? I saw a few places that looked promising."

"If you're not too hungry, there are more tea shops that serve sandwiches and such. The bakery around the corner from here makes a terrific Dundee cake." Ellie's mouth watered at the words, her favourite treat.

"Then again, if you want a proper meal, Frank's Seafood down the road a ways is popular. The fish is always fresh."

"How far is it from here?"

"I'd say a good walk. If you go now, you'll arrive before the supper rush."

Ellie stood up, wanting to be out of the house in order to process her unusual experience, to say the least. "Thanks, I'll take your advice and have some fish and chips."

"Remember, we lock the front door at eight o'clock sharp. No exceptions."

Smiling as she passed Marjorie by and went down the stairs, Ellie said to herself, *we*?

Supper was delicious, yellow perch caught fresh that day, pan fried and drizzled with lemon and pepper. Ellie salivated as the server brought her plate, noting the large wedges of potatoes and side dish of coleslaw. She realized how little she'd eaten since breakfast and determined to finish everything, just in case tomorrow morning's offering was meager. Ellie hadn't thought to ask Marjorie for a menu and then grinned at the thought of what Sandy might suggest. Dessert was served at Frank's, but in place of eating one at the restaurant, she'd already decided to buy a Dundee cake at the bakery before leaving Barrie. That was definitely too good to pass up, and she could walk off the extra calories. There weren't many other diners for the first twenty minutes before a steady stream began to arrive, clearly regulars as they were greeted by name. A few looked at Ellie and nodded or smiled briefly. Eating alone had never bothered her and she enjoyed every bite of her meal. Arriving back at the Lewis's, she walked up the front steps moments before Marjorie appeared holding a key that looked as though it was from the Victorian era.

"Did you enjoy your meal, dear?"

Ellie replied, "Yes, thank you, very much. And thank you for the recommendation, too."

Marjorie beamed. "That's fine then; you're fed and watered." She bustled around and latched the outside door, followed by locking the inside one. Reaching out a hand without touching her guest, Marjorie herded Ellie towards the stairs. "Have a good night, and we'll see you at seven in the morning."

"Thank you. I'll be down on time."

Closing the door of her room, Ellie thought about Marjorie. What a strange old lady but apparently harmless. Not too sure about the Sandy thing, however, Marjorie could pretend whatever she wished, it was her house, after all. Perhaps in the morning she'd ask about Sandy, and her hostess could fill in more of the story for her. After a quick read of the first pages of her new book, Ellie lay back on the comfortable bed and sighed, fully relaxed for the first time in almost a week. It had been a good idea, to skive off her Toronto conference for a day. She smiled, choosing between different reasons to give for being away and none of them believable. Sometime during the night, a presence woke her; at least, that's what she thought it was. Not frightening exactly, more unnerving, like realizing one was being watched from a distance. Ellie had been lying on her right hand and it prickled with discomfort as she flexed her fingers, the blood returning. There was nothing to see in the room although she couldn't shake the feeling that somebody was with her. She whispered, *Sandy*. Sitting up, Ellie was still, and after a few minutes, the presence seemed to go away. Quietly shoving the bedcovers off, she stood and walked the few steps to the window. Street lights were on and no one was to be seen. A car drove down to the end of the street and turned. The night was hushed. Ellie returned to bed and fell into a deep sleep.

A smell of frying bacon delivered her to the morning, almost sensual in its aroma, bringing her back to childhood, when Douglas would come to visit and bring food, before he and Mam became a couple. Oh, how she and Mammy dug into that food! He presented it to them like an offering, like Santa Claus, and they fell upon it shamelessly in the beginning, before they understood that there would be more again, another time. Ellie was forever grateful to the man who had helped her and Mam when they most needed it. Others had turned their backs on them, as if they were to blame for Daddy's death and their poverty. Even as an adult, Ellie could recall nights when the coal ran out, Mammy's ragged cough, the cupboards bare of food, not even enough to feed the mice. Whenever she received an award or saw records of her unbelievably high earnings, she could never quite accept it as her due. Part of her was always the hungry little girl. She'd done a story for a magazine once about children dying of starvation during armed conflict, and she'd cried every night she was there – she'd given them everything she had, sold off her own equipment to help the helpless, knowing that it would do no good in the end. Ellie knew what war was. This morning she awoke in a warm bed, hearing a bit of traffic outside the window, before she rolled over to look at her wristwatch. Eight minutes before seven, and something told her that Marjorie expected her guests to be on time. She pulled a sweater over her head and zipped up a pair of jeans before running a brush through her hair. Only a little grey so far, that's good. Ellie had no plans to dye her hair, as so many industry women did. The process struck her as disingenuous, pretending to be someone she was not. She would age with dignity, in her looks if nothing else.

"Ah, you're right on time!" Marjorie beamed.

"Breakfast smells delicious."

"I made it especially for you. Bacon, toast, fruit, and oatmeal."

Ellie went still. "How did you know what I like?"

"Oh, that's Sandy. He never steers me wrong." Marjorie winked at her guest's raised eyebrow.

Pulling out the chair, Ellie sat on a hooked rug cushion and spent the next hour chatting with her hostess. She decided that the best thing was to take Marjorie as she was, not doubting or asking uncomfortable questions. She heard the story of how Marjorie and Sandy met, when they emigrated, their experiences in Canada. Ellie listened with half an ear, as Mammy would say. Sun shone softly through lace curtains, the food was excellent, and Ellie enjoyed the moment for all its' worth.

After pouring her guest a second cup of coffee, Marjorie got up. "I'll give William a call about your ride, no need to take a taxi to the bus. It leaves just before noon."

Ellie was about to protest when the doorbell rang and she was left alone. Sighing with pleasure, she wiped the last bit of bacon grease off the plate with her finger, licking it and stifling a giggle. What would her colleagues think? Marjorie's voice took on a cadence that indicated she was fully engaged in conversation, and Ellie looked around the room carefully. Nothing strange or unexpected. On the table beside the door was a small stack of newspapers. Curious about what happened in Barrie, Ellie picked off the top one and returned to her seat, savouring the strong coffee. The news was what she expected: war in Vietnam, a windstorm, notes from the local Anglican church, a gardening column, hockey playoffs, television programming. Mentally glazing over, she turned the page leaves without reading, ending at the society news, births and deaths, legal notices. Stories about individuals had always interested her most, and what she saw in the middle of the page took her breath away. She read:

> *Notice to Creditors and Others*
>
> *In the Estate of Frederick James Dawson, deceased.*
>
> *All persons having claims against the Estate of Frederick James Dawson, late of 37 Blake Street, Barrie, Ontario who died on or about January 31, 1960 are hereby notified to send particulars of same to the undersigned on or before the 24th day of March 1972, after which date the Estate will be distributed, with regard only to the claims of which the undersigned shall then have notice, and the undersigned will not be liable to any person of whose claim he shall not then have notice.*
>
> *Dated at Toronto this 8th day of March 1972.*
>
> *John M. Bolton, Barrister and Solicitor,*
> *1407 Yonge Street, Toronto 7, Ontario*

Ellie had been holding her coffee cup in her hand while she read, and it began to shake, her whole body trembling. She set the cup onto the table without tipping it before taking one huge breath, sobbing in spite of herself. It couldn't be him. It had to be him. Reading it over again and a third time, memorizing the words. My God, died in 1960? That was twelve years earlier.

"You look as if you've seen a ghost." Marjorie was at her

elbow, startling her.

"Um, Um." Ellie couldn't speak, couldn't find any words.

"Someone you know there?"

She pointed at the notice, mute.

Taking the page gently, Marjorie read about Frederick. "Ah," she said, softly. "He was important to you."

Without stopping herself, Ellie touched Marjorie's arm. "I don't understand. Was I meant to come here? Was I meant to read this now?"

Marjorie smiled. "It appears so, my dear."

"I don't understand," she repeated. "What's happening to me?"

Marjorie moved her arm away. "It's all right. There are more things happening in this world than can be explained by our way of thinking. Would you like to know when Sandy first let me know that he hadn't gone anywhere?"

Ellie nodded. She felt as if she had been transported to another dimension. Afterwards, she had no memory of what Marjorie told her specifically, yet she retained the gist that acceptance of Sandy's ghost had made his wife's life easier, not more difficult.

The Greyhound bus back to Toronto was less than a third full, and Ellie was grateful not to have to share her seat pairing. Her traveling bag and water bottle claimed the empty space. Staring out the window to a grey sky, she unspooled her recollection back years, to the intense flush of love she'd felt for Edward. Seeing him like that in the pub, with almost an aura around him of his commitment and grace and intensity in the world. She knew they would be together, from the moment their eyes first met. He felt too much, he loved too much; Ellie saw it right away but she stayed, she wanted to feel some of that in herself after the numbness of grief. She wanted to compare the two men who'd meant so much to her, when Edward had never met her brother. Both of them gone. And Charles, grown into a lovely man but also moving away from her in more than just his body. It was right, she wanted that for him, and only lately did she understand the lonely cold of Mam and Douglas's last years, waiting for her to come home. And she couldn't do it then, she hadn't been able to go back and comfort them when they needed it. Ellie shivered involuntarily from seeing the legal notice about Frederick in the newspaper. It opened up a long-closed memory of her time in the forestry commission. Oh, how cocky she was then! Believing she could do and be anything. Of course she knew that she could turn a man's head, and at her first meeting with Frederick when she was with Aileen in the forest, Ellie acknowledged the look on his face, assessing her *that* way. She was pleased and it made her confident, and she would never give in to it, or to him. The chase (if it could be called that) made her time as a timber cruiser all the more fun. Aileen gave into it almost immediately, getting pregnant, and who's to say that she didn't have the happier ending? Maturity made Ellie realize that it was never about fun, and she was ashamed for how lightly she'd treated men's feelings in those days. All a conquest. At the same time, she'd sensed a sort of kinship with Frederick from very early on, as if they were childhood friends meeting up after many years apart. He was the only person she had really talked to during that time in her life, letting on that she was just as vulnerable as anyone. After their third or fourth meeting, she'd recognized that her feelings were changing, and she wished that they were closer in age, and that there could be something more between them. Ellie insisted on discussing his wife and family so that she wouldn't be tempted any more than she already was. Almost everybody took lovers for the duration of the war, military or otherwise, but Ellie hadn't. Edward was her first and only. Sorrow pulled her mouth into a frown as she still mourned his loss, that beautiful man full of ideals that the world couldn't hold. That's why he left. And now Frederick, whom she hadn't thought about in years. Of course he would be dead – she was now fifty-nine years old and he'd been old enough to be her father. If he'd died in 1960, he must've been in his sixties at least, although he'd never told her his age. He knew hers from her identity card that she carried to each work camp. Ellie wiped a tear from the end of her nose and wished that they had been lovers, even once, that she would have that to remember him by as well. The night after the Huntly Arms dinner when they'd walked alone in the dark and she'd kissed his cheek, it was the only time she'd dared to betray her feelings for him. Now she raised her head, the bus making a smooth rumble down the highway, back to Toronto and then onto home. There wouldn't be time to investigate Frederick's death before her return flight to London. Perhaps she would ask Ruby to find out; she could already see Ruby's eyes twinkling with glee. Ellie smiled for the first time on her journey. As the bus neared the city outskirts, she mused about Marjorie Lewis and her strange ways. What an entirely bizarre thing to have happened to her, when all she wanted was a quick break from Toronto. Someone had told Ellie once that there was no such thing as coincidence, and now she wondered. Ellie did wonder.

As expected, Ruby was more than pleased to be asked to sleuth for her friend and colleague. Ellie had been home for three weeks in London when Ruby sent her details of Frederick's obituary, found in back issues of the city newspaper. It read:

> *Dawson, Frederick James. Passed away at Sunnybrook Hospital on Sunday, January 31, 1960, Toronto, in his 65th year. Beloved husband of Kathleen Mary Dawson, dear father of James of Port Arthur. Brother of Walter, Mrs. Margaret Peake, Mrs. Annie Godfrey. Resting at the Newbigging Funeral Home. Service in the chapel Wednesday at 11:00 a.m.*

Ellie kept the notice nearby, reading it multiple times per day. It wasn't so much the man that she grieved as that part of their lives together. How ephemeral the world was. She knew that, and yet seeing the truth of Frederick's death years earlier touched her deeply. For crazy moments she contemplated contacting Kathleen or the children, but no, she wouldn't do that. And just as crazily, Ellie wished that she'd had a child by Frederick.

On a hot, sunny day in June, out in the garden, Ellie kneeled, weeding her prolific roses. Always the task ended with one or more tiny pricks from thorns. These didn't bother her as she saw them as the price of admission for touching such beauty. Perspiration trickled from her underarms down and across her abdomen, ticklish. Wiping the back of her hand across her brow, a sudden cool breeze danced across the yard, and she definitely heard the word *we* uttered by Sandy Lewis. Ellie sat back on her legs, certain that the heat was making her faint, causing her mind to play tricks on her. She still couldn't make sense of her time in Barrie with Marjorie and that odd though welcoming house. By the time she stood up and went to fetch a glass of lemonade, she couldn't prevent a smile from spreading across her face. Sandy was correct, she understood at last. While people come and go in our lives, we don't need to let all of them leave. We can carry the love they sent us in our hearts, forevermore. Mammy and Douglas, Donal, Edward and Charles. *Frederick and me*, she realized, *that's the* "*we*." Ellie grinned as she went into her house.

Epilogue

In reading this book numerous times for editing purposes, I was able to appreciate how tightly truth and fiction are woven together. I did not know my grandfather and began the writing with known facts: his military records from both world wars, copies of two hand-written letters, old photographs, and far too few anecdotes. It is not and was not enough to examine the man's life in the amount of detail that I wished. What I have written is true to the best of my interpretation, perhaps kindest to say with embellishment, considering all of the missing pieces. Soon after beginning the writing, I realized that the tale would not end with either of my grandparents' lives but with my mother's instead. Some of her more baffling behaviour was at last explained, once I knew the context of her early years. She was Margaret, Kathleen and Frederick's daughter born at Leaside (now East York, Toronto). Kathleen Dawson was the only grandparent I had personal contact with as a child, and she died when I was eighteen years old. As a youngster, I formed lasting memories of her. Kathleen was five feet, ten inches tall, towering over me, and I was afraid of her. My family saw her regularly and there were many rules: don't make any noise or sudden movements, don't speak to her first (unless spoken to), and above all, don't make a nuisance of yourself. Kathleen never hugged me (or my siblings), never sat me on her knee, never read me a story. She didn't give gifts for birthdays or Christmas. I can't honestly recall her ever smiling, much less laughing. Now that I am lucky enough to have grandchildren of my own, I cannot help my intense love and interest in them, wanting to know everything about these wondrous little creatures. I remember my grandmother with sadness now, for choosing the way that she approached her life; perhaps it didn't have to be like that. For her, the glass was only ever half empty, not half full. In the 1950s to 1970s, she lived alone in a little house with beautiful maple trees that she'd planted in her front yard, the back of the lot ringed by flower beds and more trees. Kathleen patrolled her space on daily rounds, and I believe it was one of her few outlets for creativity and peace. I'll never know. She had few or no friends, read *The New Yorker* magazine religiously and had a black and white television set that was always turned off. I felt constrained (to put it lightly) when we saw her, for an entire year of just my mother and I, before I began school as the youngest child in our family. Something frightened me (that I can't explain) around Kathleen, when I wasn't surrounded by all of my siblings, plus our father, our family like a fortress against malevolence. The dreaded silence in that house when it was just Mom and me, where I was sent to Kathleen's bedroom for an afternoon nap long after needing one at age five. I'd stand nervously immobile, in a sterile place to me after the organized chaos of my own home. It felt akin to a prison visit, going to that house, and yet we went, year after bloody year, as the British say. When we finally left each time, I could breathe again in our car on the ride home. Mom was tense and quiet – I could tell that she was upset and I didn't know why. Sometimes she would stop and buy me an ice cream cone, wanting to give kindness and attention to her own daughter, when she had not received that as child from her mother. I won't go so far as to suggest that my grandmother set out deliberately to make her daughter miserable, but that is undoubtedly what happened. What my mother experienced as a youngster is today called abuse. She was physically threatened and had love withheld from her, taught that she was a failure for even existing. In writing this book, I finally understood why Mom was the way she was, and I've never doubted her love for me. My mother was loving and kind and fiercely loyal. She also had the dark side of a wounded animal that manifested periodically. Margaret was almost manic about sticking up for anyone who was wronged, and I remember that best about her.

Kathleen never once talked about any part of her early life in front of me or when she visited my childhood home. I knew that she came from England because she talked about pounds, shillings, and pence for money, and lorries. I spent years wondering what those were because I was too afraid to ask her (in Canada, we call lorries commercial vehicles or cartage/freight trucks). For whatever reason, I can no longer recall Kathleen's spoken accent, which is known as West Country. At the beginning of each public elementary school day, children in my class recited The Lord's Prayer, sang 'O Canada' (the national anthem), followed by 'God Save the Queen.' My grandmother only ever spoke of the King (Kings George V and George VI) and that was another mystery; I thought we had a queen, not a king. My mother set me straight on that account: the Royal family had moms and dads, too. There was never a word about my grandfather, not the mention of his name, no photographs or any mementoes, as if he'd never existed. Cancel culture is not new. I was about six years of age when I began to want to know who this man was. Mom would brush off my questions, never expanding anything further about her father: that he had been a veteran of two wars, or a bush pilot, or that her parents separated permanently very soon after he returned from World War II. This lack of knowledge frustrated me. I knew who my father's parents were, even if we seldom saw them. Dad talked about his early life regularly. How Kathleen must've resented the way her daughter turned out, mostly happy. My mother married a French Canadian man, whose first language was French (black mark) and a Catholic besides (double black mark, Kathleen was Protestant). I chuckle now to think of how my grandmother might have viewed that relationship, given the context of her own childhood. She was born while Queen Victoria was still on the throne, when France was an historic enemy and Catholics certainly were (in Kathleen's mind). My father shared a *joie de vivre* typical of the French, quick to laughter, quick to anger, quick to forgive. Our home was noisy, competitive, or conflicted (between the kids), always something going on. And it was never quiet. Visiting my British grandmother was like going to a place where fun wasn't allowed. Worse still, in the last decade before her death, she would spend the entire day with us in the country (at our farm) once per month, my father driving her back and forth to the city. The few times I overhead him referring to his mother-in-law in her absence, he called her the battle-axe.

All of her life, Mom referred to her own mother by her initials only, KMD (Kathleen Mary Dawson). It was some time before I actually knew my grandmother's proper name. It was never mom or nanny or grandma to us kids, just KMD. Even as a child, I thought that was a cold reference. My father wisely stayed out of it.

This far away from the drama, I can't help but feel sad at the very premise of Frederick's relationship with his wife. According to my own thoughts or views only, it appears to me that Kathleen was determined to have her husband come crawling to her on hand and knees from very early on in their union, while he was having none of it. They were both proud and stubborn individuals from what I've ascertained. Frederick's decision to not acknowledge his own daughter was his way of letting Kathleen know that she'd failed him as a devoted and *proper* wife, i.e. one that deferred to her husband. If she wanted to play the game, so could he, and beat her at it as well. Kathleen may have wanted him to know that he was nothing special to her, and Frederick's implied return insult was that she was a fallen woman, possibly bearing a child by a man other than her husband. Personally, I do not believe that my mother was illegitimate, although it's not impossible. Both Mom and her younger brother, Jim, bore a strong physical resemblance to their mother, exhibiting what could be termed Irish colouring: dark hair and fair skin. All three had dark brown eyes. Because Frederick was geographically close to his wife when their first child was conceived and could see Kathleen with relative ease given his military duty (whenever he had a day or two off), she would've been taking a tremendous risk by having a lover. I imagine the whole scenario was just manipulation gone horribly wrong, a tragic opera. No wonder Mrs. Corp (Kathleen's mother) wanted her daughter out of the country, avoiding a potential scandal that would've affected the entire family – the rumour alone might have done it. Perhaps my mother paid the highest price, as Kathleen vented her disappointment (or disillusionment) on an innocent child. Love withheld is the most powerful weapon of all, but if that's the case, then it isn't love. Laying blame is always easier than taking responsibility. Mom never once alluded to the issue of her parentage; she believed that she was Frederick's daughter and that he simply didn't love her, neither of her parents did. She spent her entire life looking for that. I was somewhat surprised to find that the written letter of Frederick's that I have in photocopy displays penmanship that is eerily the same as Margaret's. Perhaps only a coincidence, but who knows? A story exists about Kathleen's appreciation for male attention well into the 1930s, which I will share here. According to my mom, Frederick's two great buddies at that time were George Phillips and Al Cheesman (early Canadian aviators). The three men undertook their OPAS flight training at Camp Borden, and I have a photograph of them together in 1928. Apparently, in the 1930s, one or both of these friends flew to South America, during the period when Pan American Airlines was mapping commercial flight routes in the western hemisphere. I have found no information to confirm this, so it may not be true. On the other hand, early flyers were a tightly connected group, and it is conceivable that a Canadian pilot could have piggy-backed a ride with an American aircrew at some point. Whatever the case, either George or Al went to a street market in Brazil and purchased a ring for Kathleen. Unusual, indeed! The ring is hand-made of beaten gold, with a large amethyst stone. Kathleen had been married close to twenty years when she was presented with the gift, which she kept for the rest of her life. Obviously this was important to her, and she showed my mother the ring on multiple occasions. Was it her way of saying that she didn't need her husband? Or that other men found her desirable? We cannot know. However, I think it strange that a man would bring back a beautiful ring from a faraway land for the wife of his friend.

Frederick came to love Canada, his adopted country, and never left it. By contrast, I've never understood why my grandmother didn't return to what she considered her true home in Wiltshire. For the remainder of her life, she made the long journey back to England every second year, almost until her death at age eighty-four. Surely after her husband had died, she could have lived her later years where she wished? Perhaps the complaining kept her going, I don't know. In my mind, she never loosened her grip on unhappiness and hoarded it unto herself. Looking back, I try to get a sense of her disappointment in her life and where it led to bitterness as she aged. Mom said that Kathleen always imagined herself to be a great lady, one who somehow became entangled in the mundane affairs of ordinary housewives, the fate of so many women then. KMD's attitude of being cast in a mistaken lot could be attributed to delusional thinking, perhaps as a cover for low self-esteem and depression, or some other mental health disorder. Frederick and Kathleen were married within a year of their first meeting. If a longer courtship had ensued, incompatibility might have become apparent before any wedding took place. As it was, soldiers and young women did marry on short notice during war time. It is not to say that they weren't committed or undertook nuptials lightly, but rather that getting to know one another thoroughly took place after the First World War had ended and they had emigrated overseas. And of course, some husbands were killed and never returned. Frederick was serving in the military throughout the entire period they were both in England, and he may not have been in contact with his wife more than ten or fifteen times (if that) before their marriage. The saying goes that people are always nice when they want something, and each party may have been guilty of not presenting their true selves. They were both prisoners of a common history, and I wonder if either of them gave serious consideration to what they were looking for, both in marriage and in each other. At the time of their coming together, Frederick was suffering a serious case of trench fever (untreated by today's standards) along with the psychological trauma of his twenty-two months on the front lines in France. He was just twenty years old when he left the safety of Canada, plunged into the horror of war.

I saw Kathleen shortly before her death in hospital, when she was obviously unwell. I sat at her bedside, feeling uncomfortable as a teenager with no direct experience of death yet in my own life. Grandma spent our time together telling me that she was her father's favourite and that none of her six siblings held the same affection in his heart. This was her message as she lay dying. Her father died when she was barely out of her teens, and no doubt she missed him terribly. It could be that she saw marriage to a handsome young pilot (dashing and daring!) as a substitute hero figure in place of her father, when no man could've carried it off in reality. Life can let any of us down, and we learn to adapt going forward. I wonder at Kathleen's inability to adapt. She never stopped missing England and her home there. I'm sure that she pledged allegiance to Queen Elizabeth II upon Her Majesty's ascension to the throne, but all I ever heard from Kathleen concerned the King. I do wonder whether she had any flexibility whatsoever in her thinking process. If she did imagine herself as a great lady as my mother stated, I would call that delusions of grandeur. Decades ago, many women gave up their individual dreams of solo careers and ambitions as they made a marriage pact, having children and leading entirely satisfying lives, even if it wasn't what they'd originally planned. My grandmother definitely didn't fit into that category, enjoying a happy life as a wife and mother. To end, Frederick had no part in my parents' wedding day or with any of their children afterward. I don't believe my dad ever met his father-in-law in person, and he never talked about him. Mom did not attend her father's funeral. Neither Mom nor her brother Jim ever spoke (with me) about a relationship with their paternal grandparents, John and Mary Dawson in Toronto. John and Mary both died when Mom and Jim were teenagers.

Afterword

Canadian military history has always been an interest of mine, in part because I was born less than a generation after the end of the Second World War. When I was a child, my father worked with a man who'd lost one of his legs below the knee during the Allied campaign in Ortona, Italy. This man had a different way of walking and when I asked Dad why this was, he replied, "Buster's got a peg leg." The next time I saw the war veteran, of course I stared at his pant leg, trying to imagine what that wooden leg might look like underneath. He was a very friendly man, and I couldn't picture him with a gun, killing people. On another occasion when I was perhaps five years old, my dad and I were walking in the downtown area of our small city, and there on the sidewalk was a middle-aged man, begging. Perhaps not an unusual sight, but this person had no legs at all and was seated on a piece of plywood. Two friends stood close-by protectively, and I understand now that they were almost certainly all war veterans. I was frightened by the man who ended at his bum (as I thought of him) and I took my father's hand for safety as we walked past. Dad threw some coins into the metal coffee can near the beggar and heard his thanks. While I was growing up, there were thousands still alive in Canada who'd served in the conflicts and who marked Remembrance Day very personally, commemorating all those who didn't return home. I was reciting rote prayers at school and thinking in general terms, and they were mourning the loss of so many of their close friends and comrades in arms. The specter of war in all its forms (torture, mass murder, rape, psychological warfare) was mind-boggling then, and it still goes on today, as enthusiastically as ever.

I have been ruminating on this book for a very long time, to both honour the grandfather I never knew and to explore what life was like for men and women in the military during Canada's past wars. Many of the events of this story happened more than a century ago, and one must be mindful in applying modern lifestyles, attitudes, and societal norms to those times. In writing of the deep unhappiness of my grandparents' marriage, I saw that the obvious option of leaving the union permanently may have been a difficult (even impossible) choice for either of them. Wives depended upon their husbands for financial support and to maintain their social status in society. Divorce was viewed as a personal failure, for men as well as women, and many couples stayed together for the sake of appearances. Frederick was a military officer and as such, his career demanded an unblemished record in all aspects of life, including his personal life. My grandparents never divorced, and I recall my mother telling me once that she'd found her parents' wedding certificate, mended with Scotch tape after it had been ripped up (by Kathleen, no doubt). Mom's parents lived together again only very briefly after World War II, and Frederick died in a different location, without any contact from his wife. He'd left her the sum of one dollar in his will, which was the way of cutting someone out of an inheritance intentionally, so that the will could not be challenged.

In terms of research, I needed to decide where to stop making enquiries. Family history (and all history) is a keen pursuit for me; I care about the lives of people and their stories. Frederick came from a family of ten children, eight of whom survived to adulthood. Apparently, he was close to his younger brother, Walter, and they kept in touch later in their lives. Some of the British Dawson children emigrated to the United States of America where their descendants still live. Of course I could spend potentially unlimited resources looking into all of these people as well, with their own compelling tales, but my goal was to get the book written in a couple of years rather than a decade or more. There is plenty left for whoever may be interested! My focus was on Frederick's life only. I very much enjoyed the surprises that awaited me with each package of information received from Lisette Lacroix, my researcher. For one thing, Fred Dawson was not an uncommon name back then, and there were six F. Dawsons serving with the British Army in France during World War I. To further complicate matters, one of my relative's ancestors served in France (with the 26th Battery, 7th Artillery Brigade, 2nd Division, Canadian Expeditionary Force) where he met Fred Dawson. The two became fast friends on the front lines, creating some confusion before I realized that this was not my grandfather but another man with the same name. Another point that I learned during research was the use of the term "Indian" one hundred years ago. "Indian" to the British meant citizens from the country of India, in Asia. Regiments of Gurkha soldiers fought as part of the British Commonwealth forces. Indigenous Canadians were also called "Indians" or "red Indians" at the time, terms which today are offensive. They are now known as First Nations peoples in Canada, and they had their own distinct experience of serving the country during both world wars. I encourage readers to look into this topic more thoroughly themselves, especially at what occurred when veteran indigenous soldiers returned home.

I have a copy of Frederick's application for commission in the Royal Flying Corps as a pilot officer in late 1916. The questions to be answered were standard, or ones that might be expected, except for one that startled me. It asked the applicant to confirm that he (men only, in this case) was of "pure white ancestry." I needed a few seconds to relate to the racism and colonialism of Britain at that time. My grandmother, Kathleen, often referred to the King's English when she spoke, and no one was permitted to use any form of slang or incorrect grammar in her presence. For her, fluency in any other language was a step-down; no wonder my French-speaking father (her son-in-law) didn't impress. Also, there were a few discrepancies between the passenger manifests of Atlantic sea crossings, which I could not sort out. The Canada Census record of 1921 indicates that Frederick's family emigrated from England in 1907, but the ship's manifest from their sailing is definitely dated 1905. As well, I have not got a ship's manifest for Frederick's return to Canada after the war, sometime in 1919. He is apparently missing in the records, although Kathleen's crossing is recorded, her first and when she was pregnant with my mother. Given how the marriage evolved, I chuckle at the idea that perhaps Frederick never did return. . .but no, he repatriated in 1919, I just don't know when exactly. Was either his or Kathleen's family in England impacted by the deadly Spanish Flu? I have no information about that.

I am very fortunate to own a series of black and white pictures from the time period in question, aiding in the interpretation of events. My mom was a life-long photography enthusiast, and she re-photographed some old pictures from the family albums about fifty years ago; these came into my possession after her death. There are a few things to note in the photographs: my grandmother never smiles at the camera, often doesn't look into the lens, and her eyes are off to one side. She always keeps her arms close to her body, never outward or expressive in any way. I have a single picture of her holding her baby son, James, and based upon Kathleen's body language, he was the obvious favourite of her two offspring. In the one photo of Margaret (as a toddler) with her mother, where both are sitting on the ground outside of their rural farmhouse, the two subjects are looking away from one another, and Kathleen is not touching her child. Mom told me that her father refused to be photographed with her at any time in her life, and there are no pictures of the two of them together. Neither are there photos of the four members of the Dawson family together as a group that I'm aware of. This is not unusual, as they lived in rural or semi-rural areas, where studio photography was less common. There may have been other reasons for the lack of family portraits. The two individual pictures of my grandparents (in this book) were both taken in England. In the photographs taken in Canada, Frederick appears relaxed and confident when he is alone, particularly when he's away in the bush, as we say in my area. He often holds a cigarette as he looks directly into the camera lens and smiles. In pictures of Margaret and James as children, she always rests a protective arm or hand around her little brother, and both look right into the lens. Kathleen kept tension between her children when they were adults, telling untruths back and forth to keep them apart and mistrustful of each other. After Kathleen's death, the siblings became quite close, and I enjoyed Uncle Jim's company very much until his death. Plagued by the selfishness of youth, I wish now that I had asked him much more about his early life. I believe that he got on well with his father and that they spent time together in the bush, bonding in that environment. Jim was an expert canoeist with years of experience in the northern wilderness; he ran a trapline for decades and once had prime wolf pelts sent to Montreal and manufactured into beautiful winter coats for himself and his wife.

Because I am so taken with stories and anything to do with writing, it is with regret that I acknowledge having no personal diaries or journals or anything of that nature from the time of the world wars. I have attempted to portray both Frederick and Kathleen fairly and not paint her with the villain's brush where unwarranted. There is written information about Frederick, whom I never met (he died before my birth) and I knew Kathleen personally. Everything official that refers to Frederick (primarily his military records) denotes him as well-liked, a leader, not one to shirk his duties. The dated expression that he was "loved by his men" comes to mind. No doubt some bias does enter into my interpretation. At this point, I would give just about anything to speak openly with Kathleen (today) and to hear her version of events. It is possible that Frederick may have been unfaithful in his marriage, but no evidence of that has emerged so far. I know what a cold-hearted person my grandmother was from first-hand experience, and if that were the case in her marriage, then I don't blame her husband for seeking affection or attention from another woman, morals aside. As far as I know, Frederick did not father any children outside of his marriage. Appearances are that Frederick's parents, Mary and John Dawson, had a long and happy life together, married for sixty-three years, still an impressive length of time today and considerably extended for a couple born in the 1850s. They died within a few months of each other, another possible indicator of how bereft one was without the other. I have one (photocopied) black and white photograph of the couple, and they seem to be growing into a single depiction of wedded love in their old age.

Conversations of Frederick's and of other persons in this manuscript are my own invention. I do not know the pitch or cadence of his voice, and there are no audio recordings of it. Faint or strong, richly timbred, these are things that I cannot know. Since he emigrated from England as a child, he likely would've lost at least a portion of his accent by adulthood. Kathleen came to Canada at the age of twenty-five, and so her accent was maintained. During his service in the Royal Flying Corps, Frederick may well have met a number of the flying aces of that time, perhaps such men as Doc Oakes, Len Rochford, Robert Little, and many more. I am glad that my grandfather was able to gain his commission after what he endured at the front lines for nearly two years. He was not an infantry soldier (which may explain why he survived), but nonetheless, he experienced trauma in his role in the service corps. I learned about field conditions in France through my research. The scene in the story where a soldier commits suicide near him is fictitious, but it is documented that a number of soldiers did kill themselves at the front while others shot their extremities as a way to be evacuated out of the horror. I had to stop writing for a few days during the book's first draft, when I reflected on what Frederick lived through as a young man. He shipped overseas at age twenty, still a boy in many ways. His was not a military family and he was not buffered by heroic stories from his father and uncles, for example. What Frederick experienced in World War I affected the rest of his life (not the least of which was his physical health as the result of trench fever), and I am deeply impressed by the fact that he returned to Old Blighty again in World War II when he was then in middle-age. Duty and honour, indeed, though, tongue in cheek, it would have been a brilliant way of taking a sabbatical from his marriage. Ellie, the young woman in Scotland who was Frederick's love interest for this story, is also fictitious. I wanted to introduce another facet to Frederick's time there, along with his military duties. The idea came from a single report that he wrote in 1946, summarizing the Canadian Forestry Corps' overseas operations. It is well written with a touch of humour, and he singles out the female timber cruisers from the Scottish Forestry Commission for praise. I doubt that I could identify any one group for praise, given the super-human effort that all put into the war effort. However, somebody who was a timber cruiser may well have caught his eye (most or all of them were women), and so Ellie appears in the story. I have no information as to whether he had a lady friend at the time. However, he was a handsome man, a senior military officer confident in his service role, and as one might say these days, he was in his happy place when in Scotland and working as part of a team. There is no reason to believe that he would not have been attracted to someone, or another person to him, over a period of five years. It is his wife and marriage that appear to have caused him the greatest loneliness in his life, and being an ocean away from that may have prompted him to reach out for comfort. As humans, we all need to feel loved. I have the names of the actual people who served with Frederick in District Four of the Forestry Corps, and I deliberately left them out of this book. They have living descendants whom I have not contacted, as I wanted to avoid causing offence of any kind; the families are entitled to their privacy. I do wonder if any of them kept a war diary. This story is a mixture of truth and fiction together, and it was never meant to be an academic research project or a completely truthful historic account. I ask readers to allow the liberty I've taken with specific social events which have either little or no basis in fact in terms of Frederick's life. However, the types of activities described in Scotland during the war have been documented in other sources. Reading dry military records alone would make for a very boring tale, and in consequence, I added what I felt was appropriate flavour to the times when these people lived. The research that I carried out in regards to how both military personnel and civilians lived was a great benefit to my understanding of the wars. A reference section provides a list of sources that I consulted. Names and dates of campaigns were taken from published accounts. I know where Frederick was and what he did, except I don't have it in his own words. His death notice of 1960 (*Toronto Daily Star*) and 1972 notice to creditors in the *Barrie Examiner* are accurate, published records. I have not included Frederick's place of burial here for privacy reasons although it is also published – I intend to visit his grave myself for the first time very soon. By the way, as soon as I read Frederick's death notice, I had a strong suspicion that Kathleen wrote it. Referring to him as her beloved husband, when he clearly wasn't, along with "dear father" of James only (with no mention of Margaret) is just the sort of thing my grandmother would do.

Canada is a commonwealth member country of the former British Empire. When I was young, my homeland was known as the Dominion of Canada. July 1st each year marks the current Canada Day holiday; it was called Dominion Day prior to 1982. The province of Newfoundland and Labrador did not join the Confederation (of Canada) until 1949. In 1946 the Parliament of Canada passed the Canadian Citizenship Act, which came into effect in the following year. Its purpose was to create a legal status for Canadian citizenship by both defining what that was, and by providing a community of status for all who lived in the country. Because my grandparents were past middle age by the time this Parliamentary Act was tabled, neither chose to become Canadian citizens. They remained British citizens with British passports all of their lives. From my research, I was interested to learn that since Frederick had been born in England, he could join the Canadian military in the First World War and be able to switch back and forth with the British forces quite easily, a type of secondment while in service. By World War II, the Canadian military establishment was keen to keep its serving men and women under its own command, and numerous *détentes* and rancorous meetings and discussions took place to that effect, as I found in reading more about Prime Minister Mackenzie

King and his government of the day. Canada no longer viewed itself as a vassal state of the British and wished to assert its own authority over members of its armed services. Of course, the two countries worked in tight cooperation and with positive morale in their common goal of fighting the Nazi regime in Europe. Many Canadian soldiers married British women and brought them home with them as war brides when hostilities ended. To this day, there are many links between our countries, and I am an unabashed monarchist, a trait no doubt inherited from Kathleen. While still a teenager myself, I served three years with the Canadian Armed Forces, something I've always been proud of. I kept my grandfather in mind during my training at Camp Borden in Ontario, fifty years after he'd been there, training as an OPAS pilot. We must have walked the same ground at some point. For my bucket list, one day I would love to travel to Loch Rannoch in Scotland, to a place where I know my grandfather had been during the war. And I like to imagine that his love, Ellie, was a real person.

    I make no claim whatsoever of being any sort of authority on the world wars. The amount of information available is staggering to say the least, and I am no scholar about any of it. I referred closely to the books and articles listed in my references in an attempt to try to get the dates and locations correct. These two conflicts in the twentieth century affected the lives of a large portion of the Canadian population, with reverberations that continue to this day. To all those who served then and serve now, I say, Thank You.

Bibliography

Bassett, George Henry. – *The Book of County Armagh. A manual and directory, etc. [With a map.]* British Library, Historical Print Editions. 1888.

Broadfoot, Barry. – *Six War Years 1939-1945 - Memories of Canadians At Home and Abroad.*
Doubleday Canada Limited. 1974.

Canadian War Museum – https://warmuseum.ca

Chandler, John and Peter Goodhugh. – *Amesbury: history and description of a south Wiltshire town.* The Amesbury Society. 1979.

Copp, Terry, with Richard Nielsen. – *No Price Too High; Canadians and the Second World War.* Norflicks Productions. McGraw-Hill Ryerson Limited. 1996.

Dawson, F. J. "Canadian Forestry Corps Overseas Operations." *The Forestry Chronicle.* https://pubs.cif-ifc.org

Dawson Kingston, Priscilla. -compiler.– *The Mary & John Dawson Genealogy*

Second Issue (unpublished). December 1982.

Encyclopedia Brittanica.- https://www.britannica.com

Enfield Archaeological Society - https://www.enfarchsoc.org

Fort William Daily Times Journal. Saturday, October 25, 1941.

Government of Canada Environment and Natural Resources. Station Results – Historical Data (Quebec). https://climate.weather.gc.ca

Government of Canada Publications. *Canadian Expeditionary Force 1914-1919,* No. DA3-4462E. https://publications.gc.ca

Gray, James H. - *The Winter Years.* Macmillan of Canada. 1966.

Imperial War Museum - http://iwm.org.uk

Library and Archives Canada https://library-archives.canada.ca

Mathieson, William D. - *My Grandfather's War – Canadians Remember the First World War 1914-1918.* Macmillan of Canada. 1981.

More, Alexander F. et al., - "The Impact of a Six-Year Climate Anomaly on the Spanish Flu Pandemic and WWI." *GeoHealth (AGU),* 4, 2020. e2020GH000277 https:// doi.org/10.1029/2020GH000277

Morton, Desmond. - *When Your Number's Up: The Canadian Soldier in the First World War* Random House of Canada Limited. 1993.

National Archives of the United Kingdom https://www.nationalarchives.gov.uk

Pam, David. - *A History of Enfield: A Victorian Suburb* Vol. 2, 1837-1914

Enfield Preservation Society Ltd. 1992.

Pitfield, Jane. – *Leaside*. Dundurn Press. 1999.

Queen Elizabeth I – https://www.elizabethi.org

Sharpe, Chris. – *Enlistment in the Canadian Expeditionary Force 1914-1918.*
Canadian Military History 24, 1 (2015).

Soloway, Beverley. *Throwing Good Money After Bad: The 1936 Burning of Northern Ontario*
Researchgate publication, March 2022.
https://www.researchgate.net/publication/359017267

Sunnybrook Health Sciences Centre – https://sunnybrook.ca

Sweeney, Dave (Major). – *Beasts of Burden: Horse Transport on the Western Front*
Master of Defence Studies JCSP 39 DL. (2014).
https://www.cfc.forces.gc.ca

The Canadian Encyclopedia
https://thecanadianencyclopedia.ca

The Enfield Society – https://www.enfieldsociety.org.uk

"The First Contingent – Life on Salisbury Plain".
https://canadiangreatwarproject.com

West, Bruce. – *The Firebirds*. Queen's Printer for Ontario. 1974.

Wonder, William C. – *The Sawdust Fusiliers*. Canadian Pulp & Paper Association. 1991.

Zimmerman, Ernest R. – *The Little Third Reich on Lake Superior: A History of Canadian Interment Camp R.-*
edited by M. Beaulieu and D. Ratz University of Alberta Press. 2015.

Acknowledgments

A number of people helped water the seeds in the creation of this book. I thank my relation Susan Hilliard (1923-), whose interest in our shared family history is at least as great as my own. Lisette Lacroix, researcher *par excellence*, discovered historical records and information about my grandfather's family and background which prompted more questions, as it is meant to. I owe a debt to David Ratz, CD, PhD, for his knowledge of all things Canadian military, and I am grateful for his patience with my many questions. He also deciphered old war records, something I was unable to do without his assistance. Gratitude is due to Katrina Huszarik, MD, for her insight on trench fever and its physiological effects on soldiers of the First World War. Lastly, the cheering from the sidelines by Jennifer and Lynne of Entershine Bookshop in Thunder Bay made the whole project a little easier.

Rest in peace, Granddad.

About The Author

Margaret Schweitzer is an author from northwestern Ontario, Canada. She has been writing since the age of seven and has a keen interest in history, particularly Canadian military history.

Printed in Canada